A *Just Cause Universe* Novel

Adrienne Dellwo

Local Hero Press Edition

Hero Academy: A Just Cause Universe Novel
Published by Local Hero Press, LLC
http://localheropress.com

1st Printing
Local Hero Press: trade paperback, July 9, 2018
Printed in the United States of America

ISBN-13: 9781971445120

Cover art by Scott Story
Book design by Local Hero Press, LLC

This is a work of fiction. Names, characters, places, and incidents are either the product of the author's imagination or used fictitiously. Any resemblance to actual events, locales, or persons, living or dead, is entirely coincidental.

A substantially different version of a portion of this book appeared in the anthology *Caped*, in the short story "Dax and the Red Eyes," written by Adrienne Dellwo and published by Local Hero Press.

Books by Local Hero Press

The *Just Cause Universe*

Just Cause
The Archmage
Day of the Destroyer
Deep Six
Jackrabbit
Champion
Castles
The Lion and the Five Deadly Serpents
Tusks
The Neighborhood Watch
Jackrabbit: Big In Japan
Arena
Hero Academy
The Path
Cinco de Mayo
Search and Rescue
Rooftops
Plague
Soldiers of Fortune
Just Cause Universe Compendium
Destroyer of Earth
Flint and Steel
The Club
Jackrabbit: Rinse and Repeat
Posse
Extinction Event
Rain Must Fall

Pariah of Verigo

Pariah's Moon
Pariah's War

Three Flavors of Tacos

The Guitarist
Making the Cut
The Scene Stealers

Collections

Airship Lies
High Contrast
The Good Fight
The Good Fight 3: Sidekicks
The Good Fight 4: Homefront
The Good Fight 5: The Golden Age
Muddy Creek Tales
Caped

Other Novels

Assassin
Blood on the Ice
Funeral Games
Hope and Undead Elvis
Horde
The Murder Squad (2026)
Roast Wyvern (and Other Recipes)
Starf*cker
Strings
The Oilman's Daughter
Troubleshooters

Nonfiction

Action! Writing Better Action Using Cinematic Techniques

CHAPTER ONE

Saturday, Aug. 13, 2016
Coeur d'Alene, Idaho

WyldWing zipped around one tall pine tree to see an impenetrable thicket just feet away. She angled up, whipping her head to move a stray lock of brown hair from in front of her goggles. Her dragonfly wings buzzed faster than they had in the four months since they'd sprouted from her back. She cleared the tree tops in moments, racing her unseen opponent. Below, a dense evergreen blanket stretched for miles, all the way to Hayden Lake's glistening waters. She had no time to take in the view, though—she was on a mission. She dropped down beyond the thicket, staying focused and intent on her destination deep in the heart of the Coeur d'Alene National Forest.

You have to get these plans to the secret government base before Drone finds you, her mission coordinator had told her before she set out. *The fate of the world depends on it!*

She heard a whirring sound and glanced to the side to see the black device she'd been trying to evade, the one with *Gotcha Chloe* painted on its side. The drone's pilot must've found a passageway through the thicket while she'd had to go over it. *Very sneaky, Dad,* she thought. Annoyed at herself for failing yet another training mission, she stuck her tongue out at the drone's little camera, which was trained right on her . . .

And slammed head-first into a tree.

* * *

"Chloe, how you feeling, honey?" her dad asked from the doorway. She sat propped up on pillows with a tray over her lap. It contained the wrappers from two protein bars, a tall milkshake glass, a large bowl with the remains of clam chowder sticking to its sides, and a plate covered in sandwich crumbs. Next to the plate, three dirty face wipes showed all the grit and grime that always covered her after flying. Her dad liked to tease about her reverse superhero mask—white around the eyes, where the goggles covered, and dirt-brown everywhere else.

"My head doesn't hurt as bad," she said, "but my neck's killing me. How long's this gonna take?"

Phil Wyld chuckled. "Believe it or not, hitting a tree at fifty miles an hour is a pretty big deal. Just be glad you're not frail like us wimpy humans, or you'd have a long hospital stay ahead of you." He held up her cracked helmet for emphasis. "This could have been your skull."

She sighed and shifted the wings behind her back, trying to get comfortable. She still wasn't used to leaning back against them. "Yeah, but it's just a few days until I go to the Hero Academy. I need to be on my game."

"They don't expect you to already be a top-notch hero, kiddo." He sat on the side of her bed and looked up at the gymnastics medals hanging from hooks above the headboard, next to a poster of Mustang Sally, until recently the field commander of Just Cause New York. "You're not going to Nationals—it's your freshman year. You're a noob."

"But they said there'd be testing . . ."

He put a hand up. "Just to gauge where you are. It's not a competition. They have to determine your baseline before deciding what kind of training you'll most need. Remember how much you hated balance beam, especially when your coaches made you do it twice as much as floor and bars?"

"Yes." Chloe made a pouty-face. She still hated balance beam, even though she'd never get to compete on it again.

"It doesn't do nearly as much good to train at something if you're already good at it. Coach Amy knew that. That's why you got to spend all those extra hours on the beam, and that's why it doesn't matter how good you are at flying now. There will be other areas you'll need more training in, and the Academy will design a course program to fit your needs. Now, why don't you settle in and watch that episode of *Heroes Among Us* Mom told you about?"

She rolled her eyes but laughed while she did it. "Fine, Dad, I'll be good."

"Well, that'll be a refreshing change." He grinned and winked, then handed her the remote off her nightstand and left the room, closing the door behind him.

She shook her head, then winced at the pain it caused, grabbing at taut neck muscles. "Work faster, superpowers," she grumbled as she turned on her tablet, hoping to have a message from Lindsay Malone, her soon-to-be roommate. She'd gotten Lindsay's email in an Academy welcome packet a few days ago, but Chloe didn't know what to say so she hoped the other girl would start the conversation.

Her finger hesitated above the email icon. Taking a deep breath, she tapped the screen to open it.

The first three subjects made her shrivel up inside, as she did every time she opened email these days. "Cheater," the first one said. The sender was named Flip, a poor cover for a gymnast trying disguise her identity. Chloe knew it was Jessi, her former teammate and, unfortunately, former best friend. Back in their first year of competition, their coach had nicknamed them Flip and Flop, because every time one did well, the other flopped. Whoever did better at any particular meet got to be Flip. Chloe had hated the names even then. She deleted it. The next was from the cleverly named "Anonymous" and the subject line was, "Coach is being investigated cause of your cheating." She deleted it, too.

She did hope Coach Amy wouldn't get in trouble. It wasn't her fault Chloe had sprouted wings during a meet.

She'd never forget the moment. She released the high bar and focused on "flying" to the lower one, when she felt some kind of muscle spasm in her back and realized she was hovering between the bars. Not moving forward, not falling—stuck in the air somehow. A loud buzzing sound filled her ears.

Chloe didn't understand what was happening and watched as her coach ran across the gym to her and her parents stood at the edge of the floor, staring with terrified expressions.

"What's going on?" she'd asked the coach in a trembling voice.

"Chloe, I don't know how to tell you this, but—you're flying," Coach Amy said. "You have wings."

Chloe looked over shoulder and saw them, blurred with motion, and still couldn't comprehend what was going on.

"Can you get yourself on the ground?" Coach asked.

Chloe's head spun. "How?"

Coach took her hand and pulled her down until Chloe could swing her feet down onto the mat. Everyone stared. A few people clapped while most of them sat in stunned silence.

Instead of getting to finish out the meet, she'd been taken to the hospital for a battery of tests and examinations of her new appendages. There was no question in her mind who had flopped at that meet. It was her.

The bylaws of the gymnastics association had no provision for parahumans, but it had only taken the officials a few minutes to determine that her points earned in competition were void. She had new muscles in her back, and the muscles and wings constituted an unfair advantage. They booted her off the team. With her scores nullified, it had meant the team was ineligible to compete in State for that season, which was why her former teammates were so incensed with her.

The third email, from "X" and titled *Bitch,* also went to the trash.

The fourth message raised her spirits a little. It was what she had been hoping for. Chloe clicked on it, butterflies replacing the knots from moments earlier.

Hey! It's so awesome to meet you! I saw you on the news and it's so cool how your wings came out. Flying must be the best thing ever.

Are you on ParaFrosh yet? If not you should totally get on it. Some of our other classmates are there already.

Chloe remembered seeing something in the welcome packet about ParaFrosh—an incoming-freshmen-only part of the Academy's social media site—but she'd dropped off all social media after the harassment started and wasn't anxious to get back into it.

Maybe it'll be okay, she thought, *since it's just parahuman kids, like me.* She did a quick search for the welcome email and got registered.

She accepted an invitation to friend Lindsay, whose profile pic showed a white girl with freckles and long black hair. Next, she found a list of the nine members of her class. It included photos and she recognized the name Zayden Lord right away. Everyone did—he was probably the most famous parahuman outside of Just Cause and the Champions. He was the subject of the *Heroes Among Us* episode her mom had wanted her to watch. Her stomach fluttered when she looked at his smile and bright blue eyes.

Icons next to everyone's names showed her five classmates already on the site. There was a girl named Rhiannon, with white-blond hair, deep tan, dark eyeliner, and bright pink lips. Also signed up were Isabella Machado and Jacob Cotton. His name seemed familiar, so she Googled it.

"That's right, I remember now," she murmured as headlines popped up about him rescuing kids from a flooding daycare, along with a Black Lives Matter meme in the image results. It showed a white neo-Nazi kid who'd shot up a black church and threatened police when they arrived, yet was arrested without being hurt, in a split screen with Jacob. Above the Nazi was written "Drop Out with History of Violence." Above Jacob, it said "Hero & Honors Student," and below his face, "2.5x more likely to be shot by police."

A second meme showed Jacob with cross hairs over his face. It had the N-word "AND parahuman?" written above him, and below, "Better shoot him twice."

Chloe sucked in a breath and felt nauseous. She knew how much she'd hated all the attention, both positive and negative, after her wings' dramatic appearance during the televised meet. Every time she saw the video, she wanted to run and hide. How horrible must it be for Jacob to know that meme existed?

She clicked on an article and learned he was a speedster, just like Mustang Sally. A reporter had asked what made him run into the daycare and he'd answered, "Why wouldn't I? I mean, no one would let kids drown if they could help them, right?" Chloe decided she liked this guy and marveled over having two classmates who'd already performed superhero rescues while she'd only just figured out how to maneuver in the air.

She Googled the rest of her classmates but just found social media sites, so no others had made the news, apparently.

A chat window popped up and she expected it to be Lindsay, but it turned out to be Isabella. Her profile pic featured the singer Selena Gomez.

Hey! I'm Izzy. You're Lindsay's roomie, right?

Yeah, Chloe sent back. *It's so cool meeting ppl before school starts!*

Right? I'm stoked to get to the academy. Do you know who Zayden Lord is?

Chloe's face got hot. *Ya kinda, my mom's trying to get me to watch a show about him.*

You totally should watch it, it's pretty good. And OMG, he's so cute I'm dying.

Hahaha. Srsly. Have you met him? Or anyone else in our class?

No, I just know my twin brother irl and Lindsay and Rhiannon here. Well and you now. Heehee. Plus my big sis goes to the academy.

Wow, you're all three paras? Chloe asked.

Yep. Not our other brother tho. He doesn't have the gene. Gotta go but ttyl, k?

Ttyl

* * *

From the TV series Heroes Among Us*, Season 2, Episode 7, "The Lord Family: Triumphs & Tragedies"*

Segment 1

The Lord family looked like any other, raising their sons in Lee's Summit, Missouri—America's heartland. Little did they know what changes were in store for them.

In 2009, Nathan and Anna Lord welcomed the first change: their seven-year-old son Zayden's parahuman powers revealed themselves when the family witnessed a grisly car wreck—and Zayden used his telekinesis to separate the cars so the occupants could escape, and in the nick of time. Just as the last person got to safety, the engine burst into flame.

But then, tragedy stuck. The very next day, three-year-old Daxton—previously described as a chatterbox—went silent. He was listless, eyes unfocused, and Anna rushed him to the emergency room. What doctors found remains a mystery to this day. In the ER, on one of the worst days of her life, Anna Lord says she felt attacked by medical personnel.

"The ER doctors said it had to be exposure to some kind of toxic chemical and asked me what he'd been into, like I'm a horrible parent who lets my toddler play with nuclear waste or something."

Weeks later, she'd find an ally in Dr. Preston Huxley, the country's preeminent parahuman neuropsychologist.

"Portions of Dax's brain were simply gone, as if they'd been eaten or burned away somehow. It's similar to the damage we see with high-level mercury exposure, but tests showed no trace of mercury or other known neurotoxins in his system. Right away, I suspected another cause."

The ER doctors said Dax's brain could perform only the most basic activities—those that kept the little boy alive. But Doctor Huxley disagreed, seeing activity in what remained of young Dax's brain that was anything but normal.

"You see these areas here, how they're lit up? This is consistent with Dr. Grace Devereaux's well-documented findings of parahuman brain activity. I believed from the start that, rare as it is, Dax's powers had surfaced at just three years of age. For some reason we don't yet understand, those powers destroyed these areas—here, here, and here. It's unprecedented. No one has ever seen anything like it."

CHAPTER TWO

Sunday, Aug. 14, 2016
Coeur d'Alene, Idaho

Feeling almost well when she woke up the next morning, Chloe slammed down a few bowls of cereal, a grapefruit, two bananas, and a glass of chocolate milk. She knew if she took in enough calories, she'd heal at maximum speed. In gymnastics, she had always recovered quickly from falls, muscle pulls, ankle twists, and the other myriad bumps and bruises that came from the life of a competing gymnast. She'd never once stopped to consider that her healing might be parahuman in origin, at least, not until a torn ligament miraculously stitched itself back together a few years ago. That hadn't gotten her booted off the team, but it was one more thing to separate her from her former friends and teammates.

After a quick shower, she got dressed in her training clothes—a gymnastics leotard with a deep-cut back to allow her wings freedom of movement, tights, and goggles. She'd discovered small foot movements helped her steer and control her speed during flight, so she wore five-finger shoes even though she thought they looked weird. She emerged from her bedroom into the hallway.

"Just where do you think you're going?" her mom said from behind her.

Chloe startled and spun around. "Seriously, mom, you need to wear a bell. I'm going out to train. Where else would I go dressed like this? The mall?"

Heather Wyld ran one hand through her bed hair as she closed the distance to her daughter and put an arm around her back between the two sets of wings. "Not today, you're not, Fly Girl. Dad and I agreed—you're taking the day off, no matter how good you *say* you feel."

"But, mo-o-o-om . . ." Chloe drew it out into several whiny syllables.

Heather shook her head and chuckled. "*But mom!* Nope, sorry kiddo, but you're grounded for the day." She grimaced at her choice of words. "Sorry, that was supposed to be a flight joke, but it sounded more like you were in trouble, didn't it?"

Chloe wrinkled up her face. "Probably better if you left the jokes to dad."

"Yeah, you're right." Her mom leaned in conspiratorially. "Just don't tell him I said so, okay? I'll never admit to it."

Chloe chuckled. "Deal, but only if you let me train for an hour or two tonight."

"Not fair, negotiating before I've had coffee. You know it makes me soft." Heather sighed and started toward the stairs. "Fine, one hour. Until then, get some rest."

Chloe went back into her room and changed into pajamas while wondering how she'd fill a whole day without training. After six years on the gymnastics team, then moving right into flight training, she didn't know how to do anything besides working out.

She decided maybe she'd watch that episode on Zayden Lord after all. She grabbed the remote from her nightstand, scrolled through the menu until she found it, and settled in to watch. Despite her intent not to enjoy it, she found it a lot more interesting than she'd expected, especially the more recent footage of Zayden.

As the closing credits rolled, Chloe's stomach rumbled and she smiled when her mom came in moments later, carrying a tray piled high with food.

"Oh good, you watched it. What did you think?"

Her face flushed. "Zayden Lord's really cute."

Her mom laughed. "That's your take-away, really?"

* * *

"Honey, let me do that—you should still be taking it easy," Chloe's mom said as they packed. A tower of boxes now dominated one corner of the room.

Chloe sighed and grabbed more clothes from a drawer, then arranged them in an empty box. "Mom, I told you, I'm fine."

Her phone dinged and she checked the alert. It was an email from a name she didn't recognize, something she'd learned not to trust. *Won't they ever give up?* she wondered about the girls who'd been like family until a few months ago.

"Everything okay?" Heather eyed her, worried. Chloe shrugged and tried to look casual. "Yeah, just spam."

The pinched brows let her know her mom knew better, but she didn't press.

The bedroom door swung open to reveal her dad with sandwiches piled high on a plate. "How's it going in here?"

"Good. I think we're about done with my clothes and sheets and stuff." Chloe hadn't realized she was hungry until she saw the food. She grabbed a PB&J. "Thanks, dad. Can I be off house arrest soon? I'm dying to get out and fly."

"How's your neck?" he asked.

"Totally fine." That was true, but she would've said the same thing even if it still hurt a little.

Phil looked sideways at his wife, who rolled her eyes and chuckled. "Fine, Coach Phil. You can take her out to train once we're finished here."

* * *

Chloe's phone dinged again as she stepped from the shower and shook the water off her wings, spraying droplets onto the bathroom walls that she'd have to remember to wipe dry. She'd had a short but fun training session in which she'd flown low over a beach along Lake Coeur d'Alene, racing a yellow lab who thought a flying human was the most fun thing ever. His owners, aging hippies, laughed and cheered and said it reminded them of some old Heart song, but Chloe had no idea what they meant.

When she turned on the phone, she saw she'd left her email open earlier. She stared at the unknown name next to the subject line "Winners Only" and wondered if it was yet another harassing message from a former teammate. If so, they'd found a new name and tactic. Although her anxiety spiked a little, she tapped it and read.

You're special. You're better than the people around you, yet they do everything they can to keep you down. Don't you get tired of that? Don't you want to be part of a group of people like you, who have superior abilities?

Of course you're tired of it, and of course you're looking for other parahumans—and not those with just any powers, but those with truly superior abilities. We've left the rest behind genetically, and now it's time to set ourselves apart from them in every other way. Join us now! Be part of something that will shock them into realizing how superior we truly are!

The words *join us now* were hyperlinked, but Chloe had no intention of finding out where the link went. If it was an attempt to harass her, she didn't get it. She deleted it and checked the new alert, which was a message from Lindsay on ParaFrosh.

Yay, you're here!

They chatted about their favorite superheroes and how they wanted to decorate their room. Chloe grinned over how good it felt to just talk to another girl without fear of being hurt.

So, before you meet my mom, Lindsay said, *there's something I should tell you.*

* * *

From the TV series <u>Heroes Among Us</u>, Season 2, Episode 7, "The Lord Family: Triumphs & Tragedies"

Segment 2

Despite his parents' best efforts, as well as the staff of a highly rated special-needs pre-school, Nathan Lord says Dax never spoke again.

"He eventually started making nonsensical sounds, but that was it. My wife swore he was trying to talk, but it was just wishful thinking on her part. It never made any sense."

However, he and Anna disagree on that point.

"He did speak—I understood him, even if Nathan didn't. If you took the time, had the patience to piece his sounds and actions together, you could understand what he was trying to say."

Dax's disability changed life for the Lord family. As Dax grew older, he lagged farther and farther behind other kids his age. At six, he wasn't able to dress himself. He struggled to hold a spoon. He needed constant care and supervision—with his mother shouldering the lion's share of the burden. Friends say it put a big strain on Anna—and her marriage.

"Anna was so selfless, doting on that little boy, working with him constantly. Nathan, though, could hardly be bothered to look at Dax. He put all his energy into Zayden and resented Anna for not doing the same."

In 2011, Nathan moved out and contacted a divorce attorney. Documents reveal that Nathan wanted full custody of Zayden unless Anna would consent to put Dax in an institution.

CHAPTER THREE

Monday, Aug. 15, 2016
Coeur d'Alene, Idaho

Chloe shut the back of the SUV with a thunk that felt final. The time had come to leave home and it had Chloe anxious and scared and excited and in disbelief all at the same time. It made her head spin, like she'd done one too many loop-the-loops over the trees.

Heather hugged her. "I'm so sorry I can't come with you to Denver, babe."

"That's okay, mom, I know this is a big case." She grinned. "But you better win it or I'll be super mad."

Her mom snorted and mock punched her shoulder. "I'm gonna miss you, Fly Girl."

"I'll miss you, too." Chloe blinked back tears. "I'll text you when we get to the airport and again when we land."

Phil Wyld gave his wife a long hug and climbed into the driver's seat. He sighed, looking back at his daughter, who had to sit in the center of the backseat because of her wings. "You sure you're ready for this? Leaving home at fourteen? It's a big step for anyone, superhero or not."

Chloe took a deep breath. "I guess I'd better be, huh? At least some of my classmates seem cool."

"It'll be good to have a fresh start, eh?" He gave her a wistful glance as he pulled out onto the street. "I know you could use that."

She nodded, not wanting to think about how the summer had gone. "New friends will be good. And lots of training, I hope."

He laughed. "I hope Mustang Sally can keep up with you. I still can't believe your luck, getting your idol as a combat instructor."

"Oh! I don't think I told you who Lindsay is!"

"Other than your roommate?"

"Yeah," Chloe said. "She's Katie Malone's daughter."

"Wait, the Deep Six hero? *That* Katie Malone?" Everyone knew about the one and only breakout from the parahuman prison in Montana and the woman who'd brought down a plane to end it. She'd been a rookie guard at the time but was now deputy warden. "Is everyone at the Academy famous?"

"Seems like it, right? And the ones who aren't yet probably will be someday."

CHAPTER FOUR

Tuesday, Aug. 16, 2016
Denver, Colorado

"We're pulling onto campus now! Oh my gosh, it looks so big in person," Chloe told her mom on the phone. "I'll call you later and tell you about everything, okay? Love you, too."

She hung up and stepped out of the rental car into the heat of the day. It would take some getting used to—Denver summers tended to be several degrees hotter than home, and she thought it might be a little drier as well. Chloe looked around at the brick and cinder block buildings making up The Hero Academy's campus. She had the map memorized: In front of them stood Heroes Hall, which housed the auditorium and all the administrative offices; she could see the library to the left, and behind it, the five-story dormitory; next to the dorm and behind Heroes Hall was the quad; training and academic buildings lined the rest of the quad; and beyond them all and down a hill was a small stadium.

The campus seemed enormous for just thirty-some high school students and the handful who stayed on to train for another two years. It covered at least three times the ground of Lake City High, the school of fifteen-hundred where she would've gone at home. Then again, some superhero work required a lot of space. After all, she'd covered a good chunk of North Idaho forest learning to fly.

To the east, she could just barely see the white tent-like points of the Denver Airport terminal, where she and her dad had landed last night. To the west and just a few miles away, Denver's tall buildings towered over the suburbs. Beyond the city stood the Rocky Mountains, so much taller than the mountains she was used to. The higher elevation would take some getting used to, as well—she couldn't seem to catch her breath. She had wondered if the thinner air would make flying more difficult, but some early morning experimentation had proven that wouldn't be a factor.

Chloe wore a lime green and white sun dress she thought looked good with the iridescent green in her wings. As with all her shirts, her mom had modified the back into a harness-like design to accommodate the dual sets of wings. Goggles hung around her neck. She always wore them since she never knew when she'd want to get off the ground, and taking a bug in the eye at high speeds? Not fun.

"There's the Just Cause headquarters." Her dad pointed across the field behind them at a massive building surrounded by tall barbed-wire fences, like a prison. Until they had opened Just Cause New York, the Denver facility had been the headquarters for the world's premier superhero team. Now it was just one among several facilities spread across the country.

"Wow, it's that close?" She stared at the building she'd seen so often in news reports and the butterflies she'd had all morning kicked up again.

"Yeah, this is all government-owned land." He gestured with both arms. "In World War II, the army used it for making chemical weapons."

Chloe put her hands on her hips in a classic superhero pose and added a thunderous, operatic lilt to her voice like a '60s radio announcer. "And now it's used for making weapons against crime!" Phil gave her a you-gotta-be-kidding-me look and they both burst out laughing.

"Ten bucks if you can keep a straight face while you do that." He put a hand on her shoulder and led her toward Heroes Hall, where the admissions letter had told them to check in. Inside the front door, ceilings soared above a spacious hall. An enormous blue circle around a gold HA—the familiar Hero Academy logo—adorned the center of the floor.

About a half dozen kids Chloe's age, all with at least one parent and a few with siblings as well, stood in line at a door across the hall. A sign above the door indicated it was the auditorium, and taped below it, a piece of paper said *NEW STUDENT ORIENTATION* in block letters. She stood at the end of the line, leaving a good distance between herself and the girl in front of her—Rhiannon, she remembered from the girl's picture on ParaFrosh. She recognized Jacob from his pictures as well, and she was pretty sure Izzy and her brother Miguel stood at the head of the line, but she didn't see Lindsay. Or Zayden. No one appeared to notice her, so Chloe hung back and stayed quiet. She couldn't help but notice how normal they all looked—she was the only obvious parahuman. She folded her wings back as tight as she could.

"Is it ten o'clock yet?" she asked her dad.

He checked his watch. "About two minutes till."

The door behind them opened and a girl and her mother hurried in, breathless. With their fair skin and pale eyes, they looked just alike except for their hair color—the mother had auburn while the girl's was jet black and hung in a sleek ponytail half way down her back.

"See, Mom, I told you we'd be on time," the girl said. Chloe realized it was Lindsay.

"Barely," her mother muttered.

Lindsay rolled her eyes, then saw Chloe and lit up. "Hey, roomie!" Lindsay hurried over, spread her arms and hesitated, trying to figure out how to hug a girl with four wings, then threw her arms around Chloe's neck.

Taken off guard, Chloe gave her a hesitant hug in return. "Um, hi."

"Have you met everybody yet? Who all's here?" Lindsay asked.

Chloe stammered, not wanting to say she'd been too shy to talk to anyone. To her relief, the auditorium door swung open and the line moved forward.

A deep voice greeted the kids just inside, but Chloe didn't realize who it belonged to until she stepped through the door—and her heart leapt into her throat. *MetalBlade! I can't believe it!* He was not only a legend, but a heartthrob. How many posters and calendars had she seen of the handsome black man with the beguiling grin? She'd known he was the principal, of course, but seeing him in person brought home what it meant to be here: she and these other ordinary-looking kids would someday be heroes, working for Just Cause or the Champions or even as the rare independent heroes. Despite the press coverage she'd had, she'd never been able to imagine really being famous. If Academy graduates had proved anything, though, it was that heroism came with a whopping side of celebrity status—plus criticism and hate in equal measure.

MetalBlade directed the parents to sit to the left of the aisle and the students to the center section. Butterflies again in full flutter, Chloe took a seat between Lindsay and the blond girl. She glanced to her left, past her roommate, and realized someone else had come in at the last minute—Zayden Lord! With shaggy blond hair and bright blue eyes, he was even cuter in person. Her heart raced. *How nervous can a person get without just exploding?* she wondered.

On the stage sat the faculty. Among them, Chloe spotted Icebreaker—Ingrid Jordan, Dean of Students and MetalBlade's wife. Her beauty was even more legendary than her husband's, thanks to dramatic high cheek bones and ice-blue skin. Beside her sat Chloe's long-time idol, Mustang Sally, still as blond and pretty as always, even though Chloe still missed the long braids that used to be her trademark. Head spinning, Chloe thought she just might explode after all.

"Are you dying?" Lindsay asked. "Mustang Sally, our teacher!"

Chloe giggled. "I was just thinking the same thing! I can't believe I'm in a room with a bunch of famous heroes."

"You're kinda famous, you know that, right?" Lindsay asked. "I saw the video of your wings popping out on YouTube and it had like a billion views."

"Yeah." Chloe blushed like crazy and wished she could control it. "It was so weird—I thought about flying from one bar to the next, and suddenly I was hovering there between them! Took me forever to figure out what was going on."

"That's so cool!"

"Kinda . . . but I lost the meet."

Just then, MetalBlade—Mr. Jordan, Chloe reminded herself—walked onto the stage and took his place at the podium. The murmur of the crowd died out.

"Welcome, Hero Academy class of 2020, our twentieth graduating class!" His smooth, deep voice boomed through the speakers. Everyone applauded and a few students cheered. He introduced himself and the faculty and staff members behind him. "And this year, we're delighted to have a new combat instructor—none other than the legendary Salena Tibbets, whom you probably know better as Mustang Sally."

Applause broke out again, and Chloe cheered with the rest.

Once it became quiet again, Mr. Jordan continued, talking about the relatively brief but rich heritage of the school and parahuman community. "An example of that heritage is with us here today. Katie Malone, will you stand up?"

He looked toward the parents and Lindsay's mom rose.

"Katie is with us today for a very special reason. Her daughter, Lindsay, starts school here today. Stand up, Lindsay. I hear you inherited her mother's abilities with fire, and then some. And after looking over your transcript, it looks like she passed on her intelligence, as well."

Lindsay stood, face red, and gave an awkward little wave before plopping back down.

Mr. Jordan continued. "Being a hero comes with a lot of publicity, and a few incoming students have had an early taste. Jacob Cotton, please stand up. I'm sure you've all heard of Jacob's bravery during the horrific flooding in South Carolina last year, when he used super-speed to rescue children from a rapidly flooding daycare." He broke for applause as the broad-shouldered black boy rose with a sheepish grin. "We also have Chloe Wyld, the competitive gymnast whose dragonfly wings made a rather dramatic appearance a few months ago." More applause. Chloe stood and glanced around, then sat down as fast as she could. "Last but not least, Zayden Lord, who has made headlines for no less than seven rescues in the past six and a half years." Zayden got the most enthusiastic clapping. He half stood, looking humble, then took his seat as Mr. Jordan continued. "I'm certain this class will go on to great things, as so many of our graduates have. I'll stop yammering at you now, and if you'll step back out to the foyer, the school registrar is waiting to give you your room assignments and class schedules. Then, you can get moved into your rooms, we'll have lunch, and then it'll be time to say good-bye to your families."

"Okay, that was so embarrassing," Lindsay said as they filed out.

Zayden looked over his shoulder, grinning, his blue eyes almost seeming to sparkle. "Yeah, I don't think I'll ever get used to it. I wish people wouldn't make such a big deal about everything we do."

Chloe's mind raced as she thought about his cute Midwest accent and struggled for a response that didn't sound stupid. She breathed a sigh of relief when he turned away and kept walking, which he did with a slight limp. He joined his mother, who looked thinner than she had in the documentary—too thin, actually—and moved like a skittish bird. Chloe noticed she had a strange bald spot on the back of her head she'd tried, without success, to cover.

Chloe's dad caught up to her. "Hey, how does it feel being so famous that MetalBlade even knows who you are?"

She shot him a please-stop-embarrassing-me look. "He's the principal, Dad, it's his job to know who I am." Secretly, though, she thought it was pretty awesome.

They all formed a line and each student came away with a large blue envelope. As Chloe stepped to the side to open it, Lindsay scanned a piece of paper from her own folder. "What's your schedule look like?"

They compared them as they followed the group to the dormitory and found they were almost identical, except for math—Lindsay had a more advanced class—and Abilities Training. Lindsay would be with the pyrokinetics for that, Chloe with the other winged fliers.

"So will you help me with math?" Chloe asked. "I'm kind of hopeless."

Lindsay shrugged. "Sure. You can check my spelling. Mom says she's always surprised when I get my name right."

Lindsay's mom chuckled. "She's not exaggerating."

Chloe giggled, nervous about talking to someone as famous as Katie Malone.

They walked through the dorm's front door into a small reception area where a guard sat behind a desk, a bank of monitors on one wall showing the hallways on each floor. The guard smiled and nodded as they passed by through the open door into a lounge area featuring two couches, some beanbags, and a round table with several chairs. A metal door in a direct line from the entrance opened on a staircase, but they didn't head that way—all the freshmen lived on the first floor. The hallway to the left, according to a sign, was the "Girls Wing," with the "Boys Wing" to the right.

The right side of the girls' hall contained the bathroom and an open door marked "Isabella." Across the hall, the first door said "Ava & Rhiannon" and the second one belonged to them. Several blank doors filled the rest of the hall, which ended in an emergency exit.

"Izzy, hey!" Lindsay stopped at the open door.

Izzy hurried over and hugged her. "Hey, it's so good to finally meet you! How cool is it you're right across the hall?"

"I know, right? Izzy, did you meet Chloe online?"

Chloe had already opened their door and gone in. She turned and gave Izzy an awkward smile and wave. Izzy waved back and she and Lindsay chatted like they were old friends, until someone down in the lounge called to Izzy and she jogged off that direction.

Chloe had stayed in a lot of dorms for gymnastics camps and meets, and the room was larger than she expected. She noticed Lindsay's desk had a regular chair but hers had a stool. She thought that was weird and then realized a stool would accommodate her wings a lot better. That's when she realized something odd. "Why is the furniture wood instead of metal, like in most dorms?"

"Oh, that's in case of magnetic powers," Mrs. Malone said. "Makes for fewer mishaps. Of course, Linds, you'll have to be careful with your fireballs."

Lindsay rolled her eyes. "Jeez, mom."

Chloe nodded. "Makes sense, I guess. I never thought about how hard it would be to design rooms for all kinds of crazy abilities."

Mrs. Malone sighed. "There's definitely some special challenges."

"I guess you'd be the expert on that," Phil said, referring to her job at Deep Six.

Mrs. Malone nodded. "Keeps us on our toes, for sure. The school, too. I read up on the security here, and once the doors between the wings are closed, it takes a passcode to get in, and they've got motion and temperature sensors in addition to cameras to account for things like speedsters and invisibility."

"Is there always a guard at the door?" Lindsay asked.

Mrs. Malone shook her head. "Usually just at night, and when a parent is scheduled to pick someone up, so they can sign them out. Otherwise, someone monitors the cameras from the security office."

When they went out for another load, they heard Izzy and her mom speaking Spanish across the hall. Lindsay noticed Ava and Rhiannon's door was open and stuck her head in. "Hey, guys!"

Rhiannon flashed a big smile that almost looked too wide for her face and came to the door. "How awesome is it to be here?"

"So cool!" Lindsay looked past Rhiannon to the Asian girl digging through a suitcase on her bed. "You must be Ava. I'm Lindsay and this is Chloe. We're next door. Have you met Izzy yet?"

"Lindsay, I'm gonna get more stuff unloaded. Nice to meet you two." Chloe smiled at the two girls and followed her dad back out to the car.

"So, your roommate seems pretty outgoing," he said.

Chloe nodded. "Uh, yeah. For sure."

He smiled. "That's good, I won't have to worry about you sitting alone and studying all the time."

"I wouldn't study *all* the time. I mean, I have to train, right?"

"I don't want you doing that all the time either, Chloe. This isn't gymnastics. You don't want to burn yourself out."

"I won't, Dad."

After a few trips laden with Chloe's clothes and personal effects, they headed over for lunch. They walked into the dining hall one building over to find the older students already seated around large tables. Sophomores wore regular clothes but the juniors and seniors all sported custom-made costumes featuring the Hero Academy logo. They all stood, clapping and whooping as the freshmen came in and made their way to empty tables off to the right. One girl had purple skin and burgundy hair, a muscular boy sported ram-like horns, and a guy stretched from normal height to about eight feet tall to see over the people in front. *Maybe I won't feel so freakish here, after all,* she thought. She noticed a girl pointing at Zayden and whispering to her friends as well as several people eyeing Lindsay's mom. She didn't know if she wanted anyone to recognize her or not.

"Hey, dragonfly," a boy yelled in her direction. "Lemme see your wings!"

Chloe looked for the voice's source—a tall, lanky red-head with beautiful moth-like wings spread out on full display. The top set had tan veins running through black, and the bottom set featured black spots over the same orange shade as his hair. Chloe spread out her wings, buzzed them a little, and lifted a foot or so off the ground. The closest kids put their hands up to ward off the breeze buffeting their faces. The winged boy gave her a huge grin and a thumbs-up and she blushed.

"Oh, wow, those are cool." Zayden came up beside her. "They're so loud, and they move crazy fast."

"Thanks." She searched for anything else to say. "Um, why are you limping?"

He shrugged and looked down at his feet. "Sprained my ankle last week."

Once again, she found herself at a loss for words. She sat down next to her dad, turning the chair sideways to accommodate her wings. It excited and terrified her that Zayden sat on her other side. Lindsay and Mrs. Malone sat across the table, along with Ava and her parents. Lindsay asked the others what math they were in and found no one else at the table would be in Trigonometry with her.

She sighed, looking disappointed. "Does that mean I'll be with sophomores or something? I won't know anyone!"

Her mom chuckled. "Honey, you're one of thirty-seven students here. You'll know everyone within the week. Sooner, if I know you at all."

Servers delivered food to their tables before long, and the meal exceeded Chloe's expectations. "This is nothing like my middle school lunches."

"They have to serve fresh food here to make sure everyone gets the protein and vitamins they need while training," Mrs. Malone said. "Paras tend to require more calories, too."

Chloe's dad chuckled. "Yeah, we're familiar with the caloric needs, aren't we?"

"Dad!" Chloe shot him another please-don't-embarrass-me look.

He winked. "I read something about special nutrient-packed options, too, so you don't always have to rely on volume. I might need to get those recipes before you come home for the summer."

A few staff members got up and spoke while everyone ate. First up, the tech teacher. Mr. Hutson was tall and balding with a goatee and wore loose jeans with a comic book t-shirt. He told them about Parable, the school's social media platform. Homework, club meetings, and other campus information were on there. "And, of course, you can chat and share status updates and photos. Teachers can even stream their classes live when you're sick." He said the freshmen would get invitations to download the secure app so they could upgrade from ParaFrosh.

"And now for the big announcement a handful of you have been waiting for. My freshman computer lab intern for this year is . . . Miguel Machado!" Mr. Hutson paused while everyone clapped and the boy she figured had to be Miguel cheered from the table next to them. He looked just like Izzy—same terracotta complexion and dark eyes, same shoulder-length black hair. "Congrats, Miguel, on following in your big sister's footsteps. I'd say they're hard to fill, but that sounds like I'm insulting her feet and I know better than to make Lucia mad at me."

Some of the older students laughed and someone yelled, "Smart man!"

Then Icebreaker—Mrs. Jordan—went over some campus rules, such as being careful when using powers, never using them in anger, for pranks, or to cheat, and not being a dangerous distraction to the locals by doing things like flying or running along the freeway. They weren't allowed to leave the immediate area without a parent or other designated adult, and if they did leave, she asked that they let their classmates know and mentioned Parable as a great way to do that. "You can send a private message to your friend or roommate, or post something everyone can see. It's only visible to students and staff, and we old people are just on when there's a problem or we need to get a message out." She also told them doors had to remain open when a boy and girl were in a room together, and they weren't to be in each other's wings at all after nine p.m. "I know those rules are binary- and hetero-normative and I'm sorry about that. We're working on changes to account for the full spectrum of orientations and genders."

Lunch ended, and the time had come for parents to leave. Outside, Chloe led her dad well away from the others and gave him a big hug.

"I love you, Daddy," she whispered, voice cracking.

"Love you too, kiddo." He kissed the top of her head. "We're going to miss you."

She could only nod for fear of breaking out in tears she did not want the other kids to see. After a wistful look and a fist bump, her dad tucked his hands in his pockets and ambled off toward the parking lot.

* * *

Chloe and Lindsay smiled at the replacement sign they'd hung on their door: *WyldWing & Fireball's Room.*

"It almost feels like we're real heroes, doesn't it?"

Chloe giggled. "Yeah, kinda."

They'd already covered their walls with Chloe's gymnastics medals and photos of Lindsay hiking and camping with friends in central Montana. They'd laughed to discover they'd both brought Mustang Sally posters, although Chloe had a recent one and Lindsay's dated back to Sally's first year in Just Cause. *And* it was autographed.

"Hey, guys," Ava called from the lounge. "Come join us."

When they arrived, Ava did a quick head count. "Who's missing?"

"Zayden," Chloe said right away, then flushed.

"Can you get him?" Ava asked, pointing toward the Boys Wing. "First door on the left past the bathroom."

Lindsay grabbed Chloe's arm and charged to Zayden's door, knocked, and called his name. He opened the door.

"Everyone's getting together in the lounge. Wanna come?"

"Yeah, sure." He stepped out into the hallway and stopped short when he saw Chloe. They stared at each other for a few seconds and Chloe tucked her wings in tight. Zayden seemed to recover his wits first and grinned. "Hey, did I hear you already have a hero name?"

"Um, yeah. WyldWing, with a 'Y' in '*Wyld*.'"

He cocked his head. "Yeah? Why the '*Y*'?"

Chloe's face got hot. She turned to follow her roommate back to the lounge so she didn't have to look him in the face. "'Cause it's my last name. I thought it it'd be kinda cool to keep part of me in it."

Zayden followed, shoes squeaking on the hard floor. "Yeah, that is cool. I've thought about using my last name somehow, too."

Lindsay scoffed. "Lord? Sorry, dude, that's so He-Who-Must-Not-Be-Named. No way could you use it without sounding like a villain."

He shrugged. "You're probably right. Sounds sorta pretentious, too, doesn't it?"

With the couches full, Chloe plopped into a beanbag while Lindsay lay down on the floor with her elbows on a big pillow. Zayden grabbed another floor pillow and sat next to Chloe. From the corner of her eye, she thought he was studying her but dismissed it as wishful thinking.

"Did everyone get the Parable app?" Ava asked.

Realizing she'd forgotten to, Chloe pulled out her phone and got it downloading while they went around and introduced themselves. The only one Chloe didn't already recognize was L.J. Vincent. He was tall, skinny, dressed all in black with a bright pink mohawk flopped over to one side, and sat hunched over a sketch pad.

"What's L.J. stand for?" Lindsay asked.

"Lumber Jack," he said without a pause.

She screwed up her face. "Really?"

"No." He went back to his drawing.

"So, are you guys identical?" Ava asked the twins. They looked at each other and burst out laughing. Ava looked perplexed. "What?"

Izzy stifled her laughter. "Identical twins are *totally* identical. In every way, including between the legs? Boy-girl twins are always fraternal."

"Oh." Ava squirmed.

"So who has codenames already?" Lindsay pointed to herself, then Chloe. "Fireball and WyldWing here."

"I wanted us to be Mas and Menos," Izzy said. "It's Spanish for more and less, but Miguel doesn't like it."

Her brother sighed. "Yeah, 'cause we'd have to explain it all the time."

"So?" Izzy threw her hands up. "Luc and I think our names should reflect our heritage. Once we're famous, everyone will know what it means."

L.J. put up his hand. "Mine's DaVinci. 'Cause I can make my drawings into real stuff."

"Whoa, that's awesome!" Miguel said. "So Jacob's a speedster, Zayden's telekinetic, Chloe flies . . ."

"And I heal fast," she added.

Miguel nodded. "Cool. Fireball—that's pretty obvious. What's everyone else do?"

"I'm a brick," Ava said, using the slang term for someone super strong who can take massive amounts of damage.

"Sonic scream," Rhiannon said. "How 'bout you guys?"

"I can increase someone's powers," Miguel told them, "and Izzy can shrink them."

"Sweet, so you can make me run even faster?" Jacob grinned at the thought.

"That'll be handy when I need to heal, for sure," Chloe said.

Ava looked sidelong at Isabella. "Remind me to stay on your good side."

Everyone laughed. Izzy held up a hand. "I swear, I will use my powers only for good! No making anyone weak or drop out of the sky or anything."

"What are you drawing?" Lindsay asked L.J.

"Oh, um," he held up the sketch pad so everyone could see an airplane schematic with startling detail.

"Make it real," Miguel urged.

Izzy slapped him on the arm. "No way, stupid! It'd be way too big."

"Well, not really." L.J. swiped his fingers over the paper and turned his palm up to reveal a small plane. The now-blank piece of paper showed no signs of being drawn upon. "It's actual size. If I really concentrate, I can about double it."

"So if you can make anything you draw real, why don't you just draw a million dollars?" Ava asked.

L.J. shook his head to get his hair out of his eye, but it settled right back where it had been. "It only lasts for like, an hour or so. And it's exactly like the drawing. See here," he pointed to the airplane's cockpit. "I hadn't drawn in the windshield yet, so there isn't one. Have you ever tried to draw a dollar bill? I'd make more per hour mowing lawns."

"Hey, do you have any other drawings?" Miguel asked. L.J. nodded. "What of?"

L.J. shrugged. "Some weapons, but mostly cool tech stuff."

Miguel's eyes grew big and round with excitement. "Let's go outside and see if I can help you make stuff bigger. And maybe last longer, too."

"Yeah, all right."

The two guys took off toward the door, and Jacob hopped up to follow. Miguel turned back. "Zayden, come with us."

With a glance at Chloe, Zayden got up and limped out.

Izzy rolled her eyes. "We'll never see Miguel again if he gets to play with tech stuff. He's totally envious of paras with computer or electrical abilities."

Once all the guys were outside, Ava leaned forward to whisper, "Chloe, did you and Zayden already know each other?"

"No, we just met today." Chloe's face got hot again. "Why?"

"He's so into you," Ava said.

"Why would you say that?" Chloe squirmed under the attention.

Rhiannon giggled. "She's right. He barely took his eyes off you the whole time he was here."

"He *has* started conversations with you, like, multiple times," Lindsay added.

Chloe sat there stunned, not knowing what to say.

Ava saved her from having to respond. "Does anyone know why we have to share rooms when there's all those empty ones?"

Izzy shrugged. "It's supposed to be some team-building thing, I guess." She got an apologetic look on her face. "I have my own room. I mean, someone had to 'cause there's five of us, right? But anyway, the reason I got it is to protect you guys. When I shared a room with my big sister, sometimes she'd wake up with no powers."

"What does your sister do?" Chloe asked.

"Lucia absorbs energy and can redirect it in all kinds of ways. Some of the other seniors started calling her Hoover last year, but she hates it."

"My brother Bridger's a junior," Rhiannon said. "He has super hearing, so even my quiet scream can totally mess with him. It's kind of hilarious."

Chloe sighed. "I wish I had brothers and sisters. It's lonesome being an only child."

"Yeah, it is," Lindsay agreed. "Especially growing up in the middle of nowhere. I had a whole six kids in my grade last year."

"Does everyone know about Zayden's brother?" Ava asked. "The evil little kid?"

A shoe squeaked and they looked up to see Zayden had come back in. He stared at them in silence, then turned and skulked down the hall to his room. The lounge stayed silent until his door shut.

Rhiannon winced. "Oops."

Ava rolled her eyes. "I didn't mean anything by it. Guess it's a sore subject or something."

* * *

Chloe couldn't sleep. She felt tired, but she couldn't get past the excitement of being there at the Hero Academy.

All the freshmen except Zayden had gone to dinner together that evening. L.J. said Zayden was lying on the bed listening to music and wouldn't respond to him at all.

"I suppose I should apologize to him." Ava pouted like it was a big inconvenience. Chloe didn't think she looked sorry at all. She and Lindsay agreed they weren't crazy about Ava, but the rest seemed pretty cool.

She'd called her mom before bed and told her everything. By the time they hung up, she felt exhausted enough to conk right out. She didn't, though. Fed up with lying there in the dark, she took her tablet out to the lounge to read. Before long, she dozed off on the couch.

"He's not evil." Zayden's voice startled her awake. She twisted around to see him standing in the doorway to the boy's hall wearing a white t-shirt and plaid pajama pants. He walked in and sat down at the table. "My brother. He's not evil. He just doesn't understand what he's doing."

Chloe sat up to face him, resisting the urge to smooth down her hair and wishing for a little lip gloss, but she decided that, living on the same floor, he'd see her this way sooner or later. "No one thought he was. Well, except for Ava." She rolled her eyes to let him know what she thought of her. "I saw the *Heroes Among Us* episode and thought it was really sad. He looks so sweet in all the pictures."

Zayden nodded. "Yeah, he is. Well, was. He's not much of anything anymore, just a shell of a kid hooked up to machines."

"I'm sorry." It sounded lame, but she didn't know what else to say.

He gave her a shy grin. "Thanks. You're pretty cool, WyldWing."

Chloe blushed and looked away. "So like, do you get recognized everywhere?" She regretted saying it when Zayden furrowed his brow.

"Yeah. At first, it was kind of awesome. Like I'd get free ice cream at restaurants and stuff." He sighed. "But then it got annoying. I couldn't go anywhere without someone asking me to levitate them or bend spoons or some stupid thing. Then we moved so Mom would be about half way between the Academy and Dax, and at first the new town was pretty bad, but then I guess everyone got used to me and stopped caring. It's better in a small town—you're not always running into new people."

"Yeah, I'm not so good with the blending in anymore. There's really no way to hide these things." She shifted her wings and Zayden stared at them long enough that she got uncomfortable. "So, where'd you move to?"

"It's called Hays, just a few hours away in Kansas. We used to be farther south. As soon as Dax went into the hospital in Kansas City, Mom wanted to move to be close to him, but Dad wouldn't. Once they were divorced, though, Mom and I moved right away."

"That must be hard, being away from your brother and your dad."

"I still see my dad plenty. He even brought me to Denver a couple times over the summer so I could check out the campus and see what it was like around here." Zayden shrugged. "Plus we're all in the same boat now, aren't we? We're all away from our families."

"Yeah, I guess so. It hasn't really sunk in yet, though."

Zayden stood up. "Well, I guess I should try to sleep. Good night, Chloe." He limped to the doorway and turned back. "Can I . . . touch your wings? Just to see what they feel like?"

She swallowed hard as she stood. "Uh, yeah, I guess."

She went to him so he wouldn't have to walk more on the hurt ankle. He reached out a tentative hand and she felt his finger run along the edge of an upper wing. "You shouldn't try to hide them. They're really beautiful." He flashed a heart-melting grin, punched in the code for the boys' wing, and limped back to his room.

* * *

From the TV series Heroes Among Us, *Season 2, Episode 7, "The Lord Family: Triumphs & Tragedies"*

Segment 3

While Dax's condition remained unchanged and his parents' relationship faltered, Zayden Lord continued to make headlines for daring rescues.

In 2010, the Lords attended a barbecue in a neighbor's back yard. While the homeowners and their guests ate outside, their three-month-old baby slept inside. The grill was knocked over and the house caught fire. Without a thought for his own safety, Zayden ran inside. He couldn't see for the smoke, so he concentrated on the baby's cries and levitated the baby girl from her crib and out to his arms.

In 2011, an earthquake struck Lee's Summit. Anna and Zayden took shelter in a grocery store, and when the shaking stopped, they emerged to see the roof of the pet store next door had caved in. Zayden went to work, clearing rubble telekinetically, digging the animals out. While some died in the collapse and others later succumbed to injuries, Zayden was credited with rescuing scores of puppies, kittens, and other animals as well as two store employees.

That's when the shy boy first spoke to television news cameras.

"I just want to help people, like the heroes in Just Cause."

That's Dax you hear screaming in the background of that clip. Anna held him off to the side and couldn't quiet him. Nathan thinks he knows why.

"Dax was just smart enough to be jealous of the attention Zayden got, and he tried to steal the spotlight every time. But you can hear—it's gibberish. 'Nawsay, nawsay.' What's that supposed to mean? I'm sure Anna has some silly answer to that question, but come on. It's nothing."

CHAPTER FIVE

Wednesday, Aug. 17, 2016
Denver, Colorado

Chloe kept yawning over breakfast Wednesday morning, to the point that everyone teased her about it. Lindsay imitated her in over-dramatic fashion, which just made her yawn more.

"Stop, you guys." She giggled, happy for the jovial atmosphere. She didn't know why, but she'd woken up unsettled, as if she'd had a bad dream she couldn't remember.

Then Zayden yawned, trying to conceal it behind his hand.

"Oh ho!" Ava exclaimed. "You're *both* tired this morning? Is there something you need to tell us?"

Zayden grinned, looking sideways at Chloe and making her stomach flutter. "What we talk about late at night is between us. Isn't it, Chloe?"

She blinked rapidly, stammering, unable to put words together. Lindsay saved her.

"We should get going. History's in one of the far buildings, and it wouldn't look good for the whole class to be late the first day."

They shoved final bites in their mouths, gathered up their trays, and hurried out to follow their Monday-Wednesday-Friday schedule. Chloe fell in behind Zayden on the way out and noticed he wasn't limping anymore. "Is your ankle better?"

Zayden looked suprised and glanced down. "Huh. I hadn't even thought about it today, so yeah, I guess it is."

Aram Halabi taught Parahuman History, which seemed appropriate, since he was the oldest known living parahuman. More than a hundred years old, he appeared more like twenty-three.

"Good morning, freshmen!" he boomed with a light Middle Eastern accent as they entered. Their assigned desks were in alphabetical order by last name, four in front and five in back. Chloe gave a mental eye roll at seeing she had to sit next to Ava. *Great, four years next to the one I like least.* L.J. sat on her other side, next to Lindsay, who was next to Zayden. Lindsay gave her a "sorry" look and Chloe shrugged in return.

"All history teachers over forty make the bad joke about being there for most of it," Mr. Halabi said, "but in my case, it's true. I remember hearing about the first known parahumans, courtesy of the French scientist Georges Devereaux. I remember when the Musashi genetic test became available—in fact, I was among the first test subjects in my country, and for a long time, I thought the test must be mistaken. We had no way of knowing my aging process had slowed to a crawl after I hit twelve. As powers go, it's not terribly helpful in a fight, but that's fine with me. We're not all meant to be heroes."

Next came Psychology, where the seating was still alphabetical but with the desks in a circle. Chloe didn't get why Psych was a required class until Mr. Rodriguez, an empath, told them where his lessons would focus.

"It's hard to be different, especially at your age." He stood in the center, wearing flip-flops, faded bell bottom jeans, and a weird multi-colored poncho. He reminded Chloe of the bearded Mexican stoner guy in old movies her dad liked. "The first U.S. military parahuman squad was called The Freak Show—did you know that? No one wants to be a freak, right? And even for those who are lucky enough to gain celebrity status . . ." He gave Zayden and Jacob pointed looks. "The pressures of fame can be tough to handle." He turned to L.J. "Did you color your hair or did it come with your powers?"

L.J. looked up from his sketch with the characteristic hair flip. "Oh, uh, I did it."

Mr. Rodriguez's eyes landed on Chloe next. "Even in a room of parahumans, you stand out, don't you, Miss Wyld? And I'm going to guess that's not always easy."

She smiled and nodded, but she wanted to shrink away to nothing.

He went on to talk about the psychological impact of combat, being responsible for millions of people's safety, and the guilt and grief that came along with the job. Chloe had never considered those things and left class feeling more stressed than when it began.

Language arts came next. "Finally, a normal subject," Lindsay said as they hurried to a different building.

"Normal's boring," L.J. said. "I want to get to Combat Training." Several others agreed as they filed in. Other than being their blandest teacher, Shoshana Zimmerman did impress them by already knowing their names, powers, and other details like where they came from.

"Is it true you remember everything you've ever read?" Ava asked.

Mrs. Zimmerman nodded. "Everything I've read, heard, seen, thought, or experienced. And that includes grammatical rules, so keep your semi-colons in their place and don't dangle those participles." An expectant pause revealed that she thought they'd all laugh. Instead, she got a nervous titter from Lindsay before continuing.

The bell may as well have been a starter pistol with how they all took off at the end of class, heading for the largest enclosed building on campus—the training hall, a massive, five-story tall gymnasium holding a full-sized track surrounding a military-style obstacle course. What hung above them caught her attention more—an aerial course comprising multiple gymnastic-like apparatuses. It beckoned. *Wow, I've found where I belong.*

A door to a small office off to the side opened and they came face to face with the teacher they'd all been waiting to meet: the legendary Mustang Sally herself.

She was shorter than Chloe expected. "Good morning, freshmen! I feel like I'm one of you, being back here after so long." She looked back and forth at them as they stood in a rough semi-circle. "I know most teachers go in for that mister and missus stuff, but please, just call me Sally." She showed them to locker rooms. "You won't get official costumes until your junior year, but you'll get a school uniform, customized for your abilities and physique, in a few weeks. Let me know if you have ideas about what safety features you need." She directed those who needed special clothing to go ahead and get changed.

Chloe put on a leotard and warm-ups along with goggles and the helmet she'd gotten to replace the one she'd shattered against the tree.

"We're going to start by testing you each individually, so I can get a feel for your powers and where you are with them," Sally said once they were all ready. "Jacob, you're up first."

"Man, running for Mustang Sally. I'm not sure if it's a dream or a nightmare," he muttered, then stepped onto the track and bent into a starting position.

Sally counted down and yelled, "Go."

Jacob took off, a blur as he ran circles around the gym.

"And . . . stop!" she yelled. He slowed, once again visible, flailing his arms and stumbling as he tried to stop for another half lap. "Impressive." Sally looked at her stop watch. "You're a little faster than me at your age, but you do need to work on stopping. You won't always have the luxury of this much space and you don't want to spend your career smacking into brick walls. Speaking of . . ."

She had Jacob run the obstacle course next. He clipped his shoulder a few times while trying to go faster than he could control and she promised to work with him on finding a balance between speed and agility. "You're breathing hard—is the altitude getting to you?"

Jacob nodded.

"All of you with athletic powers will notice that, I'm sure. You'll adjust pretty quickly, though. Training at this altitude will improve your stamina better than you would believe."

Next, she had Zayden telekinetically toss around some basketballs and tackling dummies, then hurl some arrows at a target across the gym. The first one arced too much and hit low, the next one bounced off the side of the target, and the third one stuck in an outer ring. "Not bad," she told him. "You seem to adapt quickly." Then she had him stack bricks. When his tower collapsed, she told him his individual training would focus on precision but he seemed ready to go for basic combat techniques.

Chloe flew cleanly through the aerial obstacle course until Sally had Zayden and Ava throw some dodge balls at her. She evaded the first few, but then Ava threw one that slammed hard into her feet. She spun off course and headed for a wall, moving too fast to stop. The memory of smashing into the tree back home loomed large and she was determined to avoid the same fate. She changed direction but clipped the tip of a delicate wing on an obstacle, which compromised her flight. She reached up and grabbed a swinging bar with one hand. Her body jerked to a stop and her shoulder screamed in pain as it dislocated. She flung her other hand up to grab the bar, ignored the pain enough to get swinging, and launched herself forward with decent momentum. That gave her time to get horizontal and spread her wings so she could glide to the ground. *Holy crap, that was ugly*, she thought, half expecting her classmates to hold up score cards with low numbers.

"Not bad at all," Mustang Sally said. "Good quick thinking. All that time in gymnastics paid off."

"Really?" Chloe felt like Sally was humoring her. "I got hit and totally lost it."

Sally chuckled. "It's about survival, not pretty. Getting yourself out of a bad situation means you live. That's a win where I'm concerned."

"You sound like my dad," Chloe said, sheepish. She winced and grabbed her shoulder as it ground itself back into place.

"When multiple people tell you the same thing, it usually means you should listen." Sally gestured toward the injured shoulder. "Need some help with that?"

"No, it'll be fine in a minute."

Next, L.J. manifested a small dagger, which Sally admired and promptly confiscated, and then a revolver. For safety reasons, he'd drawn it without a trigger. He'd forgotten ammunition, though, and the bullets he sketched under pressure didn't fit.

"In combat, your power is going to be all about forethought." Sally held out her hands and he turned over the gun and over-sized ammo. "Plus, we need to find a way for you to carry around a bigger notebook. You might want consider finding a space manipulator to make you a bag or something."

"Miguel can help me make stuff bigger, too," L.J. said.

"Great! Miguel's up next, then. What else have you got, L.J.? Preferably not a weapon."

He whipped out a jetpack with Miguel next to him, concentrating. The pack went from notebook-paper sized to more than three feet tall. L.J. strapped it on and zoomed around the ceiling. They all watched, cheering him on, then saw his face go from exhilarated to terrified—the machine sputtered out.

First Sally, then Jacob became blurs of accelerated motion. Chloe left the ground the next instant, making a beeline for L.J. She almost missed him but managed to snag his arm with her uninjured one. His additional weight strained her wings beyond their lifting capacity, though, and they spun downward together like a deflating hot air balloon.

"Let go!" Sally yelled from below. After hesitating for a moment, Chloe put her trust in the legendary hero and released L.J. He didn't plummet, as she expected, but made a slow, gentle descent into a net Sally, Jacob, and a few others held below.

Chloe landed and caught her breath as L.J. untangled himself and unstrapped the jetpack.

"Guess I made the fuel tank too small," he said, pale and shaking.

Sally let out a long breath. "Okay, let's look at what we did right there, and what we could've done better. Jacob, excellent job getting in place beneath him. What was your plan?"

Jacob shrugged. "Catch him, I guess?"

Sally nodded. "You're certainly fast enough to pull it off, but you both probably would have sustained severe injuries in the impact, or worse. Am I right?"

"Yeah, I guess so."

"Noble of you to think of him and not yourself, but two team members down during a fight is never a good thing. I had an advantage—knowing the environment—so I could grab the net. If I'd been the only one in place, though, it wouldn't have done any good, so at least you got there." Sally turned to the others who'd grabbed the net in time. "Rhiannon, Miguel, and Izzy. Especially well done, since you don't have the advantage of super speed. And Zayden, excellent use of your abilities, slowing his fall. Chloe, if you hadn't intercepted him, we wouldn't have had the net out, and Zayden might not have had time to react." She grinned at them. "What we have here is the beginning of one kick-ass superhero team."

"I'm sorry I didn't do anything useful," Lindsay said. "I tried to get to the net, but I was too slow."

"That's all right, your training will help you learn to think on your feet. Ava, how about you?" Sally asked.

Ava blushed a deep red. "What was I supposed to do?"

Sally looked around at the class. "Anyone have an answer for Ava?"

"You could've tried to catch him," Jacob said. "You wouldn't get hurt."

"But he still would have, and anyway, I couldn't have gotten there in time." Ava crossed her arms, tone defensive.

He shrugged. "You could've tried. These guys got here quick enough."

Ava started to respond, but Sally cut her off. "We all have our strengths and weaknesses, and I think this was a good opportunity for everyone to learn about their own. When you find a weakness, it's not a reason to feel bad or get defensive—it's an opportunity to work on it. Okay, who's next?"

Rhiannon volunteered. They all went into a long padded room and donned hearing protection. Rhiannon opened wide and screamed, shattering a pane of glass. Then Izzy shrank her next scream to just above a whisper.

"Miguel and Isabella, can you affect more than one power at a time?" Sally asked.

The twins shook their heads. "I've tried," Izzy said, "but it's never worked."

Sally turned to Lindsay next. "Let's see what you can do, Miss Malone." Sally directed the others into an observation booth and took Lindsay into a big room with several targets painted on the stainless-steel walls.

Lindsay held up a hand and a gout of flame rose from her palm. She rolled it between both hands, shaping it into a roiling sphere, then wound up like a softball pitcher and threw it. It smacked the wall at an angle and skittered along for a few yards before falling to the floor. She snuffed it out with a wave. Her next few hit the targets, and then, finally, she got a bull's eye and cheered. Then Sally tossed in a straw-stuffed dummy. Lindsay launched two fireballs in rapid succession and, in a flash, reduced the dummy to cinders. She extinguished the remaining flames with another wave. Sally gave a thumbs up from behind the glass.

Back out in the gym, Sally turned to Ava. "So, do you do martial arts or anything?"

Ava looked offended and made a disgusted noise. "What, because I'm Asian?"

Sally looked taken aback. "No, not at all—because you're a brick. Have you had any kind of fight training?"

Ava sighed and crossed her arms. "Why do I need training when I'm already stronger than everyone?"

Chloe's eyes went wide. She'd have been grounded for life if she'd talked to her parents that way, and it had never occurred to her to act like that toward a coach or teacher.

Sally's smile looked forced. "A few years back, in New York, I went up against a speedster who was as fast as me plus a well-trained fighter. Before then, I'd always relied on my speed to keep me out of combat, but I learned that day what a bad idea it is to rest on your abilities. She kicked my ass." She paused, eyes locked with Ava, who wore a so-what's-your-point expression. Sally sighed and went on. "What I'm trying to say is, you're not the only para in the world with super strength, and when you come up against another brick who *has* been training to fight—and most of them love to—you'll regret every hour you didn't spend working out." She rolled up a garage door in the far wall to reveal a junked car and told Ava to do her worst.

Ava sauntered over and ripped a door off, gave it a casual toss, and kicked in a fender without any real enthusiasm. After a minute or so she quit and walked back over to the group.

"Are you worn out?" Sally asked.

Ava shrugged. "No. I just figured that would show you what you need to know."

"Let me decide that next time," Sally said with a tight jaw. "I'm sure you guys are all starving now—why don't you head to lunch a few minutes early?"

They went to the dining hall exhilarated and talking about how amazing everyone's abilities were. "How are we supposed to focus on math and science after that?" Miguel asked. Then it got quiet as they pounded down as much food as they could before the bell rang.

"Wish me luck." Lindsay headed off with the twins to Trigonometry.

As predicted, their afternoon classes had them yawning, in spite of Mr. Reyes, a.k.a. Shrink Ray, demonstrating his shrinking ability and Mrs. Mathis making a vine grow around Rhiannon's legs.

After their last class, they went back to the dorm, where some did homework and chatted in the lounge while others went to their rooms. Chloe decided to take a nap before dinner.

* * *

Fire. Black smoke. Fear. Chloe inhaled, breathing the heat from the fire and the smoke from the air. Somewhere, people screamed.

A girl in a yellow swimsuit on a high dive. She'll hit her head!

A balloon in the wind.

A pole fell. Daddy who wasn't her daddy pinned, his pain louder than the screaming below.

Eyes burned.

Coughing out the smoke. Can't let them die!

She knew she wanted to help, but she was doing all she could and feared it wouldn't be enough. It was hard, since she wasn't even there. The harder she worked, the more her eyes burned.

Chloe woke up feeling anything but rested, remembering fragments of the dream at first. By the time she got out of bed, it had evaporated from her memory and just left her anxious. She kept rubbing her eyes and had no idea why.

* * *

From the TV series Heroes Among Us, *Season 2, Episode 7, "The Lord Family: Triumphs & Tragedies"*

Segment 4

Nathan and Anna reunited in early 2012, shortly before tragedy struck once again.

A car hit a power pole in front of their house one summer night, and when Nathan rushed to help the woman and child inside, the pole slammed down onto the roof and pinned him face down on the passenger seat. Zayden, surrounded by neighbors in the front yard, tried to lift the pole off his father but was thwarted—by Dax, who stood above them all, looking out a second-story window. The glass had broken out, and witnesses say they became terrified of the little boy that night.

"I couldn't believe it. Little Daxie had always seemed so sweet, but the way he looked, standing up there making these strange sounds, his eyes blazing red? He was focused right on that pole when it fell, I saw it, and Zayden begged him to stop, to let him help their daddy. And when Zayden got the pole off, Dax started screaming and clawing at his face like some kind of crazy person."

Nathan would recover, but not without extensive surgery and months of painful rehabilitation. Dax, for reasons doctors don't understand, permanently lost his vision that night, his brown eyes and even his pupils turning white. He also became listless again, slipping in and out of consciousness, and stopped making even the few sounds he'd been capable of.

Police and reporters began asking about the numerous calamities the Lord family had witnessed, giving Zayden so many opportunities to be a hero— wondering if those so-called accidents hadn't in fact been caused by Dax.

"Lock him up, lock him up." *Neighbors overheard and began picketing the house, saying Dax had to go away—somewhere, anywhere—so he wasn't a danger to anyone else.*

It was time for Anna to face a truth no mother wants to confront.

"That night, Zayden came and curled up in my lap. He was so scared, and I thought it was because of Nathan's injuries. But then he asked me, did I think Dax would hurt him like he'd hurt Daddy. And I just knew I had to put Dax in an institution, to protect his brother."

CHAPTER SIX

Thursday, Aug. 18, 2016
Denver, Colorado

Tuesdays and Thursdays meant a lighter schedule. The freshmen had Intro to Criminal Law together, then split up for foreign language classes and Abilities Training.

Their law teacher, Jamal Kirby, demonstrated the proper procedures for taking a suspect into custody by pretending to apprehend and arrest a mirror image of himself. It got confusing trying to keep the two of them . . . two of him? . . . straight, until Lindsay noticed the backward monogram on duplicate's shirt pocket.

Next, Chloe went off to Spanish with Zayden, L.J., and Rhiannon, the twins and Jacob headed to Japanese, while Lindsay and Ava went off separately for their first customized Abilities Training class.

Lindsay chewed a ragged fingernail as she walked by herself into the stainless steel room off the main gym, where she found a tall, fit woman in athletic wear setting up straw targets.

"Hey, you must be Lindsay," she said. "I'm Michelle Donovan, I'll be working with you and the other fire users. Have you met Austin and Kaci yet?"

Lindsay shook her head. Two older students entered the room, looking fit and ready to burn some things. Austin Mann, a tall Native American with compact muscles, had black hair pulled back in a short ponytail. Kaci Taylor had spiky blond hair with red and orange tips that resembled flame. It really popped against skin so fair it was translucent. She exuded a powerful aura despite her willowy frame.

"Let's just sit and talk for a bit about what each of you can do." Ms. Donovan had them sit on the floor in a circle. "Kaci, why don't you go first?"

"I can start fires, obviously. I have a limited range—only twenty feet or so, but I'm working to increase it. Plus I can put them out. And I can sense flame, too."

"Can you put out fires that aren't yours?" Lindsay asked. Kaci nodded. "That must be nice—I can only control mine."

Austin went next. "I can torch anything I can see, put out my own fires or others if they're not huge, and I can direct them, too."

"I create fire from my hands." Lindsay demonstrated with a flame on one fingertip. "And I can shape them into fireballs and throw them. That's really all, though. Once I throw it, I can either put it out or let it burn, nothing else."

Donovan nodded. "Interesting range of abilities, here. It'll be fun to see how you can team up to make the most of them." She told Lindsay she was a power mimic, able to take on other paras' abilities for a short time by touching them. She borrowed Lindsay's powers and they threw together for a while so she could get a feel for it. Austin directed Lindsay's fireballs as well a small fire Kaci set. Kaci attempted to extinguish the fireballs while they were in flight. It didn't work at first, so Ms. Donovan switched her mimicry to Kaci's powers and showed her how to aim where the fireball would be rather than where it was at that moment. She called it *leading the target*, and likened it to a quarterback throwing a football to the spot where a receiver would be on his route. By the end of class, Lindsay had already made some improvement and was thinking about how she, too, could lead targets by throwing fireballs ahead of them.

"Good job today," Ms. Donovan said after the bell rang. "Think about what your limits are and next time we'll come up with strategies for expanding them."

The three pyros high fived and went to have lunch together.

* * *

Sophie LeBlanc called herself LeMot, French for "The Word." She had a unique parahuman ability called omnilingualism. With only a few sample words, she could derive an entire language and understand it with better than eighty-percent accuracy. She could have worked for any corporation or government and named her price, but she preferred teaching at the Academy instead. The students challenged her and she switched effortlessly back and forth between Korean, Navajo, and Gciriku, which she said was a Bantu dialect out of Africa. L.J. asked if maybe the woman was putting them on, because how could they know if she was speaking real languages? Ms. LeBlanc smiled and said they should worry first and foremost about passing her course.

After language and then lunch, Chloe and the others split up for their two hours of Abilities Training. She headed down the hill to the open-air stadium to find Michelle Donovan awaiting her, goggles around her neck. The moth-winged red-headed boy and a short, stocky African-American boy with jet-black bird wings were already there, limbering up their wings. They stood in the middle of the large space, which would be an athletic field at any other school. The sun beat down on them, making sweat bead up on Chloe's forehead, but she couldn't wait to get into the air—she loved feeling the sun on her wings.

Ms. Donovan asked them to introduce themselves and Chloe went first. "Chloe Wyld. WyldWing."

"Charlie O'Neal," the moth-winged sophomore said.

The junior with feathered wings and aviator sunglasses nodded. "Justin Sharp."

"You each fly in slightly different ways," Ms. Donovan said, "determined by your wing type. Still, you have a great deal in common and can learn a lot from each other. Later in the year, we'll have some competitions with the non-winged fliers, who do things totally differently." She looked at Chloe. "I've never had dragonfly wings before. If I can touch your arm, I can mimic them and get a better idea how to work with you. Is that okay?"

Chloe shrugged. "Yeah, sure." She started to ask if Ms. Donovan's shirt would accommodate the wings when the instructor took off her hoodie to reveal a close-fitting athletic top with an open back.

Ms. Donovan put a hand on Chloe's upper arm for a few seconds and sprouted identical wings. She experimented, giving them a little buzz before lifting off, then making a clumsy circle overhead. "These are tricky. Any advice?"

"Um, have you done any gymnastics?" Chloe asked.

She nodded. "A little when I was young."

"You want to be in pencil body. Really rigid. Kind of like planking."

The instructor nodded, lifted off, and, doing much better this time, dove back down toward them and stopped to hover five feet off the ground. "Wow, these have a really different feel from moth or butterfly wings. Do you tilt your entire body to maneuver?"

"Yeah, that's what works best. The tighter and straighter I stay, the better I do."

Ms. Donovan nodded. "Okay, let's see how your speed and maneuverability compare to these guys. Justin, why don't you lead us in a few formations? Chloe, just follow along."

Justin flapped his wings with a *whoosh*, generating a strong breeze. Charlie pulled up the goggles from around his neck and settled them in place. The plastic rims looked like burnished copper and seemed old fashioned.

"What kind of goggles are those?" Chloe asked.

"Steampunk," he said, which meant nothing to her at all. "Pretty cool, huh?"

He fluttered his wings and took off after Justin. Ms. Donovan gestured for Chloe to go next. Goggles up, she lifted off with a buzz, the instructor close behind.

It didn't take long to see the differences in how they each moved through the air. Justin banked wide, tipping his wings and gliding around curves, while Charlie and Chloe could change direction on a dime. Chloe could also raise or drop several feet in an instant as well as fly backward. The two guys moved at around the same speed, but Chloe and Ms. Donovan soon found they were faster, zipping past without a problem.

Chloe grinned and flew loops around them but got blown off course once when she got too close to Justin's powerful wings. She rolled head-over-heels away from him and struggled for several seconds before recovering.

"Let's race!" Ms. Donovan called. Chloe pulled up alongside her. "To the flagpole and back." The instructor pointed to the immense American flag on the stadium's upper rim. "On three." She counted.

Chloe darted forward, buzzing at top speed, and took the lead. She made a mistake and looked back over her shoulder, which sent her off on a slight angle and allowed Ms. Donovan to make up a lot of distance. Chloe doubled her effort and focus, and in moments she arrived at the pole. She flew around it and streaked back toward the starting point, seeing she didn't have the lead she'd hoped for. The two guys watching from the ground appeared little more than a blur. Moments later, she reached the starting point and turned around.

Her brow furrowed when she didn't see any sign of Ms. Donovan in the air. She looked down toward the guys and realized the instructor lay on the ground near them. Chloe zipped down. "Are you okay?"

"I'm exhausted." Ms. Donovan gave a tired chuckle. Chloe helped her up. "It was amazing, though—I've never flown that fast without propulsion. I can't get over how fast those wings move." She looked at the guys. "Sorry boys, we've got an aerial speedster here now. You just became the rear guard."

"That was some crazy flying." Charlie fist bumped her.

Justin smiled and shook his head, his inky black wings arched high over his shoulders. "Damn, girl. I get up over forty-five miles per hour and you were crushing me."

"So, Chloe, do you have any more bursts in you?" Ms. Donovan asked.

"Sure." She shrugged. "I can go for a couple hours, usually. Not *that* fast, but close."

Ms. Donovan went to a closet and came back with a radar gun. "All right, WyldWing, let's see just how fast you fly. Give me a few laps at a normal speed, and then really push it."

Chloe took off around the stadium, saving energy for a burst of speed on the last half lap. Winded, she touched back down.

"Your first few laps, you were streaking along between forty and fifty." Ms. Donovan raised an eyebrow. "But in the final sprint, you hit sixty-three miles an hour."

Charlie whistled through his teeth.

* * *

Thursday, Aug. 18, 2016
Kansas City, Missouri

Misteya Michaels perched on the edge of a stiff-backed leather chair facing Dr. Huxley's zebra wood desk and stifled a yawn. The intern had yet to adjust to the early morning schedule he insisted upon, but it didn't dampen her determination to impress him. As the first African-American woman to snag an internship in this department, she'd make damned sure her performance didn't bar the way for the next one who applied.

"So, Misteya, what are your conclusions regarding our young patient?"

Wishing, as always, that he'd just call her Misty, she slid her glasses up and pushed a stray hair back. A few ultra-curly brown wisps had escaped their braids, and the air conditioning vent above her head made them wave around her face.

Her mentor knew she'd spent the last three days pouring over Daxton Lord's records, including brain scans from the past four years and Dr. Huxley's meticulous notes, jotted down in neat, even script that defied every stereotype of his profession.

"I believe the advisory panel is mistaken in their diagnosis. The excess activity in his brain can't be explained simply by those parts taking over his vital functions. He's shown double the activity and quadruple the connectivity necessary for homeostasis in a healthy brain. That's not just abnormal, it's exceptional. I've compared his scans to those from known psionicists, and his levels are consistent with parahuman abilities like telepathy and telekinesis. With those abilities documented in his history, I don't see how I could come to any other conclusion." She leaned forward, intent. "He's reaching out."

"You're not just saying so because it meshes with my opinion?" Huxley asked.

Her mouth twisted into a wry smile. "Not at all. Actually, Doctor, I'd love nothing more than to prove you wrong, but my own research seems to support your hypothesis."

He chuckled. "Your advisor mentioned you had a reputation for that. He said it like it was a bad thing, but it's why you're here. In my opinion, that should be the goal of all scientists, at all times." He leaned forward, his elbows on the desk. "Back to Dax, now. What do you make of the recent changes in his scans?"

She rifled through the folder on her lap and pulled out a newer scan. "This much activity here and here?" She pointed at areas lit up like the Vegas strip. "It has to be a surge of his abilities, and since nothing is flying around the hospital, that rules out telekinesis. My conclusion is he's either using telepathy in a new way, or we're seeing something new and undocumented before now. Has anyone reported strange things in the hospital?"

"I've asked the administration and department heads to notify me immediately if they hear anything, and no one has." He shook his head. "Once again, we're in agreement. We may have to bring in a ringer just to give us someone to argue with. I believe Dax is trying to contact someone, and he's either dictating a novel or not having much luck."

Misty nodded. "That makes sense. That much cerebral activity suggests a lot of effort on his part. Poor kid is screaming and maybe nobody is listening." She frowned. He raised an eyebrow. "What is it?"

She considered the best way to word her response, taking the time to appraise the doctor sitting across the desk from her. He was unusually intuitive, to the point where she wondered if he was a secret parahuman with empathic abilities. "I had another idea, based on . . ." She rifled through the folder again, pulling out another brain scan and pointing at different spots as she talked. "This, right here, where it's all orange, and the red on the rim of this region. I saw something similar in the Periscope case report from Dr. Devereaux last year."

Preston Huxley owed his career in parahuman neuropsychology to working in Paris alongside Grace Devereaux, who'd founded the field and remained its leader. He perked up, intrigued. "And?"

"Periscope is a remote viewer, which is one of the rarest abilities. Here, I brought a couple of his scans too." She pulled them from the folder and laid them on the desk alongside those of Daxton Lord. Even accounting for normal variation between human brain activity, there were clear correlations and pattern similarities between the two. The difference, though, would have been obvious even to a layman. If Periscope's brain scan was a candle, Dax's was a searchlight. "Even when he worked the hardest, Periscope's brain didn't generate near the activity we're seeing in Dax's brain." She paused for several seconds, studying Dr. Huxley as he cocked his head, eyes narrowed. "Is it possible, based on what you know of Dax, that he has this power as well?"

Dr. Huxley drummed his fingers on the desk as he looked over the scans. "Given the levels of his telekinetic and telepathic abilities—in as much as we've been able to measure them—a third ability, and a strong one at that, would make this little boy one of the most powerful parahumans on the planet."

* * *

"Here just three months and you're already the pet intern." Rachelle poured another cup of coffee and sat down to a stack of charts. She was the ward nurse and Misty's closest work friend. The fluorescent light above them flickered and started to hum.

Misty snorted. "I don't think that's true at all. He can't even remember to call me 'Misty,' even though I've told him to probably a dozen times."

Rachelle chuckled. "It's precisely because you're his pet that he calls you by your full name."

"What do you mean?" Misty asked.

Rachelle sipped some coffee and winced as it burned her tongue. "Damn, that's hot. You know how in every movie and TV show where a researcher or professor has a female intern, they're having an affair?"

Misty laughed. "Yeah. Even though in real life most of them are gross?"

"Exactly." Rachelle rolled her eyes. "Dr. Huxley hates that stereotype and he's paranoid someone will suspect him. So he's excessively formal with all the young women in the hospital—especially the ones he likes."

"But he's gay," Misty blurted out without thinking.

Rachelle's eyebrows went up. "What? He is?"

Nice one, idiot, Misty chastised herself. "Uh . . . well, I thought so. My gay-dar, you know? Just a vibe I get or something."

"Well, if he is, you're the only one who knows it. Besides, why would he hide it? Who even cares, anymore?" Rachelle slid the coffee cup over and grabbed the top chart, then glanced up as the light flickered again. "Damn, that's gonna drive me crazy."

Misty stood up and climbed on a chair. She didn't know the full story behind why Dr. Huxley hid his orientation, but she got a feeling it had to do with his mother, an ultra-conservative evangelical. His "friend" Victor had called once while she visited, and while he looked calm and cool, she knew he'd just about panicked. Huxley had never said anything about it, but Misty didn't need to be told aloud to know. That was her special gift.

"What in the world are you doing?" Rachelle asked.

"Sometimes you just have to tap it." She hit the butt of her hand against the light fixture and delivered a covert burst of electricity. The light brightened, nice and steady, and the humming stopped.

"Thanks, you saved my sanity." Rachelle sipped her coffee, swore as she burned her lip again, and focused on the charts and forms in front of her.

Misty wandered down the hall and went in to Dax's room. "Hi, Dax!" She made her voice bright and cheery. Silence greeted her. She sat on the stool beside his bed, rubbed her palms on the metal side rail to discharge any residual energy she might have accumulated, and then took his hand. "What do you have for me today, Daxie?"

She felt a tingle in the center of her brain and closed her eyes, focused on the sensation. A few moments later, an image began to take shape. Misty reeled, dizzy as the feeling of forward movement overtook her senses. Whomever Dax was watching hurried along a dark hallway. The walls were close, the ceiling low, but the edges of his field of view were fuzzy, and details were indistinct, like she was watching through a lens smeared with grease. His feelings came through loud and clear, though: Dax was upset about the person being there and desperate for someone to stop the stranger, but she couldn't feel why it was so important to him. After a few minutes, she got flashes of intense heat and fear—things he'd sent her before. Then Dax's mind withdrew from hers, and refocused on his obsession, watching through someone else's eyes. Whose eyes were they? He was calling out, transmitting an urgent message, but why? And what was the message? It was like he was broadcasting on an empty radio channel, desperate for someone to hear his call, but the only reply was silence.

CHAPTER SEVEN

Friday, Aug. 19, 2016
Denver, Colorado

Chloe awoke with a start, heart racing. She sat up on the side of the bed, shaking all over, and leaned forward with her head in her hands, afraid for a moment she might puke.

Breathe, she told herself, *nice and slow. It'll all be over in a few minutes.* The mantra had always helped her during gymnastics meets, and while it automatically kicked during times of stress, she didn't understand why she needed it now. She figured it must've been a dream, but she couldn't remember it.

As she calmed down, elusive fragments tried to break through the haze in her mind. Black smoke. Intense heat. Someone familiar. *But who?* The fleeting memories vanished a moment later. She checked her phone and she'd awakened forty-five minutes before her alarm would sound. It was no use trying to get back to sleep, she decided, so she slipped on a robe and flip flops and headed across the hall to the girls' bathroom. She figured she might as well shower before the morning rush.

Just as the bathroom door swung closed behind her, shoes squeaked on the tile floor in the lounge. Wondering who would be coming in at this hour, she peeked back out around the edge of the door to see Zayden's back to her as he punched in the code to the boys' wing.

What the heck? He'd been up late their first night on campus, and now he was up early on the fourth morning. It seemed weird, and then she realized she only knew that because she'd been up at those times, as well. *I guess he's having some trouble getting adjusted, too,* she thought. Still, she couldn't shake an uneasy feeling and decided it must be because he'd startled her.

* * *

"How'd your exam go?" Lindsay asked when Chloe got back to their room that afternoon. Each of the freshman had been pulled out of class, one after the other, for start-of-the-year physicals.

Chloe shrugged. "They poked at my wings and back muscles a lot, told me to look for the high-protein options in the dining hall, and that was about it." She grabbed her training clothes out of the closet. "I need to go work the obstacle course. I feel like I've really slacked off this week."

Lindsay gaped. "Slacked off? I've never trained so much in my life. Of course, I can't exactly throw fireballs just anywhere."

Chloe laughed. "Yeah, I can see you off in the woods, just chucking fire around, having fun."

"Right? We're working on control and precision in Abilities Training, but there's only so much you can do with it."

"I've spent the last few months out flying almost every day," Chloe said. "And before that, it was nine years of gymnastics, six on the competing team. Flight and Combat Training are awesome, but I need more physical activity. Sitting around is the worst." She changed into a modified leotard and warm-up pants and headed over to the gym, excited about getting to spend serious time with the aerial obstacle course at last.

As she walked in, she found Sally heading out. "Hey, Chloe. Did you need something?"

"No, just here to train." Chloe stripped off the warm-ups and stretched her wings and back.

"On a Friday afternoon?" Sally's eyebrows went up. "Wow, that's dedication. Good job, you. Me, I'm done for the week. Netflix is calling my name." She winked. "Until I pass out. Sleeping has always been my hobby."

Chloe's face went hot, wondering if Sally thought she was being an overachiever or a suck-up. Nevertheless, Sally wished her a good weekend and left. The silence of the massive space reminded her of the early mornings at the gym she'd always loved. She needed to get here as often as possible, she decided. This wasn't the time to get soft.

After a quick stretching routine, she took off and went to one end of the course and plotted some paths through it. The options boggled the mind, she realized, when one approached it with three dimensions to travel. She went through it at a nice, easy pace several times, exploring different routes and methods. After her warm-up laps, she picked up speed for several passes. She pushed herself to react faster and maneuver through difficult areas with greater efficiency and economy of motion.

On the floor, the gym was already hot. Up around the ceiling it was sweltering, and the higher temperature soon had her dripping with sweat. "Ugh, time for a shower," she muttered, but then had a better idea. On the flight into Denver, she'd seen a small lake not far away, in the middle of the government reserve where nobody would stop by to hassle her except maybe some curious deer. She headed outside. In spite of the blazing sun, the fresh air felt cool as she flew up over buildings and toward the shimmering water in the distance.

She reached the lake in minutes, even at an easy cruising speed. From the air, she snapped a pic of the water and posted it to Parable without a comment. *Let them figure it out*, she thought. Something in the center of the lake caught her eye and she swooped down to check it out.

A concrete rectangle jutted three feet above the surface. It was big enough for two people to stretch out upon so long as they were good friends. A rusted pulley sat along one edge and a ladder poked up from the water beside it. After two circles around the platform, she gave in to the promised coolness of the water.

She skimmed low across the surface, her wings kicking up spray that tickled her bare arms and legs. She couldn't fly with wet wings, but she could dry them in seconds the way she did after a shower. She angled down, tucked everything in tight, and plunged through the glassy surface. A moment later, she allowed herself to bob up, and rolled over onto her back. With her wings splayed out to the sides like they were pontoons, she could float forever.

Feeling cooled and refreshed at last, she stared up at the blue sky and the top fringes of the sparse trees at the lake's edge. She marveled at how quickly flying had become normal for her. While she hadn't had a choice about leaving gymnastics, flying was a better rush even than standing on the podium to receive a first-place ribbon. At the Academy, she felt less pressure than she'd been under for all those years on the team. Most of her life had been a constant push for perfection. Now, the luxury of moments like this made her grateful for the changes her wings had caused.

Chloe decided to head back to land and let the warm sun dry her wings instead of vibrating them dry when she heard a loud splash. She turned and saw what she first mistook for a mermaid. The lithe figure breached the surface in a graceful leap, hung in the air for a moment, and then splashed back down. She didn't have a fish tail—just legs held tight together. *Good form,* Chloe thought as she swam toward the girl, who surfaced a moment later.

"Hey," Chloe called as she pulled her goggles down. "Sorry if I startled you."

The swimmer wore her black hair in a pixie cut emphasizing her angular cheekbones and large, dark eyes. As she got closer, Chloe noticed blue-tinged scales along the girl's hairline, the color fading into a skin tone that suggested Asian ancestry, and ruffly-looking gills down the sides of her neck. "I sure didn't expect to see a flier out here. Not exactly your element, is it?"

Chloe laughed. "I got overheated working the aerial obstacle course and thought this would be a good way to cool off. I'm Chloe. WyldWing."

"Clara Sato, but I prefer Ondine."

"That's pretty. What does it mean?"

"It's a type of fairy. A water sprite." Ondine shook her head and water flew off like crazy.

"I take it you can breathe under water?" Chloe asked, gesturing toward the gills. "Must be why I didn't see you sooner."

"I was down on the bottom when a shadow went over me and I came up to see who was here."

"Do you know what that concrete thing is? Out in the middle?"

Ondine nodded. "It's a hatch. You know how they used to make chemical weapons here? I guess they kept them underground, and they built this lake—and the hatch at the bottom—so they could flood the tunnels. As a safety precaution."

"Cool, I wish I could see it better, but I'm guessing that would be tough without gills." Chloe squinted at the structure. "It must be awesome to stay under as long as you want."

"Yeah, it is. I speed-swim, too, so the pool on campus is way too small—I can hardly get going before I have to turn around." She headed for the shore and Chloe followed.

"Yeah, I know the feeling. I feel cramped inside, even with how huge the training gym is."

"How fast can you go?" Ondine's speech and movements had a slow, deliberate pace as they walked up on the rocky shore. It lent her a stately and serious demeanor.

"Ms. Donovan clocked me at sixty-three miles an hour in a sprint, but it's usually more like somewhere in the forties. How about you?"

Ondine looked impressed. "Water has a lot more drag, and no matter how good my form, humans just aren't very hydrodynamic. I can hit just over twenty-eight. Doesn't sound that fast compared to you, but I could probably beat a great white head-to-head, especially over long distances."

"Nice!" Chloe's stomach grumbled and they both laughed. "Well, as you hear, I'm starving. I guess I should head back."

"Hey, have you heard of the Obvious Club?" Ondine asked. Chloe shook her head. "It's for those of us who can't hide—the ones people point and stare at. We meet on the senior floor Fridays after dinner. You should come."

Chloe wasn't sure how she felt about that but said she'd consider it. They exchanged good-byes and Chloe watched as Ondine walked back out into the deeper water and disappeared beneath the surface. After buzzing her wings for a while to get them good and dry, she headed back to the dorm.

When she was almost there, she remembered leaving her shoes and pants in the gym, so she went back to grab them. As she walked out, Zayden came from between buildings on the edge of campus. He looked surprised but smiled.

She smiled back. "Hey, where you been?"

He shrugged a shoulder. "Just taking a walk, looking around. Didn't get enough training this week, I see."

"Yeah, I'm a glutton for punishment. Find anyplace cool out here?"

He stopped and looked thoughtful. "I did, actually. Want to see?" He took a few steps backward, waiting for her to catch up to him, then turned around. They went around the building and she followed him up a stairway to a balcony on the third floor that stretched the full width feet of the building. It held a rickety wicker love seat and an overturned bucket for a table, plus a few old soda bottles given new life as ashtrays. Zayden sat and motioned her over. She sat next to him, on the edge of the love seat because it didn't accommodate her wings. She was sure she looked awful.

"It's pretty, isn't it?" He looked out at the view. She turned to see and caught her breath. Over the edge of the hill, they had a spectacular view of the mountains looming beyond a ground-level residential neighborhood.

"Wow. Why would the maintenance building get this, when my room overlooks the oh-so-scenic dining hall?" she asked.

Zayden looked at her for a long time before answering, which didn't help the awkward feelings. "This was the first dorm, back when they never expected to have more than three or four students per grade. They didn't have room to expand it, so they built a new one."

She looked away, unable to keep eye contact for any longer. "The sunset from here must be amazing."

"We should come watch it sometime." He spoke in a soft, intimate tone that gave her goosebumps.

"Yeah, that'd be cool."

They sat in companionable silence for a while before Zayden spoke again. "So what do you want to do with your life, WyldWing?"

She smiled, liking the way her chosen name sounded in his voice. "I guess I want to help people, do good things with my abilities. I mean, that's pretty much the gig, right?"

"You make it sound like we don't have a choice. We do, though. We can do anything normal people can do, and then we get all these other options that are only for us."

She looked at him, forcing her nervous eyes to stop flickering away. "So what do you want to do, Zayden?"

One corner of his mouth turned up and his eyes narrowed as he looked out at the mountains.

"Something big. Something no one will ever forget." He turned to face her. "I'm gonna make history. Maybe we both will."

* * *

"Told you he was into you," Ava said when Chloe told the girls about their conversation on the balcony. She'd taken a quick shower and joined them for makeovers in Ava and Rhiannon's room. Rhiannon, the unquestioned makeup expert among them, sported shiny orange lips and bronze eyeliner. The number of eye shadow pallets, liners, tubes, sticks, brushes, and applicators strewn across her desk overwhelmed Chloe, for whom makeup had never meant more than a little blush, mascara, lip gloss, and—for gymnastics meets—glitter hair spray.

"Okay, maybe he does like me." Chloe sat on Ava's bed and pulled a pillow into her lap.

"How lucky can you get?" Izzy shook her head. "The only hot guy in our class, and he's already famous, and he's into you right away."

Rhiannon paused, mascara brush inches from Lindsay's lashes. "I wouldn't say he's the only hot one."

Ava squealed with delight. "Ooo, who do you like, roomie?"

"L.J.," Rhiannon muttered, ducking her head and going back to Lindsay's eyes.

"Somehow, shipping you two makes total sense," Lindsay said. "And Miguel and Jacob aren't exactly *bad* looking. Pretty decent, in fact."

Izzy made a puking noise. "Gross, don't talk about my brother like that! Seriously, though, Zayden's the catch."

A knot formed in Chloe's stomach as she wondered whether Izzy was jealous and if it would cause problems between them. She felt nervous enough already. "So, what do I do?" she asked. "Okay, this is totally embarrassing, but I've never had time for like, a boyfriend or anything."

"Um, go for it?" Rhiannon suggested.

Lindsay shrugged. "Flirt like crazy?"

"I say make the first move. Get him alone and kiss him." Ava gave her a suspicious look. "I mean, you've at least kissed someone, right?"

Chloe shook her head.

"Girl, get over here and let me give you the evil fairy treatment," Rhiannon said. "That'll get his attention."

Chloe examined Lindsay's makeup job. She looked exotic with bright red lips and eye makeup resembling sparkly flames. Ava had bright pink rectangles around her eyes and down her cheeks in an abstract style that somehow managed to look pretty decent. *They're bricks,* she realized, and it dawned on her that their makeups reflected their powers. She'd mistaken the mark on Izzy's forehead for a weird bindi, but it was actually a stylized minus symbol above dark, smoky eyes.

She smiled at the evil fairy idea. "Okay, sure."

Lindsay hopped up from the chair and Chloe took her place. After using various beauty blenders to get her foundation just right, Rhiannon picked up an acidic green eye shadow that made Chloe shy away.

"What?" Rhiannon said. "It's in your wings and it'll make your eyes pop."

"My eyes are boring brown. They never pop."

A well-drawn eyebrow arched. "Oh, they will when I'm done with them."

Half an hour later, Chloe had to agree. Greens and purples shimmered around her eyes, which she'd never known could look so good. Dark contour under the cheekbones and a deep plum lipstick gave her a dramatic appearance. Rhiannon topped off the look with a high ponytail.

"Wow, Chloe, you look fantastic, like a super model," Lindsay said.

She stared into a hand mirror. "I don't even look like me, it's crazy. Rhiannon, this is your real super power."

Rhiannon gave them a smug grin. "Told you guys I was good. Should we go show it off?"

"Yeah, but a selfie first." Chloe pulled up her camera as the girls gathered around. She snapped a few pics and sent one to her mom.

As they all flounced through the lounge, Chloe could tell they felt extra confident and . . . something else she couldn't put her finger on until Ava did the stupid thing with licking her finger and touching it to her butt with a sizzling noise. *Oh my gosh, I feel sexy!* She hadn't known she could.

They stopped in the open door to the boys' wing. Rhiannon motioned for them all to cover their ears and then yelled, in a medium volume for her, "Hey, guys, let's go to dinner!"

Jacob's head poked from his open bedroom door and his eyes went wide. "What happened to you guys?"

The door closest to the girls opened and L.J. stood in frozen shock, taking a moment to contemplate each of their faces. "Huh. Nice job. Rhiannon's work, I'm guessing?"

Ava giggled and Rhiannon went red.

"How'd you know?" Izzy asked.

L.J. shrugged. "She always does interesting makeup." He squeezed past them into the hall as Zayden stood up from his desk. He turned toward the door and stopped short. Even Chloe couldn't mistake the look on his face this time.

"Whoa. Chloe, you look, uh . . ." he stammered, ". . . wow."

She resisted the urge to chew her bottom lip. "Rhiannon calls it *evil fairy.*"

"Yeah, you look like a sophisticated super villain." He couldn't take his eyes off of her.

Chloe tried to deflect his gaze. "Everyone looks great, don't they?"

He seemed to notice the others for the first time. "Oh, yeah. Cool."

"You look weird, Izzy," Miguel said as he came down the hall toward them.

Izzy sighed and rolled her eyes. "Wow, really? Chloe gets *sophisticated villain* and I get *weird*?"

"Your eyes are awesome," Jacob told Lindsay, making her turn as red as her lips. "You look cool, too, Izzy. You guys all do."

"You're not going to dinner like that, are you?" Izzy's twin asked. She glared at him and turned away, stomping toward the door.

In the dining hall, once they had their food and sat down, two older boys Chloe didn't recognize joined them. "You've been busy, Rhi," said the one with big ears sticking out through long blond hair.

"Guys, this is my brother, Bridger." Rhiannon introduced everyone.

"What's L.J. stand for?" Bridger asked when Rhiannon got to him.

"Ludicrous Jerkwad," L.J. replied, not missing a beat.

"Don't bother trying to whisper anything while Bridger's around—he's a total snoop," Rhiannon said.

"I'm Solomon," Bridger's friend said. He had short black hair, a long nose, and piercing dark eyes that he turned on Miguel. "And you should probably get over yourself because your sister likes how she looks and will probably be wearing more makeup from now on."

Miguel looked shocked and offended and Izzy choked on her root beer.

"Sorry." Bridger pointed at his friend with a french fry. "Telepath with boundary issues. You'll get used to it."

A few minutes later, Chloe looked at Lindsay's eye makeup and got a mental flash of flames and black smoke. She flinched. Solomon's head snapped toward her and she returned his gaze with wide eyes.

You felt that, didn't you? she heard in her mind, startling again. *But* you're *not a telepath. What's the deal?*

"Hey, knock it off!" Zayden's voice boomed. He glared at Solomon and leaned as much as he could between the telepath and Chloe.

Sol stared at him with a disinterested expression and said nothing. Nothing aloud, anyway. *Your boyfriend has a temper. Be careful with that one,* he told Chloe.

"It's okay, Zayden," she said. "He's just joking around, it's not a big deal. Just startled me, is all."

Sol continued staring at him. "You heard me even though I wasn't 'pathing you, and you know how to block me. What's up with that?"

"Yeah, my brother's a telepath. I didn't want him in my head, either." Zayden picked up his tray and stormed off.

"His brother's not crazy, Ava. Cut him some slack." Sol turned to look at Ava, who hadn't spoken. "He's got neurological damage from his powers coming on too early."

Ava went pale.

* * *

Chloe shivered. The gentle afternoon breeze had turned cool and gusty while they ate and ripped the door of the dining hall right out of Lindsay's hand. Ominous clouds swirled overhead.

"Brr!" Jacob, accustomed to balmy southern weather, shivered just before streaking off with super speed, making for the dormitory.

"He's got the right idea. Stand back, everyone." Chloe got her wings buzzing as everyone threw up their arms as shields, and she flew off after the speedster. The others ran after her, hoping to outrace the incoming cloudburst. Moments after the last of the kids made it inside, violent rain smashed against the windows.

"Glad I went flying earlier. I've never seen rain like this!" Chloe flopped onto a big bean bag. She liked the way it molded itself around her wings—way more comfortable than a regular chair. Everyone but Zayden —who she assumed had come back ahead of them— gathered in the lounge.

"Yeah, a blizzard I can handle, but this is crazy!" Lindsay nodded, eyes wide. "So what should we do? I don't want to spend Friday night studying."

"We could play a game, I guess," Izzy said.

Lindsay looked around. "Anyone bring any games?" No one had.

The door to the stairwell banged open. "Any freshman freaks around?" a strange voice bellowed.

Chloe looked up to see the boy with the curling ram's horns standing next to Charlie.

"Hey, Chloe," Charlie said. "Obvious Club's about to meet. Want to come up?"

She hesitated, not sure she wanted to sit around and dwell on being weird, but then she decided it would be cool to get to know Charlie and Justin better, since she trained with them, and Ondine from the lake, too. "Yeah, sure. Right now?"

"Yep." Charlie offered a hand up and she took it, relieved Zayden wasn't there to see.

"See you guys in a while," she said as she left.

"Freak show's about to start," the horned guy yelled when they got to the fourth floor. "We picked up the frosh bug."

"Just ignore him," Charlie muttered. "He played football without a helmet a few too many times—before the horns came in."

Chloe stifled laughter as they walked into the senior lounge, already full of chattering students. Suddenly, she felt too normal to be there. She held back for a moment, stunned by the strangeness of the group and the cognitive dissonance that *she wasn't a freak; she didn't belong among them* even as her wingtips brushed the sides of the doorway. She sat down at the table next to Charlie and hoped no one had noticed her reaction. Ondine nodded from across the table, black hair so shiny it still looked wet.

Justin raised a hand to her from the couch, which was mostly occupied by his wings. "Okay, let's get started." Conversation tapered off. "This is Chloe—WyldWing. If you haven't met her before, introduce yourself." He turned to a girl with yellow cat eyes and hair with orange tabby stripes.

"Hey, Chloe." She spoke with a heavy southern drawl. "I'm Cori, but everyone calls me Cat, for obvious reasons. I've got night vision and I'm a shapeshifter."

The obnoxious guy with the horns leaned up against the wall between couches. He thumped himself on the chest and belched out, "Ramage."

"Way to keep it classy, Jack." Justin shook his head, turning to Chloe. "He's a brick. Big shocker, right?"

"You know the twins," the girl with the purple skin and burgundy hair said. "I'm their sister, Lucia,"

"Oh, wow, you don't look like them," Chloe blurted out, regretting it right away. Everyone laughed.

"No, not so much anymore." Lucia chuckled, not seeming at all offended. "I can absorb energy and use it some cool ways."

"Hoo-ver," Ramage burped.

Lucia whipped around and pointed at him. "Don't call me Hoover, seriously!"

"Okay, now I see the family resemblance." Chloe laughed. "That sounded just like Izzy. If you don't mind me asking, why is your skin purple?"

She shrugged. "No one knows. It just got more purple every time I absorbed something, until I ended up this way."

Beside Lucia sat a boy who looked like a candle gone soft. "I'm Isaac. You can call me Stretch." He reached out to shake her hand, elongating his arm by six feet in order to do so. Chloe shook it.

Justin looked at Ondine.

"We met earlier today, at the lake," the swimmer told him. "She swims pretty good for a bug."

Charlie shuddered.

"You don't like the water?" Chloe asked.

"I can't fly for a couple days after getting wet. It damages the powder—well, scales, to be accurate—and really messes with my wings."

"I can shake the water off of mine, no problem," Justin said, "but they're so heavy they just drag me down."

"Yeah, so's my head," Ramage said.

Cat laughed. "Even without the horns." Lucia leaned over for a fist bump.

"So, Chloe, Mr. Rodriguez suggested this group a couple years ago, and most of us thought it was kinda dumb," Justin said, "but after he got us to meet a few times, we started to see it as a good thing. I mean, we're the freakiest of the freaks, and even other paras sometimes get weirded out by us."

"Word." Lucia leaned back, arms crossed.

Justin continued. "One of our first members was Humbug. You know, with the Champions? She's probably the buggiest looking bug out there—antennae, the faceted eye thing going on, crazy stuff. You got a lot of attention after your wings came in, right?" he asked Chloe. "How big a town are you from?"

"About fifty-thousand people, but we get a ton of tourists, too. Of course, with all the publicity at first I'd practically get mobbed any time I went out. It got so I didn't want to go to the lake, or out to dinner, or anywhere but out in the woods, to train with my dad."

"They made you quit gymnastics, right?" Charlie asked.

"Yeah. My healing factor kicked in when I was a lot younger. They discovered it when I healed from a torn ligament in about an hour. The gymnastics association determined that it didn't give me an unfair advantage, so they let me compete." She sighed. "Not everyone agreed. A lot of parents asked for appeals, especially after I beat their daughters. Then when the wings popped out, they had an excuse to walk it back and cut me immediately. They said the extra muscles in my back plus being able to fly *did* give me an advantage." She sighed. "They were probably right."

"That blows," Ramage said, not sounding like a jerk for the first time. "I got kicked out of football and wrestling, and just when I got really good."

Ondine put up a hand. "Swim team. 'Course, it wasn't exactly a challenge anymore."

"I was never a jock," Isaac said, "but the basketball coach sure tried to recruit me."

They talked for another hour or so and Chloe decided she liked this group. The other kids did seem to understand certain things her classmates didn't.

"I like your makeup," Ondine said as people drifted out. "You match your wings now, the way Charlie's wings match his hair. Doesn't it look good?" she asked Charlie.

"It's cool, I guess." Charlie shrugged, looking down at Chloe. "But you look best when your cheeks are all pink from flying."

Chloe didn't know what to say and wished Lindsay were there to save her.

Cat walked up to them. "Hey, Charlie boy, when y'all starting the game up?"

"Tomorrow. Chloe, you should join us."

"What kind of game?" she asked, pretty sure he was just being polite.

"Tabletop RPGs. I'm not sure what system yet."

Chloe blinked. "I'm sorry, I have no idea what any of that means."

Ondine laughed and waved good-bye as she drifted away from them.

"Role-playing games," Cat said. "Y'all come up with a character and the game master gives you situations to deal with. It's pretty fun."

"You mean, like, Dungeons and Dragons?" All Chloe knew about those games is that the geeky kids at school played them.

Charlie nodded. "Yeah, that's one of them. Every Saturday at one, second floor. We'll be building characters tomorrow. Think you can make it?"

"Yeah, maybe." She shrugged and excused herself, saying she had a lot of reading to do. Mostly, though, she was tired from training and the lake and hoped to see Zayden before turning in early.

* * *

Chloe awoke with a start around one a.m. She'd fallen asleep in the lounge, reading *Lord of the Flies* on the tablet propped up against the back of the couch.

Silence filled the dormitory. She got up and headed toward the girls' hall when something wet soaked through her socks.

Grimacing, she looked down and saw water drops on the tile floor, along with muddy footprints leading toward the guys' door. She peeked through the window and saw they led into Zayden and L.J.'s room. The prints came from athletic shoes, so they had to be Zayden's. L.J. always wore the same black boots.

It started raining after we got back from dinner, though, she thought, *and Zayden came back before then.* She realized she'd assumed he was in his room. Plus, the floor wouldn't take hours to dry. She decided either Zayden had gone somewhere else after dinner, or he'd left the dorm after she fell asleep. Either way, he couldn't have been back for long. She hoped she hadn't been drooling or snoring or anything.

Maybe he went back to the balcony, she thought, getting butterflies as she remembered being there with him. Maybe she'd suggest watching the sunset tomorrow.

CHAPTER EIGHT

Saturday, Aug. 20, 2016
Denver, Colorado

Zayden slept through breakfast Saturday morning, then said he was going to do some training with another telekinetic after lunch. Chloe decided not to bring up the whole balcony-at-sunset thing unless it seemed convenient. She went to work on the obstacle course for a while after lunch and then did homework—with the door open, hoping she'd hear when Zayden came back.

When she realized dinner time had crept up and she hadn't seen him, she checked Parable. He hadn't signed in anywhere or mentioned going off campus. However, she did see an invitation, for earlier, to Charlie's game. She winced, feeling bad for forgetting. She hit the reply button and swiped in, *Sorry, got too busy.* She wondered if she should say more but decided he probably didn't even notice she wasn't there. After all, he'd only invited her because Cat brought it up while she was standing there. She erased the response, figuring she didn't need to call attention to it.

Also on Parable, she came across an announcement from Mr. Jordan. On September 11, the school always had a memorial for those killed in the terrorist attack on the World Trade Center, including the Just Cause members at their headquarters in one of the towers. Over the past few years, it had become a tradition to include an awards ceremony as well, where they honored recent graduates and staff members. This year would be extra special, the announcement said, because Mustang Sally would be getting a lifetime achievement award. Celebrity superheroes past and present would be attending.

"Wow, did you see the announcement?" she asked Lindsay, who hadn't. Chloe filled her in.

"Oh, my God," her roommate said. "Can you imagine how many heroes will be here? I did bring my autograph book, right?" She rummaged through a trunk at the foot of her bed.

"Yeah, you showed it to me when we were moving in."

"Okay, good. 'Cause if I missed that opportunity, I'd never forgive myself." Lindsay didn't find it in the trunk, so she dug around in her desk drawers for a minute before pulling it out. "You go on a shelf," she told the book, adding it to the row of texts above the desk, right on the end, where it was nice and visible.

Chloe squinted, trying to remember something. "Isn't there some policy about not having too many superheroes in one place? To prevent stuff like Destroyer's attack that killed Sally's dad?"

"Uh, yeah, but that's only for Just Cause members."

"Dinner time!" Rhiannon yelled from out in the hall, making them jump and rattling their window. Chloe was pretty sure the whole dorm heard it.

* * *

Zayden joined them part way through dinner.

"Where you been?" L.J. asked.

"My mom drove into town for the weekend and surprised me," he said. "We had lunch and did some shopping in Denver, but she went to see an old friend for the evening."

"You didn't say anything on Parable," Chloe blurted out, then turned red. Not only did she sound nerdy spouting the rules, he'd know she'd checked.

Zayden squirmed. "Oh yeah, I forgot. I'll let you guys know next time." He flashed Chloe a smile and she grinned back, cheeks still burning. She wanted to mention the sunset to him but decided not to do it in front of everyone. She didn't want anyone tagging along—it should be something special between them.

Back at the dorm, she noticed the sign-in book lying open on the desk, with Zayden's name and his mother's signature in small, tight script. She managed to grab a moment alone in the lounge with him and had just worked up the nerve to ask about the sunset when he asked her something first.

"Are you ready for the math quiz on Monday?"

"Oh, uh, not at all." She giggled.

He grinned. "Want to study together?"

Her stomach did a flip. "Yeah, sure. I'll get my book and meet you back here."

Minutes later, they sat next to each other on one of the couches, going over equations. Their feet or legs would touch now and then, and each time it sent an electric tingle through Chloe's gut. Miguel and Isabella sat out there for a while to study Japanese, but they didn't stay long. Jacob came in, took one look at them, and mumbled about needing something in his room. Lindsay peeked in at one point and asked if they'd seen Rhiannon, but Chloe knew she just wanted to see how things were going. A few minutes later, Chloe's phone buzzed and she checked the alert—she had a group message from Lindsay, Rhiannon, and Ava.

Chloe and Zayden, sitting in a tree . . .

She turned off the phone as fast as she could so he wouldn't see.

By the time he yawned and said he was going to bed, Chloe felt more prepared than she ever had for a math quiz. Zayden had been really helpful. Then she realized he hadn't needed help at all. *Did he just want to spend time with me?*

CHAPTER NINE

Sunday, Aug. 21, 2016
Denver, Colorado

Sunday morning, Chloe woke up to find a Parable alert, just to her, from Zayden: *Hanging out with my mom today. Should be back for dinner. Tell L.J. for me?*

She checked email, which still made her stomach clench after the summer of harassment, even though no one from home had her school address. Even so, the top message gave her a start. The subject line read "Winners Only," just like the one she'd gotten before leaving home. She clicked on it and read:

You're special. You're better than the people around you, yet they do everything they can to keep you down. Don't you get tired of that? Don't you want to be part of a group of people like you, who have superior abilities? Of course you're tired of it, and of course you're looking for other parahumans—and not those with just any powers, but those with truly superior abilities. We've left the rest behind genetically, and now it's time to set ourselves apart from them in every other way. Join us now! Be part of something that will shock them into realizing how superior we truly are!

Lindsay came in the room wearing a bathrobe and a towel wrapped around her hair. "Is something wrong?" she asked, seeing Chloe's confusion.

"Take a look at this. I got one like it at home, too." Chloe handed Lindsay her phone.

Lindsay's eyebrows drew together as she read. She handed the phone back to Chloe and hung her towel over the rod on the side of her closet. "Okay, that's weird. What do you think it is? A scam or something?"

Chloe shrugged. "It sounds like some weird para-supremacist thing." She got nauseous just thinking that a group like that would try to recruit her. Growing up in North Idaho, she knew all too much about the area's long history as a white supremacist hotbed. The big group that had plagued the area for decades broke up years ago, but several factions remained. A few had even established small compounds in the dense, remote wilderness of the panhandle. She'd seen enough fliers on windshields and doorknobs to recognize the language. "Do you think we should tell someone?"

"I don't know." Lindsay brushed out her long, black tresses. "Maybe?"

Chloe considered going to Mr. Jordan and decided she'd feel silly if it was just some stupid spam thing, but she'd also had "see something, say something" drummed into her head forever. *I'll tell Mr. Rodriguez tomorrow, or maybe Sally,* she thought. They'd be better judges of whether to take it to the administration.

* * *

Zayden didn't come back for dinner, but as they ate, Chloe's phone dinged.

Want to meet me for the sunset? It was from Zayden.

Yeah, that'd be awesome, she sent back.

7:50. You know where.

Chloe couldn't help but smile down at the phone.

"What's Zayden have to say?" Ava gave her a knowing grin.

Everyone stared and her face went hot. "Stop it, you guys!" Chloe wanted to deny anything was going on. She had to admit, though, that yes, Zayden did seem to like her. She didn't get how that had happened so fast. But she knew she liked him back.

Rhiannon batted fake, jewel-tipped eyelashes. "Ah, young love!"

Jacob, who'd been across the table from Chloe, appeared over her shoulder. "Ooo, they're meeting to watch the sunset."

Everyone laughed and made teasing noises. Chloe whirled around. "Jacob, oh my gosh!"

"Sounds romantic, roomie," Lindsay asked. "Where you going?"

"I'm not telling, so you guys can't show up there and ruin it." Chloe hit the thumbs-up icon and tucked the phone away.

L.J. looked around the table and shook his head. "Wow, guys, you're being seriously uncool. Knock it off."

The laughter subsided, much to Chloe's relief. "Thank you, L.J."

She went back to the dorm with everyone and tried to study, but for the most part, she just watched the clock until about 7:35.

"I'm gonna go fly around campus for a few," she told Lindsay, "before I meet Zayden."

Lindsay grinned. "On the balcony, right? Don't worry—I won't tell anyone. Good luck!"

Chloe thanked her and headed out, leaving her goggles behind, since she didn't want rings around her eyes.

The moment she hit the cooling evening air, she took off and circled the quad, keeping an eye out for Zayden. After a few minutes, she decided that would make it awkward when he did come back, so, squinting into the lowering sun, she flew up over the maintenance building roof. When the balcony came into view, she got a surprise —Zayden already sat there, waiting.

She touched down in front of him. "I didn't expect you to be here already."

He smiled. "I didn't want to be late, so I came straight here when my mom dropped me off."

She wondered how she'd missed seeing his mom, but then Zayden patted the seat next to him and all other thoughts went out of her head. Since she couldn't lean back, he scooted forward so they sat shoulder to shoulder, eyes fixed on her face.

She couldn't meet his eye, so she kept her gaze pinned on the distant mountains and the glorious streaks starting to fill the horizon. "It's so pretty." Her voice trembled.

"So are you."

Her heart and stomach did some complicated flips. "Um . . . thank you." To her relief, he turned and looked out toward the sunset.

"You're special, WyldWing. I hope you know that. You're so much cooler than the other girls."

"How do you know?" she blurted out without thinking, then had immediate regrets. "I mean, we're all just getting to know each other."

"I did my homework on everyone before school started. Everyone I could, anyway. I've seen every video of you online, and read every article about you, too."

"Oh. Wow."

"The training and dedication it takes to be a gymnast, the crazy skills, all the medals you earned." He turned back to her. "And now you can fly. You're like an aerial ninja."

She giggled and forced herself to meet his eye. "You've done some pretty incredible things, too. All the people you've saved? I mean, we all want to be heroes, but I have no idea whether I've got it in me. You, you already know. You're the real deal."

His mouth quirked into a half-smile she couldn't read the meaning of. "You know, Izzy and Miguel have pretty special abilities, too. Imagine the four of us teamed up, what we could accomplish. With our abilities boosted and our enemies' reduced? There'd be no stopping us. All we really need is an opportunity to show what we can do."

"I'm sure we'll get one, eventually. It'd be awesome if a bunch of us could be in Just Cause together, wouldn't it?"

He shrugged. "Or if we started our own group."

"Can we even do that anymore?" She was fuzzy on how things worked now, with government oversight of parahuman groups increased. Just Cause had spread to more cities, and the Champions filled the role independent teams used to occupy.

"Sure we can. Like anyone could stop us?" He raised an eyebrow. "I mean, it's still a free country. For now, anyway."

She laughed. "I suppose we can daydream about whatever we want, right? So yeah, it would be cool to start our own group. Maybe all nine of us, since we'll be working as a team for the next four years."

"Well, we'll see who measures up, anyway." He sat in silence for a few seconds, looking at view. "I'm glad you agreed to meet me."

"Me, too." She took a deep breath, working up courage. "I was really happy you asked."

He gave her a smile that made her weak and turned back to the last remaining rays of the sunset.

It grew dark and they walked back to the dorm. Chloe noticed Zayden's mom had signed him in after all wondered how she'd missed seeing her. *The timing must've just worked out,* she decided.

"I'd hang out more, but I have some homework to finish for tomorrow," Zayden said as they entered the lounge.

"I've got some reading to do, too. See you tomorrow."

He leaned in and, for a moment, she thought he meant to kiss her. She froze, not knowing whether she wanted him to. He just whispered in her ear, though. "Thanks again for meeting me. I really like you, WyldWing."

"Uh, yeah, um. I . . . I like you, too."

He grinned and turned away to go to his bedroom. She all but sprinted to into her room, then leaned back against the closed door, not caring that she smushed her wings against it. "Lindsay, oh my gosh!"

Lindsay lay on her stomach doing math. She dropped her pencil, sat up, and hugged her knees to her chest. "Tell me everything!"

Chloe plopped down on her own bed and summed up what had happened on the balcony and what he'd just said in the lounge.

Lindsay listened with wide eyes. "Oh my God, so are you, like, his girlfriend now?"

"I don't know, exactly, but I kinda think so."

Lindsay gasped. "You guys could be just like Mastiff and Mustang Sally! Only, you know, without the part where he dies super young." Sally's husband, Jason, had been killed three years ago fighting an alien invasion of New York City.

Chloe grimaced. "So . . . maybe more Desert Eagle and Crackerjack?" Desert Eagle led Just Cause-Dallas, and her husband, Crackerjack, had retired after decades as a successful hero—and well-known heartthrob.

Lindsay nodded. "Yeah, them. That's way better."

CHAPTER TEN

Monday, Aug. 22, 2016
Denver, Colorado

"Crap, I forgot my Psych notebook!" Lindsay noticed it wasn't there as she put the *History of Parahumans* text in her bag.

"Is your homework in it?" Chloe asked, leaning around L.J.

Lindsay nodded. "I'll run back to the room—you go ahead without me."

"I can fly back and get it for you," Chloe offered. "It'll be faster."

"I don't want to make you late. Thanks, though!" Lindsay hurried out, sleek black ponytail bouncing behind her.

About two minutes after the bell rang in Psych, the door opened and a red-faced Lindsay rushed in, leaving the door open.

"That's your first warning about being late, Lindsay." Mr. Rodriguez sounded apologetic. "You just get two, then you'll have detention—not my rule, but I have to enforce it."

"Sorry, Mr. Rodriguez. It won't happen again."

"Close the door and join us, please."

As Lindsay hurried to her seat, she tripped over her feet and bashed a shin into Zayden's desk. His water bottle toppled over and rolled off the desk—then stopped midair and rose until he grabbed it and set it back in place.

Lindsay's face grew redder than Chloe had ever seen it and she tried to catch her friend's eye to give her a reassuring look. Lindsay stared at the floor, though, and chewed her bottom lip.

They'd just gotten their papers handed in and started the day's lesson when an alarm rang throughout the building. Mr. Rodriguez startled at stared up at the speaker above the blackboard. "Fire drill? I must've missed the memo. Let's hurry, guys, or they'll make us do this again in a few days."

"Does anyone else smell smoke?" Jacob asked as he headed toward the door.

Zayden sniffed. "Yeah, I do."

Jacob put his face up to the narrow window in the classroom door and peered out. "The hallway trash can's on fire!"

Everyone gasped. "Out the window." Mr. Rodriguez rushed across the room to open it.

"Lindsay, can you put it out?" Chloe asked as they hurried toward their teacher.

Lindsay shook her head. "Only if I created it."

"Where's an extinguisher?" Jacob asked.

"At the end of the hall." Mr. Rodriguez pointed the direction away from the fire. "The teacher closest to it will—"

But Jacob had already turned into a streaky blur and bolted out the door, which he left open. Zayden took the lid off his water bottle and, without moving, sent the bottle sailing out into the hall and emptied it on the flames, putting a good dent in them. A moment later, Jacob arrived with the extinguisher and put it all the way out, the sound of the spray mingling with the alarm. In another blink, he joined them back in the room. "It didn't have time to spread, so it's all cool."

"Still, everyone out—that's the policy." Mr. Rodriguez directed them out one by one, and ushered them to a grassy area well away from the building, where other classes already congregated. "Jacob, it's cool you got it put out so fast, but you gotta think before rushing in like that."

"But—" Jacob protested.

Mr. Rodriguez held up a hand to cut him off. "Think about it for a sec. The breeze you make when you run could've spread the flames and made things a lot worse. Do you get what I'm saying?"

Jacob's shoulders drooped and he shoved his hands into his hoodie pockets. "Yeah, I guess so."

Mr. Rodriguez looked around at them. "Remember, almost everyone here is a para, and lots of us have way more real-world experience than you guys. Let us deal with stuff when we can, okay? We don't want you guys getting hurt." He clapped a sympathetic hand on Jacob's shoulder before wandering over to where the other teachers gathered and talked.

"That rocked, dude," L.J. told Jacob once Mr. Rodriguez was out of earshot.

Jacob gave him a sheepish grin. "Thanks."

"Yeah, it was cool. I mean, aren't we supposed to be learning to think on our feet?" Miguel asked.

"I gotta wonder what started it," Jacob said. "I mean, it was mostly empty judging by what was left. Why would the garbage just burst into flames?"

"You don't think . . ." Zayden started, "I mean, nobody would set it on purpose, would they?"

Chloe thought she saw some looks flicker in Lindsay's direction and a protective instinct rose up. "No, I'm sure not. Maybe a teacher threw a cigarette butt in there or something." She glanced at Lindsay, who looked like a cornered animal.

Izzy gave an awkward shrug. "Yeah, maybe."

"Maybe one of the pyros wanted out of class," Ava said as if she'd stumbled on some choice gossip.

Lindsay's hands went to her hips, face red. "Seriously, you're going to accuse me of this?"

Ava rolled her eyes. "I didn't say anything about you."

"No, but there's exactly three of us at the school with fire powers, and Kaci and Austin are both in Combat Training right now."

Ava looked away, arms crossed. "Well, I didn't know that. How did you know it, anyway?"

Lindsay sighed. "Remember me stopping to talk to them before breakfast?"

"Yeah, I do," Chloe said. "Ava, I think you should apologize to Lindsay."

Ava made a disgusted noise. "I didn't mean anything by it. She just needs to chill."

Mr. Rodriguez came over and told them they could go back in. Amid all the excitement, Chloe forgot what it was she'd intended to tell him. Oh well, she thought, she'd think of it sooner or later.

* * *

"I freaking can't stand Ava!" Lindsay whisper-yelled in their room after class. Her ponytail hung low and limp, so she yanked out the band and ran a brush through it. "A fire starts, so it has to be someone with fire abilities. Can you believe her?"

Chloe shook her head. "It was so rude. Seriously, way uncalled for. If it's any consolation, though, I'm pretty sure no one likes her. Even Sally, and she's super cool to everyone."

"Right? Her attitude sucks." Lindsay gave the ponytail tie one last wrap and it broke, snapping back against her finger. "Ugh!" she yelled and threw the thing down. Her eyes crackled with red sparks.

"Um, Lindsay? You okay?" Chloe asked, a little frightened. She thought over escape routes and the locations of fire extinguishers—half way down each hall plus one at the guard station, if she remembered correctly. Then she felt guilty for even considering it. She wondered if Lindsay ever ignited things by accident when she got mad or frustrated, like she'd been earlier when arriving late to class and then stumbling into Zayden's desk.

Lindsay closed her eyes and whispered. "One, two, three . . ." When she got to ten, took a deep breath, and opened her eyes, now back to their normal blue. "Sorry. I'm good. My mom says I have a redhead temper in disguise." She gave an uncomfortable laugh.

Chloe chuckled, still a little nervous. As much as she liked Lindsay, she had to keep in mind that they'd only known each other for a few days. As she'd learned after her wings' surprise appearance, she couldn't count on people to be who she thought they were. Even after years of friendship, some girls had turned on her in a heartbeat. Or at the flap of a wing.

As she and Lindsay settled in to do some homework, Chloe tried to push the gymnastics team from her mind. They'd known about her parahuman status for three years. It was hard to miss rapid healing in a sport that led to near-constant injury. After the first time she'd been investigated, and found eligible to compete, her best friends on the team, Jessi and Faith, had cheered and hugged her.

After her wings came out, though, they sang a different tune. "How can it not be an unfair advantage?" Jessi had asked. "You can *fly*."

"Yeah, but it's totally obvious when I'm using my wings, and they'll be tied down any time I compete. If anything, they're in my way and a huge disadvantage." Chloe looked to Faith for support.

Faith shifted uncomfortably. "Still, how do we know it's your only power? You could have super strength or something, and that's not fair."

Bursting into tears, Chloe yelled at them. "I don't! They tested me!"

They stared at her, contempt on their faces. "That's what you said before, and then you got another power. I mean, you have extra back muscles. That's *cheating*." Jessi said, and they'd turned and walked away.

That's what had clinched it for Chloe—she decided at that moment to apply for the Academy instead of going to a regular high school. At least at the Academy, everyone was weird and maybe not so judgmental because of it. She'd have given up gymnastics even if she hadn't had been forced to. Her wings were a serious hindrance, and she didn't want to win championships when people would always question whether she'd done it through hard work or *cheated*.

After she'd worked on math and then Spanish for about an hour, someone knocked on their door. Lindsay got up and opened it.

"Hey, can we come in?"

Chloe looked up to see Zayden and L.J. standing there, looking apologetic.

"Yeah, I guess." Lindsay's tone was frosty. She plunked down in her desk chair.

Chloe sat up on the bed and tried to contain the smile that broke out any time she looked at Zayden. He sat next to her on the bed, which she wasn't sure she liked. "What's up guys?"

L.J. straddled Chloe's stool and flipped the pink hair out of his face. "Lindsay, we wanted to let you know we don't think you started the fire, and we should've said so when Ava was being such a bitch about it." He kept his voice low, not wanting to be heard through the open door.

"Yeah, we're sorry we didn't have your back," Zayden said. "We will next time."

Lindsay looked away, blinking hard, before speaking. "Thanks, guys. That's really cool of you to say."

* * *

Chloe and most of the other freshmen gathered together and then left for dinner. As if by silent agreement, no one suggested knocking on Ava and Rhiannon's door. Chloe felt a little bad for Rhiannon, but not bad enough to risk having to deal with Ava.

In the dining hall, they sat at a table with Charlie and Austin, one of the pyros, which left just one empty chair. Before long, Ava and Rhiannon came toward them and all those seated at the table gave Ava a you're-not-welcome look.

"I'm gonna go sit with the other bricks," Ava said, ostensibly to her roommate but loud enough for everyone to hear. "Come on, Rhiannon."

Rhiannon gave her an uneasy look, then glanced at the others. "I see my brother. I think I'll go hang with him for a while." She took off in his direction, leaving Ava to huff and go find the bricks on her own.

"Some drama in Frosh-land?" Charlie asked.

Lindsay rolled her eyes. "Did you hear about the fire in Devereaux Hall this morning?"

Austin's eyebrows went up. "Uh, yeah, that was pretty big news." Lindsay shared details about the confrontation between her and Ava afterward. Austin shook his head. "So not cool to automatically blame us. We get enough crap from normals, it shouldn't happen here."

Charlie nodded in agreement, mouth too full to speak. His tray held more food than Chloe's, and Jacob's came close.

Chloe swallowed a bite. "I have to say, I love how so many people here eat like I do. It was way awkward at home, eating like triple what my parents did, and at school, I pretty much starved because I didn't want to gorge myself in front of everyone."

Charlie laughed. "I remember during the Olympics, they made this huge deal over how much Michael Phelps eats when he's training. I was like, yeah, so?"

"I used to be chubby," Jacob said. "Now, my doctor keeps telling me 'you're too thin, eat more.' I have to down protein shakes all the time just to keep weight on."

Izzy smirked at Lindsay. "Don't you wish you had their problems?"

"Right? Eat a whole pizza and then be like, 'oh, I'll go fly a hundred miles and burn that right off.'"

"After worrying about my weight for so long with gymnastics, it's seriously a relief to just eat," Chloe said.

"I used to kind of like it when I got hurt because healing takes so much extra energy."

"Do you miss it?" Zayden asked.

The question caught Chloe off guard. "Gymnastics? Yeah. A lot." An awkward silence fell among the freshmen at the pain in her voice. "But I have training here to replace it now, and I love to fly, so it's cool."

General chatter around the table picked up, and Zayden leaned over and whispered in her ear. "Sorry I brought it up."

His warm breath on her cheek made her heart pound. "It's okay, really."

"Chloe, do you think you can make it this weekend?" Charlie asked.

"Sorry, what?"

"For gaming? I . . . uh, we missed you Saturday. I was just thinking, training here's probably way less intense than what you're used to. Gaming's a great way to pass the time, and it's sort of like mental training, really."

"Uh, yeah, maybe." She tried to sound genuine even though she had no real interest.

"We can't handle more than one or two more people without it getting too crowded." He looked around at the others, sounding apologetic. "If a few of you guys want to learn how to play, though, I could probably run another game for you."

"That sounds cool," Chloe said. "Let me see how much homework I have, though."

He nodded. "Sounds good. You're welcome to come up Saturday to just check it out, if you want."

Her mouth full again, she gave him a thumbs up.

CHAPTER ELEVEN

Wednesday, Aug. 24, 2016
Denver, Colorado

"With the memorial ceremony coming up, we're going to jump ahead to September 11, 2001," Mr. Halabi said. "I want to make sure you all understand the date's significance in both American and parahuman history."

They all knew several Just Cause members were among the nearly three-thousand people killed that day. The original team headquarters had been in one of the twin towers since the 1970s, when the buildings were new.

"Look around at your classmates." Mr. Halabi paused while they did so. "I would imagine you've had time to start forming some real friendships and seeing how you could work together as a team. Rest assured, those bonds will only deepen over time.

"Just Cause had ten members before that day, the same number as are in this room if you include me. Now imagine four of us, gone, in an instant. That's what the attack did to the most powerful superhero team in the world."

They eyed each other, the gravity of it sinking in. Chloe thought about how they'd treated Ava since her careless words about the fire two days ago and felt guilty. They were supposed to be a team, not splitting apart in their second week of school. Then again, Ava had rubbed everyone wrong since their first day on campus, and she'd never apologized for anything—not for calling Zayden's brother an evil little kid, not for accusing Lindsay of setting the fire, nothing. Still, Chloe wished she knew how to fix everything.

Mr. Halabi went on to cover the attack's aftermath and how the surviving heroes relocated to the Just Cause Second Team headquarters before coming to their current location, just across a field from where the Academy had stood since 2000.

He then had them draw slips of paper from a hat. On them were the names of the four heroes killed that day—Timekeeper, Javelin, Foxfire, and Imp. "Find the other one or two of your classmates who drew the same name. That's your team for a project, which is to put together a presentation teaching the class all about that person. You'll have two weeks to work on it."

Chloe drew Javelin, as did L.J. and Miguel, who immediately geeked out over Javelin's sweet tech. She had a sneaking suspicion she'd have to do a lot of wrangling to get this project done, but at least they had enthusiasm for the topic. She saw Zayden had to work with Ava and felt bad for him, but at least it wasn't Lindsay.

"So here we talked about what happened," Mr. Halabi said after the bell rang. "In your next class, Mr. Rodriguez will help you understand what the survivors went through."

When they got to Psych, the desks were all pushed against the wall and nine big pillows sat in a semi-circle around one pillow, upon which Mr. Rodriguez sat in meditation. Uneasy, they all went in and sat on the floor around him, waiting for him to notice they were there. When the bell rang, he opened his eyes.

"Welcome. I understand your history lesson today focused on one of the biggest tragedies to ever hit our country as well as the parahuman community." He looked them each in the face without saying anything more than long enough to make them uncomfortable. A few couldn't hold back nervous titters. "How are you all feeling right now? Is anyone upset by the lesson?"

Everyone sat and stared at each other until Lindsay broke the silence. "It's hard to think about losing four people you're close to all at once. I mean, I've only lost one person—my grandma on my dad's side—and I wasn't very close to her."

He gave her a thoughtful look. "Lindsay, tell us about your grandma. What was she like?"

She grimaced. "I was pretty young. I don't remember much."

"Tell us something you do remember, even if it doesn't seem important."

"Mostly I remember how she smelled like parsnips and dogs, but that's not very nice to say." She thought for a moment. "I remember baking cookies once when we were visiting. I woke up really early in the morning and cried 'cause I didn't know where I was, and she came and got me out of bed. Her yellow and white kitchen, like, glowed when the sun shined in through the windows."

"That's beautiful." Mr. Rodriguez smiled and nodded as though she'd said something profound. "Who else wants to talk about a loss they've suffered?"

Chloe glanced sideways at Zayden. His head hung way down.

Izzy said something about a middle school friend who'd died, but no one else volunteered anything.

"Loss doesn't have to be a death," Mr. Rodriguez said. "It can be a divorce, or a disability, or even being here instead of at home. Anything." He gave Zayden and L.J. pointed looks, but Zayden kept his head down and L.J. just stared straight ahead. Chloe wondered what the teacher knew about L.J. that the rest didn't. After a while, she couldn't take the uncomfortable silence.

"Giving up gymnastics was really hard," she blurted out.

Mr. Rodriguez turned to her. "Good, Chloe. Tell us what that meant to you."

"I guess I get the whole team thing, like with Just Cause," she began. "I mean, that's obviously way worse, but the girls on my team were like family. They were the only really good friends I had 'cause we were training all the time, and traveling together, and competing together."

"And you lost it all because of your powers?" he asked.

She nodded, emotion welling up and making her wish she hadn't said anything. "I got kicked off the team, and it sucked, but even worse, my season scores were voided, which meant our team didn't qualify for the Finals. My teammates—my *friends* blamed me for it, and turned against me. I lost my sport, everything I'd worked for since I was four years old, and my friends all at once."

"Let's talk for a moment about the concept of 'team' and 'teammates.'" Mr. Rodriguez stood up and meandered as he spoke. "'Teammate' is a specific word for a specific relationship. It's not the same as 'classmate' or even 'friend'—no, in some ways it's much more intimate. Your teammates are people you intrinsically rely upon. You're all supposed to have the same goals, and you're all supposed to work together to achieve those goals. You're supposed to care about and protect each other."

Chloe's guilt over the Ava situation grew.

The teacher went on about the particular difficulties of losing teammates, especially when one felt responsible for protecting them, as well as survivor's guilt. Just thinking about it got Chloe's heart hammering in her chest. She closed her eyes and thought of flying. Soaring through the chill morning air above the woods not far from home. Folding in her wings and diving toward the ground at incredible speeds, then spreading out and gliding. She forced the first few images but then her mind took over, flowing from one to the next. Sticking a landing. Winning a meet. Getting the Academy acceptance letter. Calmer now, she pictured Zayden's smile. Sudden images of black smoke, heat, and fire flooded her mind. Fear sent her heart racing again.

Before she knew what she was doing, she'd run from the room and down the wide hall. She hit the bar to open the exterior doors with her hands stretched out in front of her and only then realized she was flying. The breeze hit and she angled up, flying past the roof, and higher and higher still. Something hit her left eye and it teared up, stinging. That jerked her back to reality and she hovered while putting her goggles in place.

Oh my God, I just ran out of class like I'm crazy or something, she realized as her head cleared. Looking down, she spotted Mr. Rodriguez and her classmates standing outside the building and angled down, free falling for a few seconds and then going into a wide spiral to keep from building up too much speed. Mr. Rodriguez waved the others back inside and she touched down moments later, grateful she didn't have to face them all right away.

"Welcome back to the ground, Chloe. Are you okay?"

She pulled the goggles down. "Yeah, I just got overwhelmed. Sorry to take off like that."

"I'm sorry I wasn't more aware of your feelings. I guess I focused too much on students with more obvious losses, and I shouldn't have. You've lost a lot, too." He gave her a kind smile. "Ready to go back inside?"

She nodded and followed him back to class. Lindsay caught her eye with a concerned look. Chloe mouthed *I'm okay* as she sat down.

Mr. Rodriguez apologized to the class for letting things get too intense. "Let's end class early today, but please, anyone who'd like to talk, stay behind or come find me later today. And please, everyone, be there for your teammates."

Ava strode out ahead of them.

When they got outside, Lindsay tried to put her arm around Chloe's shoulders but kept smacking her wings. "Help me out here, I'm trying to hug you!"

Chloe took Lindsay by the wrists, wrapped them around between the upper and lower wings, and hugged her back. "Thanks," she whispered.

When she drew away, everyone stared like she was fragile. Zayden hovered near by, looking unsure what to do.

"I'm fine, guys," she said. "Just had a little freak-out moment."

"It was kinda getting to me, too," Izzy muttered.

Zayden shoved his hands in his pockets and looked at the ground. "Yeah, me too."

"Hey, uh, I forgot my sketch pad." L.J. headed back inside. "I'll meet you guys in Language Arts."

They had about half an hour to kill, so they went and sat in the grass on the quad.

"I really hate that class," Miguel said.

Zayden sat beside Chloe and nodded. "If it's gonna be group therapy, they should call it that."

"I don't know, I think it's kinda good for us." Lindsay gave them an apologetic look. "I mean, yeah, some things are hard to deal with, but that's the point, right? If we actually work as heroes, we're gonna have to deal with a lot of hard stuff. Like, a lot harder than this, probably."

"Do you think L.J. really forgot his pad or went in to talk to Mr. Rodriguez?" Jacob asked.

"I hope he went to talk," Zayden said. "I think he could use it."

"Why?" Lindsay asked.

Zayden thought for a second. "It's not my story to tell. I'm sure he'll fill you guys in at some point."

"Maybe there needs to be another support group, like Obvious Club but for people who've been through other stuff," Chloe said.

"Does Obvious Club help?" Lindsay asked.

Chloe shrugged. "I mean, I've only been once, but yeah, it's nice to be around people who understand what it's like to go out in public when you stand out."

"Welcome to my life." Jacob sighed.

"You grow up in a white neighborhood, too?" Miguel asked.

Jacob snorted. "Only black kid in my elementary school, one of four in middle school."

"That sucks, man," Miguel said. "Things have been so much worse with the election coming up, too. A kid I've known forever told me to go back to Mexico. I'm like, bite me dude, we were born in the same hospital."

"I think it's actually better for Lucia now that she's purple," Izzy said. "I mean, a few people have called her a freak, but at least they don't think she's illegal. Some people treat her like a celebrity."

"Maybe this is our support group, right here—and maybe that's the whole point of what Mr. Rodriguez is doing," Lindsay suggested.

Jacob considered it. "Four of us are brown, if you include Ava. Chloe's an obvious, Zayden's got a disabled brother and divorced parents, L.J.'s got . . . whatever it is." He gestured to Lindsay and Rhiannon. "You guys got much going on, other than being parahuman?"

"Well, I've had it easier than you guys," Lindsay said, "but my parents are divorced, my dad's a jerk, and my mom has a totally dangerous job. So life hasn't exactly been perfect."

Rhiannon just sighed and looked away, her lips pressed together.

Jacob nodded. "So yeah, I guess this is our group."

* * *

Wednesday, Aug. 24, 2016
Kansas City, MO

"What's going on?" Misty dropped an armful of charts, staring at the frantic medical team working on Dax.

Dr. Huxley pulled her out to the quiet of the hallway. "He had an acute anxiety attack and it escalated into a cardiac event."

She looked at him, stunned. "Anxiety attack? What could've triggered that?"

"I've no idea. He was alone in the room and all his readings were what we've come to expect, and then his heart rate and blood pressure spiked."

"He's stabilized," called one of the nurses. "Pulse and respiration are returning to normal."

Misty struggled to hold back her emotions and appear professional. She cared too much about Dax. "Want me to call his parents?"

"No, it'll be better coming from me. I'd like you to stay with Dax for the afternoon. You seem to have a calming effect on him."

"I do?" She retrieved a coffee cup from the nurse's station. When she pushed her glasses up with the same hand, she managed to steam up a lens.

"I noticed some distinct lulls in his readings and checked the logs." He gave her a penetrating look, as if diagnosing her. "They consistently happen while you're in with him. Any thoughts as to why?"

"Oh, um, maybe because I sing?"

"You sing?" He appeared skeptical.

"Yeah, I like to sing when I'm alone." She actually hated singing because she couldn't carry a tune. "I'm not very good, but I figure Dax doesn't mind." She shrugged. "I guess he finds it soothing."

One of the crash cart nurses called Dr. Huxley into the room to update him on Dax's status. Misty took a moment to retrieve the charts she'd spilled all over the floor. She missed part of the conversation but caught the gist—Dax had been in real danger for a while but was now stable. They didn't think he'd been without oxygen long enough to do further brain damage.

Dr. Huxley left to call Dax's parents and review the morning's readings to see if anything strange had happened leading up to the anxiety attack. Misty got her stack of work settled onto the small desk a few feet from Dax's bed, then turned and wheeled the stool over to the bedside and took his hand. "What's going on in there today, buddy? What's got you so worked up?"

The mental flash she got jolted through her body, making her legs go rigid and rolling the stool back several feet. Misty looked at her fingertips, almost expecting to see them singed and smoking, cartoon-style.

She'd had the sensation of flying straight up into the air in a mad panic, cool air buffeting her face, a brief stinging pain, and free falling before the speed slowed enough to be in control. Misty glimpsed mountains in the distance, and what looked like a small college campus below.

"Who are you watching, Dax?" She hesitated before taking his hand again. Nothing. She peered at the monitors and saw only the brain activity of deep sleep. He hadn't responded to her presence at all.

CHAPTER TWELVE

Thursday, Aug. 25, 2016
Denver, Colorado

Chloe wiped sweat from her forehead and bent backward, stretching her tired flight muscles. Beside her on the stadium grass, Justin bent over with his hands on his knees, and Charlie lay on his stomach, wings pooling on the grass to either side.

"Good workout today," Ms. Donovan said. "Chloe, you're getting more agile already."

Chloe flushed. "Oh, yeah. I've been working the obstacle course a lot."

Ms. Donovan nodded. "Nice. Maybe you need to take Moth Boy with you, eh?"

Charlie craned his head to look at her. "My wings are too broad for that thing."

"How about outside, then?" Chloe asked, always happy to have a training partner. "There's a few decent clumps of trees over by the lake."

He sat up, stretching his wings. "Fine, but not today. Maybe Saturday, after gaming?"

"Make it Sunday after breakfast and you've got a deal," Chloe said.

"You get up for breakfast on Sundays? Not sure I can hang with that." Still, he smiled as he heaved himself up off the ground.

"I'll go easy on you the first time," she teased as they headed out of the stadium.

He laughed. "Where are you headed right now? I thought maybe we could talk about what character class you wanted to be . . ."

"I have to meet L.J. and Miguel to work on a history project. They're trying to re-create some of Javelin's tech while I do all the research." Chloe had to admit they pulled more of the load than she'd expected, at least when it came to the visuals. "L.J.'s drawings were looking really cool last night. Want to come see?"

"L.J.'s the kid who makes his drawings real, right? Pink hair?" Charlie asked, excited.

Chloe nodded. "And with Miguel's help, he can make stuff bigger, too."

"Yeah, I'll totally come see what they've got going. That sounds awesome." He seemed to have perked up considerably.

They walked to the quad to see the guys already out there, working with help from the tech teacher, Mr. Hutson. He looked up as they approached. "Oh, hey, Charlie. I've missed you in the lab this year."

"Yeah, I've missed it, too."

Chloe figured Charlie must've had the tech internship last year, like Miguel did now. He knelt down and looked over the drawings. "Whoa, L.J., these are crazy. You can make this all real?"

L.J. nodded. "Just have to focus a little, and then I can pick it up."

"Awesome power, man. So what's L.J. stand for?"

"Learning Japanese," L.J. said without glancing up.

Mr. Hutson gave them a wry look. "He told me it was Lame Jokes. Probably because I'd just told one."

Charlie gave Chloe a quizzical look and she chuckled, shaking her head. "L.J., you've got a bunch of those, don't you? Just sitting there waiting for someone to ask the question."

"Yup." L.J. flipped his pink hair and continued drawing, putting the finishing touches on a schematic. "Okay, Miguel, gimme a boost."

Miguel put his hands out toward the drawing as they both focused and L.J. picked up a three-dimensional, burnished gold gauntlet blaster from the paper and laid it on the grass, then grabbed the sides and stretched until it was big enough to cover his forearms. Miguel and Mr. Hutson high-fived.

Charlie's eyes just about popped out of his head. "Holy crap!"

"Pretty cool, eh?" Chloe said.

"I've seen a lot of cool stuff at this school, but that's right there with the coolest." He shook his head, marveling at the fully operational device L.J. had sketched into being. "I wish I'd had something like that for my presentation last year. I would've done a lot better."

"Hi, Zayden," Chloe called as he walked out of the dorm.

Zayden shot Charlie a suspicious look, then dismissed him and peered over at Miguel and L.J.'s project. "Hey, Chloe. What are they working on?"

"Javelin's tech. For History."

Zayden rolled his eyes. "Meh. Javelin didn't have any powers, he shouldn't be counted as one of us."

Charlie did a double take. "Dude, seriously? Do you know how hard normals have to work to hang with paras? I've got mad respect for Javelin. Then there's Destroyer—one of the toughest super villains of all time, even took on the Hind, all 'cause he's a great engineer."

Chloe shivered, thinking about Destroyer. Sure, a few years ago he'd helped save the Earth from an alien invasion, but his attack on Tornado's funeral in 1985, while inside his super-high-tech armored suit, killed five heroes, including Mustang Sally's dad.

"But that's just it," Zayden countered. "I mean, given the time and resources, anyone could build a suit, so he shouldn't be classified as a super villain. He's just a really good villain, is all."

Charlie shrugged. "I don't think it matters where the power comes from, dude, just how powerful it is. And Javelin and Destroyer? Both seriously freaking powerful."

Zayden opened his mouth to respond, but Charlie cut him off. "I'll see you tomorrow, Chloe. Thanks for showing me this." He turned and headed toward the dorm.

"Yeah, you bet. See you." She turned to see Zayden's receding back as he walked off in the other direction. She almost followed him but then realized she'd be the one bailing on the group project. She sighed and plopped down on a bench, dug out her tablet, and did some more research.

Before long, she decided she had enough information gathered to start paring it down into a biography. The guys had tested the blasters and discovered some flaws, so they went back to work on the drawings. She didn't want to leave while they worked, so she checked email to kill time.

She read one from her mom and responded briefly, then saw the weird para-supremacist message and remembered guiltily that she'd meant to show it to a teacher. Mr. Hutson could be the best person to tell, and he was right there. He'd just said good-bye to the guys and headed off toward the computer lab, so she hurried after him.

"Mr. Hutson?"

He turned around. "What's up? It's Chloe, right?"

She nodded. "I got an email I thought maybe I should tell a teacher about."

"Come with me to the lab." He looked concerned. She fell in step beside him, hurrying to keep up with his long strides. "Is someone harassing you?"

"No, not exactly. I mean, it's like an invitation, but it's totally fishy."

They walked into the lab and he perched on a stool. "Show it to me."

She handed him her tablet.

"Oh, wow, I see what you mean." He scanned it once more. "Can I forward this to myself? Mr. Jordan needs to see this."

She nodded and a minute later he gave the tablet back. "What do you think's going on? Is there really some creepy group trying to recruit me?"

"That's what it looks like on the surface. Have you clicked on the link?"

"No, no way. I know better than to click on something sketchy like that."

"Good. Do you know if any other students have received emails like this?"

Chloe shook her head. "No, but I haven't really asked anyone else."

"Let me get together with Administration and we'll figure out the best way to proceed. In the meantime, if you receive any more messages like this, please let me and Mr. Jordan know immediately."

"I will, I promise. What do you think it means?"

"I don't know, but I'll check it out, see what's going on. Thanks for bringing this to me, Chloe."

CHAPTER THIRTEEN

From the TV series <u>Heroes Among Us</u>, *Season 2, Episode 7, "The Lord Family: Triumphs & Tragedies"*

Segment 5

Once Dax was admitted to the hospital under his care, Dr. Huxley realized Dax's parahuman abilities went well beyond what anyone had suspected.

"We knew Dax was a powerful telekinetic based on what he'd been seen doing, but in interviewing Zayden, we learned he's also telepathic. His brother said Dax would whisper threats to him as he tried to sleep, from his bedroom down the hall. That also told us Dax's mind could understand and use language, so his inability to speak must be physiological and not due to cognitive deficits."

The Lords' already-troubled marriage wouldn't survive the strain of it all. Nathan and Anna's divorce became final less than a year after Dax went into the psychiatric wing of Bedford Hospital in Kansas City. There he remains to this day, and it's where he's expected to live out what remains of his life—which, according to his mother, may not be long.

"Dax has gotten weaker and weaker. It doesn't seem to matter what the doctors do, how often we visit him, nothing helps. Zayden sits and holds his hands for hours—after everything, he loves and misses his little brother."

Nathan also believes his youngest son's days are numbered. "He stops breathing sometimes, has to be fed through a tube. The doctors say one of these days his brain just won't be able to keep his body going anymore."

Meanwhile, Zayden is a shining light in his parents' lives, continuing to use his powers to help people, whenever he can.

The most dramatic rescue was only weeks before this episode was filmed, when he ran inside a burning office building. He moved debris off of people, burst pipes to help douse the flames, lowered three people to safety from upper-story windows, and carried an injured women out to the waiting paramedics.

All this, before he's even old enough to apply for the Hero Academy. With his fourteenth birthday drawing near, however, it likely won't be long before Zayden Lord enters the hallowed halls of the school that's produced some of the greatest parahuman heroes the world has ever seen.

* * *

Friday, Aug. 26, 2016
Denver, Colorado

Chloe woke up certain she smelled smoke. Whipping off her covers, she sat up and looked around but saw nothing. She crept to the door and peeked out into the hallway, where yellow emergency lights and green exit signs provided enough illumination to see everything appeared normal. Plus, if there had been smoke, she figured an alarm would've gone off, for sure.

Adrenaline pumping, she knew she wouldn't be able to get back to sleep, so she threw on a robe and slippers, grabbed a book for Language Arts, and went down to the lounge. Her face went hot when she saw Zayden sitting at the table, reading something on his tablet. He looked up with a start when she walked in.

"Oh, hey, Chloe. Trouble sleeping again?" He switched off the tablet and pushed it aside.

She padded over to the nearest couch. "Yeah, I think I had a bad dream or something, but I don't remember what it was."

"That sucks."

She nodded, not sure what to say. The awkward silence stretched out. "Well, I guess I'll read until I can get back to sleep."

"Cool, I was just thinking I'd to head to my room." Zayden stood up, paused, then sat next to her. "If you want to talk about . . . you know, stuff . . . being different, having to give up gymnastics, whatever. I get all that stuff. I've been dealing with it for a long time, and I just wanted to let you know."

She gave him a shy smile. "Thanks, Zayden."

"There's . . . there's something I've been wanting to ask you. Since the sunset." He paused and swallowed hard. "Will you . . . do you want to be, like, my girlfriend?"

Her heart pounded and she felt dizzy. "Oh, I . . . um. Yeah, I'd like that."

He let out a breath and grinned. "Cool. I'd like it too. So, uh, good night. Hope you get back to sleep okay." Zayden put his hand on hers for just a moment, and left.

At his touch, excitement overwhelmed her. Her mind reeled.

Then images flashed through her mind, dousing the euphoria.

Fire. Screaming, coughing.

Black smoke.

A girl on the high dive.

The sound of cars crashing.

Fear. Fear that (she) wouldn't be able to save them this time, that they would die.

Chloe shook her head, disoriented and near panic. All of a sudden, she remembered seeing those images before, in the dreams she couldn't remember. *Why would Zayden's touch make me remember that?* she wondered. Could he be telepathic too, like his little brother? Wouldn't he know it, though?

She tried to brush it off and be excited about being his official girlfriend, but she was unsettled. She tried reading to take her mind off of it, but after scanning the same page three or four times without anything sinking in, she went back to bed only to toss and turn the rest of the sleepless night.

CHAPTER FOURTEEN

Saturday, Aug. 27, 2016
Denver, Colorado

"Oh, my God, he did?" Lindsay exploded with excitement for her roommate. It was Saturday, so they didn't have to rush off to class.

"Shhh!" Chloe hissed, eyes darting to the door.

Lindsay plopped down on the end of the bed where Chloe sat cross-legged, dropping her voice to make sure no one heard them. "What did you say? What did you do? Did you kiss him?"

"No! I totally froze. He squeezed my hand and smiled and I just sat there."

Lindsay's head fell back, eyes closed. "He's the one who's done everything. You don't want him to think you're not that into him, do you? It is so time to kiss him! Don't you think?"

Chloe squirmed. "I'm not sure I'm ready to."

Her roommate stared, jaw slack. "You. Are. Kidding me. Girl, you've been all gooey-eyed for him since orientation."

"I know, but . . ." She sighed. "Something weird happened, after he left." She told Lindsay about the images in her head and how she'd dreamed them earlier. "So now I'm really, I don't know, uneasy."

"It's probably just 'cause you were freaking out. Brains are bizarre—you get them all flooded with adrenaline and hormones and all kinds of things happen. That's why most parapowers first appear during puberty and when we're under stress, just like your wings popping out during a meet, right?"

"I guess that makes sense." She felt a little hopeful, as if maybe she was over-reacting.

"Okay, so you'll kiss him? Or at least do something to make sure he knows how much you like him?" Lindsay attempted a stern look that made Chloe burst out laughing.

"Only if you promise never to make that face again."

"Deal." Lindsay held out a hand, pinky extended.

Chloe linked pinkies with her. "Deal."

As they got ready for breakfast, they heard noises in the hallway and Lindsay looked out. It turned out to be Miguel knocking on his sister's door. "You guys going to breakfast?" she asked.

"Yeah," he said, "if Izzy's up."

Izzy opened the door, long dark hair sticking out all over and eyes just slits in mounds of puffiness. "Gimme two minutes." She ducked back inside.

Jacob strolled into the lounge, wearing running clothes, a sheen of sweat on his dark forehead. "Hey, someone's finally up! I thought you guys were gonna waste the whole day."

"You've already been for a run?" Lindsay gave him an incredulous look.

He grinned. "Just a couple twenty-mile sprints, no big."

Chloe grabbed her student I.D. and room key and joined the growing group down in the boys' hall, where they knocked on Zayden and L.J.'s door. Zayden opened it and his eyes landed on Chloe right away.

"Oh, uh, good morning."

"Uh, hi." Chloe looked away, unable to meet his eye, and saw Lindsay's eyes riveted on something in the room. She glanced over to see L.J. pulling a skinny pant leg down from his knee—over something that wasn't a leg. He looked up and caught their stares before they could avert them.

"Guess that cat's out of the bag." He came out to the hallway. "Is everyone here? I only want to do this once."

Lindsay swallowed hard and tried to look casual. It failed worse than the stern look she'd given Chloe. "Not quite. Izzy said she'd be right out, and we haven't heard from Rhiannon or Ava."

Jacob zipped down the hall and knocked on their door. "You guys up? Wanna come to breakfast?"

"Some of us are trying to sleep!" Ava yelled from inside.

Jacob put his hands up and backed away. "Whoa, sorry!"

The door opened just enough for Rhiannon to slip out, looking uneasy. "Can I come with you guys?"

"Yeah, sure." Miguel glanced at the closed door. "*You* haven't been a total bitch to everyone."

She gave them a relieved smile. "Cool."

Izzy opened the door. She'd managed to get her hair back in a messy bun and her eyes were more open.

"Okay," L.J. said, a determined, almost agitated, edge to his voice. "Before we go, I have something to show you guys. Like I said, I'm only gonna do this once and I'll talk about it until we get to the dining hall, and that's it." He bent down and slid up his right pant leg, revealing the white prosthetic underneath. It came up to four inches below his knee. It appeared 3D printed, with a woven look and lots of open areas revealing a hollow center. The five who hadn't already seen it gasped. "It's fake, obviously. I was in a bad car wreck a couple years ago and it got crushed. Then it got infected real bad and they had to amputate." He pushed the pant leg back down, then turned and headed out the door.

Everyone followed, quiet. Lindsay spoke up first. "Did you draw that? And make it with your powers?"

"I make prototypes that way, but they don't last very long. Once I get one I like, I print it out."

"Why don't you just have one made?" Rhiannon asked.

L.J. sighed. "One, it's seriously expensive. Two, I've grown really fast and this way I can replace it whenever I want. Three, mine look way cooler." They'd reached the dining hall. L.J. stopped outside the door and turned to face everyone. "Any more questions?"

"What's L.J. stand for?" Lindsay asked.

"Licking junk."

Everyone laughed.

"Anything else?" L.J. asked.

They all shook their heads.

"Good." He gave a final hair flip and went inside.

"Chloe," Zayden called as she moved toward the door. She turned back to him. "I'm sorry if I made you uncomfortable. You know, last night. I'm cool with being friends if you don't . . ."

"No, I'm not, um, I mean—" She stammered, gaze flicking to him and then away, "Okay, I am kinda uncomfortable, I guess, but that doesn't mean I don't want to be your girlfriend. 'Cause, yeah, I . . . I really do." She forced herself to look him in the eye.

He grinned, blue eyes lighting up. "Cool." Neither knew what to do next, so they just stood there awkwardly. "Should we, uh . . ." He gestured to the door.

"Oh, yeah. I'm starving."

* * *

Chloe closed her math book and stared at the history text waiting to be read beside it on the table. "My brain is fried. I need a break."

"Yeah, me too," Lindsay said from the couch.

Zayden looked up. "Uh huh."

"Want to go upstairs and check out Charlie's game?" she asked them.

Lindsay shrugged. "Might as well. It gives us an excuse to do something besides study, anyway."

"I don't know." Zayden looked skeptical. "It sounded kinda nerdy, didn't it?"

"Kinda, I guess. We don't have to stay very long, but I spaced it last week and I think it kinda hurt his feelings. He's really cool to me in Flight Training, so I don't want to be rude."

Zayden took her hand as they climbed the stairs. She tensed, both from the emotions it stirred up and in preparation for the dream images to resurface, but none did. She sighed with relief and decided Lindsay must've been right about it being a weird over-loaded brain thing.

In the second floor lounge, they found four sophomores and two juniors crowded around the table. On the table lay a big map drawn on graph paper with tiny figurines placed around it. Each player had a clipboard and some weird-shaped dice. Charlie had some kind of folder thing with a bunch of charts on it standing in front of him, shielding a large collection of dice and stack of papers from the players.

"Roll your will save," he said to Solomon, the telepath who'd upset Zayden at dinner the other night. Sol rolled a die with lots of tiny facets. It landed on a one and he winced and groaned.

Cat, sitting next to him, laughed. "Serves you right for spying on the GM's brain."

"Hey, Chloe. Cool, you made it." Charlie grinned, but then his eyes fell on her hand in Zayden's and his expression clouded over. "Did you want to join us?"

"Oh, not right now. We just thought we'd check it out." She glanced at the paper on Cat's clipboard, which held an overwhelming amount of information. She grimaced. "It looks complicated."

Bridger, Rhiannon's brother, looked up. "It is, especially this system, but you don't have to know everything. We can mostly just tell noobs what to do until they get the hang of it."

"Sol will tell you what to do even if y'all don't want him to," Cat teased in her southern drawl.

Sol gave her an arrogant look, one eyebrow raised. "That's because I know when you're confused and just too proud to admit it."

Cat wrinkled her nose and hissed at him. He rolled his eyes.

"Why don't you sit down and watch for a while?" Charlie suggested. They sat down on the couch.

Charlie described a scene to the players and then had them say what they did in response. Sometimes they'd roll dice to see how well they did it, and then Charlie would go back to his descriptions. Chloe got caught up in the story. "Wow, Charlie's really good at that!" she muttered to Zayden.

"Huh?" He seemed to come out of a daze. "Uh, yeah, I guess."

She turned to Lindsay and found her nodding off. Chloe nudged her awake. "Do you guys want to go?"

Lindsay nodded with an OMG-get-me-out-of-here expression.

Zayden looked at his watch. "Yeah, I'm supposed to meet a couple guys for training pretty soon, anyway."

They stood up and she told Charlie good-bye.

"Want to talk about building a character sometime?" he asked.

"Yeah, sure. See you Tuesday, if not before," Chloe said. They headed downstairs. "I think I might want to join the game. What'd you guys think?"

Lindsay shook her head. "Sorry, I thought it was boring."

"Not my thing, really." Zayden shrugged. "But you should, if you want."

She was disappointed but didn't think she'd want to play without at least one of them there.

Zayden left for training, so Chloe decided to head over to the gym for a while. On the way, she got a Parable alert and stared at the name, wondering why Bridger would message her.

Charlie says you're pretty cool so I wanted to talk to you. Rhiannon's really confused about the whole thing between Ava and everybody else.

Chloe walked into the gym and sat on a bench. *I feel really bad for her and totally get her trying to keep things cool with her roommate. Lindsay's suuuper pissed at Ava, but I'll see what I can do, k?* She took off her shoes and warm-ups.

Really appreciate it, he replied. *Btw, don't tell her I talked to you. She'd be pissed.*

Chloe sent a thumbs up and focused on the obstacle course, coming up with a new route to push her agility. However, between not sleeping well, things developing with Zayden, and worrying about Rhiannon, she was distracted. On her second pass, she clipped a wing on a stout metal bar and spun off course, slamming her hip and thigh into another obstacle. She fell halfway to the ground before she got control and slowed enough to glide down for a soft landing on the padded floor. She sat, shaking and sore, and decided she should be done for the day. She thought it might be time to get some protective gear, like stuff people wore for skateboarding. Or roller derby.

Chloe limped over to the bench and messaged Rhiannon. *Want to get together and talk, away from the dorm and everybody?*

A message came back immediately. *Yes! Thank you! Where?*

Meet me in the gym? I'm there now.

Rhiannon sent back a thumbs up. Chloe lay down on the bench, on her un-injured side so her wings could hang off the edge, and closed her eyes. Her energy dropped as her body re-directed resources to healing. Five minutes later, when Rhiannon walked in, she already felt a little better. Another hour, two at most, and she'd be fine as long as she didn't push it.

Chloe stood and Rhiannon hugged her. "Thank you, Chloe!" She bumped the injured wing, but Chloe didn't let on that it hurt.

"Hey, no problem. Want to take a walk?"

Rhiannon nodded, looking a little teary. They went out and walked past Heroes Hall, toward the lake—the other directions would either take them past the dorms or over near the maintenance building, and Chloe wanted to keep that spot between her and Zayden.

"So I know things have been rough this last week and I wanted to let you know we all totally like you. It's just, Ava's so . . ."

Rhiannon sighed. "Ava can be such a bitch. She knows it, too, but she can't seem to stop herself."

Chloe nodded. "If she'd just apologize to Lindsay, maybe things would be okay."

"I don't think she will. She's cried a couple of times, but mostly, she just gets madder and madder. And she doesn't let me see her cry. It's only when she thinks I'm asleep."

"Okay, well, I don't know if we can fix things between them, but I'll try to figure out something to at least make things better. We can't spend the whole year —or the three after it—excluding Ava from everything."

"Oh, my God, I can't even think about that!"

"I know Ava would probably see it as choosing sides, but the rest of us want you around," Chloe said. "Maybe you could tell her if she doesn't apologize, you can't keep trying to be neutral."

Rhiannon shrugged, looking miserable. "Maybe. It's hard, though, living with her. I'll think it over."

"Cool, I'll see what it would take for Lindsay to get past everything." Chloe thought maybe she'd talk to Zayden about it, too. He was so understanding, she was sure he could come up with a way to fix things.

Before long, they circled back toward campus. They hadn't made it anywhere near the lake—it amazed Chloe how much longer it took to walk anywhere than to fly.

"I really appreciate this, Chloe," Rhiannon said as they neared the dorm. "I think I'll come sit with you guys at dinner whether Ava likes it or not."

Chloe grinned. "Cool! I'll message you before we go."

She didn't get a chance to talk to Zayden alone before dinner and figured she'd grab him afterward. Before she had a chance, though, his mom called and they talked for a long time. L.J. said it seemed to be about his little brother. He didn't come back out before Chloe couldn't keep her eyes open any longer and went to bed.

CHAPTER FIFTEEN

Sunday, Aug. 28, 2016
Denver, Colorado

Charlie cheered as he cleared the tree tops seconds before Chloe. "Outmaneuvered you that time, Wyld!"

Chloe laughed, wiping sweat off her forehead. "Yeah, you got me. One out of—what, seven?"

"With how fast you are, I'll take it." He grinned, face red with exertion. "Damn, I'm getting worn out."

"Race you to the lake!" Chloe took off in a flash and Charlie did his best to keep up. Still, she beat him there and landed on top of the concrete pillar in the center, shading her eyes from the sun and watching as he descended.

He flew a wide arc to decelerate as he approached. Just as she expected him to touch down, he smirked and swept a wing forward to knock her off the edge. She shrieked at his audacity, then sucked in a breath before she splashed into the cool water.

A moment later, she bobbed back to the surface and spread her wings out to help her float. "Feels good, you sneaky jerk. Come on in!"

Charlie threw his head back and laughed. "No way, I'd be grounded for days."

She swam over to the ladder and climbed part way up, stopping to shake off her wings. "It sucks you can't get in the water. It's nice—even when you get pushed in."

He gave her a hand up from the top rung. "So, that Zayden kid, are you, like, going out with him or something?"

Chloe blushed. "Um, yeah. It's all official and everything."

He turned and looked off toward the trees. "That happened pretty quick, eh?"

"Yeah, I guess." She squirmed, trying to think of a way to change the subject.

Charlie turned back to her. "This has been fun, but we should probably head back." Something in his tone made her feel like he wanted to get rid of her.

"I think I'll stay and swim a little. See you Tuesday, if not before."

He nodded, looking out at the lake again. "Yeah, see you later, Wyld." He lifted off and she watched him fly away.

Does he like me? she wondered. But then she decided she was being vain or silly, or maybe both. *Just because one guy likes you, now you're thinking everyone does,* she told herself. He and Zayden had clashed the other day over the whole Javelin/Destroyer thing, so she figured Charlie probably just didn't like him.

CHAPTER SIXTEEN

Monday, August 29, 2016
Denver, Colorado

"Protect civilians by drawing combat away from them," Lindsay said.

"Good! Next." Sally stood inside a circle of freshmen and whirled to point at Jacob.

"Uh, use the terrain to your advantage."

The teacher nodded. "Good! Ava?"

"Observe the . . . um, the weaknesses of your opponents?"

"Not quite," Sally said. "Who can help her?"

"Observe the abilities of your opponents," L.J. and Miguel said together.

"Yes!" Sally spun again. "What's next, Chloe?"

Chloe realized she'd been staring at Zayden and not paying attention. She scrambled to mentally catch up. "Next is . . . uh, seek and exploit weaknesses."

"Quicker next time, but yes. Izzy, give us the last one."

"Retreating is not cowardice, because . . ." She scrunched up her face, trying to remember.

"Outta time!" Sally pointed at Zayden.

" . . . Because you can't win every fight."

"Good! We got through it." Sally stood with her hands on her hips. "Remember, the Cardinal Rules of Combat aren't something to be memorized for a test and then forgotten. I said them in my head during many a fight, and they saved me more times than I can count."

The door to the gym opened and Sally turned to see Mrs. Jordan. "Ingrid, what's up?"

"Could I have a moment to talk to your class, Sally?"

"You bet." Sally motioned for them to sit down on the benches along the wall.

Mrs. Jordan—who Chloe still thought of as Icebreaker—stood in front of them. "One of your classmates reported a strange email, one that appeared to be recruiting for a para-supremacist organization."

"Whoa," Jacob said under his breath. The twins looked at each other with matching furrowed brows.

Mrs. Jordan read a portion of it. "We're investigating to see if we can figure out where it came from, and in the meantime, we want to ask all of you to let us know if you receive one of these emails or have in the past."

Ava's hand went up. "I got one."

"When was that?" Mrs. Jordan asked.

"Just after school started. Like maybe the second or third day?"

"Anyone else?" She scanned the line of them, but no other hands went up. "Ava, can you forward that to Mr. Hutson?"

"Sure." Ava pulled out her phone.

"Again, if anyone else receives one, please let me and Mr. Jordan know, and forward it to Mr. Hutson right away. It goes against everything we believe here at the Academy. Plus, considering the current political climate, we can't afford to have this kind of movement take off. It would only add fuel to the fire of those who fear parahumans and want to take away our rights because of it." She turned and nodded at Sally. "Thanks for the time."

* * *

"A brick and a flier? I totally get it," L.J. said over lunch. "I'm just saying, it makes strategic sense to go after you two. If I were putting together a team, it's what I'd do.

Of course, I'd want Lindsay, too, but considering where your mom works, it's too risky to go after you. And Jacob, but you've had notoriety as a good guy and, you know, probably wouldn't be into any kind of supremacist thing. What I don't get is why they're not pursuing Zayden and the twins."

Izzy paled. "Why would you say that?"

L.J. shrugged and flipped his hair. "Telekinesis? No brainer. Then you guys," he gestured to Miguel and Izzy, "you have powers that are obviously beneficial in a lot of situations. Plus, hey, two for the price of one, probably."

Lindsay shuddered. "The whole thing just gives me the creeps."

"Seriously," Jacob said. "The election's got enough hate stirred up, this is the last thing we need."

"Are you okay?" Chloe asked Zayden under her breath. He stared at his tray as he ate, not saying a word.

He glanced up at her and sighed. "I didn't want to say anything, but my brother had a heart attack or something last week."

Chloe gasped. "Oh, my gosh."

"He's okay now, but I guess I'm worried about him."

The bell rang and they all headed to class.

CHAPTER SEVENTEEN

Tuesday, Aug. 30, 2016
Secure Chatroom

Chupara: *Who turned us in?*

LB: *Don't worry about it. I expected as much.*

Chupara: *Don't worry about it?! How can I not worry about it? The Jordans are investigating. Did you forget they ran a Just Cause team like, forever?*

LB: *There's nothing to tie us to it. Trust me.*

Chupara: *We should shut it all down. At least for a while.*

LB: *No! This is the most secure way to talk and we need to keep plans moving forward. If you don't have the stones for this . . .*

Chupara: *Screw you, you know I've got the stones! I just think we need to be smart now so we're not sorry later.*

LB: *We've been smart all along. That's why we don't need to panic now. Just stay chill and ride this out.*

Chupara: *Ok, but you better be right.*

CHAPTER EIGHTEEN

Friday, Sept. 2, 2016
Denver, Colorado

"I'm exhausted from Flight Training, but otherwise, great," Chloe told her mom over the phone. "Grades are good, things with Zayden are good, I love my roomie . . . Really, it couldn't be going any better."

She could hardly believe that Hero Academy life felt so normal after such a short time. Everyone had settled into a routine, and other than the recruiting weirdness—which she didn't think had anything to do with the school anyway—life was good.

Her mom chattered about everything that had happened at home and Chloe only became more convinced that, as much as she loved her parents, she wasn't missing anything there. She was where she belonged and happier than she'd been in a long time.

CHAPTER NINETEEN

Monday, Sept. 5, 2016
Denver, Colorado

Zayden had seemed distant on and off since getting the news about his brother last week, and it worried Chloe. She couldn't help eyeing him in Psych, where they sat in a circle, and she briefly wondered whether she should say something to Mr. Rodriguez. Then she decided she should let him go to someone he was comfortable with if he needed to talk. Like L.J., or maybe her. She hoped he'd come to her.

As they headed to Combat Training, alongside the grassy quad, Ava hurried past Lindsay and bumped her, knocking into her arm and making Lindsay drop her soda. It splattered on the ground and spilled sticky fizz all over her shoes. Ava kept going without so much as a look back.

Lindsay picked up the can and hurled it at Ava's back, but not hard enough to hit her. "Excuse you, Ava!"

A riding lawn mower on the quad exploded without warning, throwing the driver several feet. Flames shot from the engine.

"Jacob, no!" Zayden yelled, grabbing the speedster's arm. "Let me try first."

"But that guy's hurt!" Jacob called, pulling out of his grasp.

Zayden focused and water erupted from the sprinklers, rising higher and higher until it inundated the mower. It doused the flames in seconds, revealing the grounds keeper lying on the grass. He screamed and writhed in pain.

Izzy called 9-1-1 as security guards ran from the dorm.

"Thanks for boosting me," Zayden told Miguel as they all sprinted toward the mower. Their shoes squelched in the wet grass.

"No problem, man," Miguel said. "Glad you acted so quick."

Chloe grabbed Zayden's hand. "That was awesome."

He grinned, eyes sparkling.

"Are you okay?" Lindsay asked the grounds keeper.

He moaned in pain. His clothing smoldered where flames had licked at him.

"Help's on the way," Lindsay said.

People converged on the site from everywhere. Even the administrative staff rushed out from the back of Heroes Hall. Mrs. Jordan knelt beside Lindsay and used her icy touch to soothe the injured man's burns.

"Who was it turned on the sprinklers?" a security guard asked. "That was quick thinking."

The freshmen all looked at Zayden, but he didn't speak up.

"It was Zayden," Chloe said, "with help from Miguel."

A bunch of people congratulated him, some applauding.

"I'm just glad I could help." Zayden squirmed at the attention. "Miguel's really the one who got the fire put out so fast—I couldn't do it on my own."

"Well done, boys." Mr. Jordan put a hand on each of their shoulders. "All you students need to move well back. Emergency personnel are on the way."

As if his words had called them, sirens screamed and a fire truck from the station down the road came into view. Chloe's vision wavered and smeared, as if watching one movie projected over another. The fire truck raced toward the quad to stop on the grass near the injured groundskeeper. Paramedics hurried over to check the groundskeeper's wounds.

But also . . .

The smoke burned (her) lungs as she tried to draw the heat from the fire. (She) felt a hopeless fear, certain this time (she) wouldn't be able to save them, that he would get his way. The world swayed as (she) tried to flail her arms, frustrated something kept them from moving, hearing the beeps and alarms of the things attached to (her). To (her) left, a teddy bear stared at (her) with cold black eyes and above in the ceiling, a building burned. (She) smelled the smoke, felt the heat, and yet the smoke didn't cross an invisible barrier between the room and the side of the building. (She) noticed it didn't build up against the barrier, either, but appeared to just vanish once it got there. (She) breathed in more heat and the flames receded, and then someone came through the front door carrying a hurt woman. A gust of wind blew the smoke away and (she) saw Zayden's face, covered in soot . . .

And everything returned to normal, leaving Chloe trying to catch her breath. Mr. Jordan ordered them all to get back to class as the paramedics took the groundskeeper off on a stretcher.

"Chloe, you okay?" Lindsay asked. "You look like you're gonna puke or something."

"What? Oh, no, I'm fine." She shook her head to clear it.

Zayden looked concerned and took her hand. "Are you sure? Did his leg make you feel sick or something?"

She gave him a weak smile. "Yeah, I guess so. I'm not used to seeing stuff like that."

They started once again toward Combat Training. Chloe walked a little slower than the rest so she and Zayden would fall behind.

"So I've been meaning to ask you . . . are you just telekinetic, or are you telepathic, too?" she asked him.

He shook his head. "Just telekinetic. Why do you ask?"

She shrugged. "I got a flash of something back there, of like, a burning building or something. I wondered if it was from when you rescued those people from the office building."

"No, couldn't have been from me." He looked serious for a minute. "The fire probably triggered a memory in a telepath close by, and you somehow picked up on it. I used to get flashes like that from my brother sometimes."

"Yeah, that must've been it." She tried to sound casual. *But that wouldn't explain why I saw you, would it?* She didn't know why she hadn't told him that part, but something told her not to.

They walked into the training gym, where Sally and everyone else waited for them. Sally eyed their linked hands and the corner of her mouth quirked. Embarrassed, Chloe let go.

"Let's talk about what just happened out there on the quad," Sally said. "Jacob, how do you feel about Zayden stopping you from running in?"

He shrugged. "I wanted to help, but it was probably the smart thing to do. Mr. Rodriguez lectured me about it after the fire in the trash can."

"It's never good to add wind to fire, it's true," Sally said. "Believe me, I know how hard it is not to rush in—I had to learn some hard lessons in the field—but it does pay to think a little bit first."

Ava's hands went to her hips. "So are we going to discuss the elephant in the room or not?"

Sally's eyebrows went up as she swung her head toward Ava, who stood apart from the group. "There's an elephant?"

"I'd say so." Ava turned and stared at Lindsay. "Every time Miss Pyro gets her widdle feels hurt, something starts to burn."

"It wasn't me!" Lindsay shouted. "Not either time!"

Sally put herself between them. "Why don't you two stay after class and we can talk, okay? If any of you ever have concerns about a fellow student, do bring it to a staff member, but try to do it in private rather than calling them out in front of everyone."

Ava pouted at the admonishment. Lindsay glared, eyes flashing with red specks.

"The school will be looking into it, though, right? Two fires on campus, a few days apart?" Rhiannon asked.

"I assure you, the administration started looking into the trash can fire right away, and you can bet they'll investigate this one, too. We've spent enough class time on this. Let's get started on a simulation."

She split them into two groups, heroes and villains, and let them loose to see what they could do when opposing each other. "No real punching, so Ava, you're basically playing tag. Lindsay," she tossed her a can of tennis balls, "pretend these are fire. Rhiannon, yell 'scream' and point to where the blast would go. Everyone, it's like laser tag—when they target you, you have to react as if you just got hit with the real thing. Chloe, if something would knock you out of the air, just land. You don't have to plummet to the ground. And Izzy, don't really shrink a power if it would put someone in danger."

"I read something about how some powers can't take away natural abilities," Lindsay said. "So I was wondering whether Izzy could shrink, like, Chloe's flying ability, since it comes from wings."

Sally looked at the twins. "Have you guys tested yourself against anything like that?"

They shook their heads.

Sally nodded. "Good thought, Lindsay. I'll try to figure out a safe way to test that sometime. Now let's get going."

Toward the end of class, Chloe was the only remaining villain. Ava lobbed tennis balls as L.J., on a flying carpet, tried to drive her into a corner. Chloe dodged a ball and surprised L.J. by dropping down and flying backward, right under him. "Yank!" she yelled as she grabbed the carpet.

"L.J., you lost your carpet!" Sally called. "You're out!"

L.J. flew off to the side and landed with the others.

"Simulation over!" Sally waited for Ava and Chloe to join them. "I have to declare the villains the winner."

Ava crossed her arms. "That's not fair! I was still in —we tied."

Sally waggled a finger. "Sorry, but you can't fly. In a real situation, once there's no one to pursue a flier, odds are they'll be out of range before you can do anything."

"I didn't know you could reverse like that," L.J. told Chloe.

She grinned. "Dragonflies are tricky."

"It's true," Sally said, "most winged insects have to turn around, but not dragonflies, and not some self-propelled fliers, either. 'Observe the abilities of your opponents'—remember that? It's the third Cardinal Combat Rule for a reason. In fact, let's make that your homework for the week—two pages on the different types of motion possible with different wings. Look at birds, bats, butterflies, moths, and, of course, dragonflies." She looked at Chloe. "I'm guessing this is an area you've already studied?" Chloe nodded. "Okay, I still want a paper from you, but I also want you to give us a full demonstration of your abilities. Because while it's important to know your opponents' abilities, you need to know those of your teammates even better."

An older student walked in just as the bell rang and handed a note to Sally, who then motioned Lindsay up and whispered something. Lindsay's face went white. "Ava," Sally said. "I'd still like to talk to you for a minute." She and Ava walked back to Sally's office together, Ava looking sullen.

"What's going on?" Chloe asked Lindsay.

"Mr. Jordan wants to see me. Looks like Ava's not the only one who thinks I'm a frigging arsonist."

* * *

Lindsay didn't join them for lunch, so Chloe saw her next in the hallway between math and science. She hurried to catch up.

"What happened?" Chloe asked. "Is everything okay?"

Lindsay shrugged, looking glum. "Yeah, I guess. I don't want to talk about it."

After class, Lindsay dashed out before Chloe even put her notebook away.

As soon as she walked into the dormitory, Chloe heard loud music coming from their room. She slipped in to find Lindsay crying, face down on her bed.

"Oh my gosh, what's wrong?" She sat on the edge of the bed and put her hand on Lindsay's back. "Do they think you did it?"

Lindsay turned down the music. "Mr. Jordan said he believes me that I didn't do anything . . . intentionally." She put sarcastic emphasis on the last word. "But they want to do some tests to see if I could be having trouble controlling my powers when I'm upset."

Chloe's eyes fell closed. "That sucks. I'm sorry."

Lindsay looked up with puffy eyes and red cheeks. "I know it's your room and everything, but can I be alone for awhile?"

"Yeah, sure." Chloe stood up, feeling a little stung. "I'll just go down to the lounge."

The music went back to blaring as Chloe passed through the lounge to the guys' hall to see what Zayden was up to. Through the open door, she saw him sitting on his bed, looking at something on his phone.

She leaned on the door jam. "Knock, knock."

He smiled and motioned her in. Chloe didn't feel comfortable joining him on the bed, so she sat sideways on the desk chair. "Lindsay needs some time to herself, so I'm kinda kicked out of the room. Where's L.J.?"

"He and Miguel went out to test some designs."

Her mind spun, trying to come up with something to talk about, and she remembered the topic she'd been waiting to bring up. "You know how it's like, everyone against Ava?" She kept her voice low, glancing out to the hallway. Zayden nodded. "I was thinking. We're supposed to be thinking and acting like a team, and we're all going to be together for four years—at least. Who knows which of us will end up working together."

He looked thoughtful. "That's a long time to hold a grudge against someone."

"Exactly, but I don't know what to do." She sighed. "Ava's certainly not doing anything to help the situation, and no way is Lindsay going to be all buddy-buddy with her."

Zayden scooted toward the foot of the bed so he could take her hand. "Why don't we sit down and talk to Ava, let her know we want to be friends if she can apologize and be cool?"

Chloe beamed. "That sounds awesome. You'll do it with me?"

"Of course." He stood up and went to the door. Thinking he intended to go to Ava's room, she stood up and followed him, then bashed into him when he closed the door and turned around.

Chloe's heart hammered and she stumbled back. Zayden closed the distance and leaned in to kiss her, a hand on her arm.

Images of smoke and flame flooded her mind. He emerged from the burning building and the sight triggered an onslaught of emotion she didn't understand—terror, hate, resentment, profound weariness, desperate yearning.

She yanked her arm away and stepped back, stumbling over his backpack. She reeled, trying to catch herself, but knew it was a losing battle. Zayden lunged forward and grabbed her around the waist, pulling her back up onto her feet. Once she was steady, he held her there, one arm mashing her wings painfully into her lower back, the other at her waist. He moved in for a kiss again.

She twisted in his arms. "Zayden, my wings. That hurts."

He didn't respond. Her fear ramped up and she tried to push him away. Anger flashed in his eyes and she wondered, with Lindsay's music so loud, whether anyone would hear her scream.

At last he released her, expression cold. "I thought you wanted to kiss me."

Shaking, she backed away a few steps, stretching out her wings. They ached but didn't seem damaged at all. "I think maybe I'm not ready yet. I . . . I'm . . ." She broke off before apologizing, realizing she didn't owe him being ready for anything. "I should go." She started for the door and he stepped in her way. Fear gave way to anger. "Zayden, let me go."

He grabbed her wrist hard enough to hurt. "I thought you liked me."

She stood tall, shoulders back and head high. "Seriously, Zayden, we can talk later, but right now, you need to let go." Her voice trembled and she cringed inside at how weak she sounded.

He stepped in close and grabbed her other wrist. "And if I don't?"

He's strong, she thought, *but I'm pretty sure I'm stronger.* She twisted her arms toward each other as hard as she could and broke his hold. Surprise flashed, then the unsettling cold glare returned.

Just then, his phone rang and he glanced away. Chloe shoved him aside, charged out of the room, and slammed the door. Trying to contain her emotions, she pulled up her goggles, ran outside, and took off. She flew over the quad and saw the scorched grass plus L.J. and Miguel making what looked like a miniature jet. She continued up over Heroes Hall and spotted the lake shimmering in the distance. She headed for it at top speed. The wind rushed against her face, flowing over and under her wings as they beat up and down in a frantic rhythm.

At the edge of the water, she dipped down to the cooler air just above the surface. Spray from her wind kicked up against her shorts-clad legs. Her jumbled emotions began to simplify, clarify, and she slowed. The beauty of the sunlight on the water, the warmth on her wings, the trees on the shore helped her fear and panic fall away. Her anger no longer raged and bubbled, but mellowed to a simmer.

What would he have done if I hadn't resisted? If I hadn't stood up to him?

She couldn't believe he would've hurt her or forced anything on her. He was Zayden—everyone's hero—and he cared about her. Didn't he?

Did I over-react? she asked herself. Going over it all, she decided she hadn't. It was one thing to try to kiss her. If it hadn't been for the weird memory flash, she might have been okay with it. Grabbing her to keep her from falling? Sure, great.

When she pulled away, though, he should've known she didn't want to be kissed. Trying again, holding on when she squirmed and told him to let go . . . not okay. Grabbing her wrist and everything after? Not okay at all. Even if he'd just made a series of innocent mistakes, which is what she hoped, it scared her that he didn't *know* all that was wrong. *And that look in his eyes . . .*

Chloe knew she had to end it. She circled around to head back to campus. As soon as her eyes fell on the dormitory, though, she got choked up. *It was all so perfect,* she thought. *He's so cute and seemed so nice, and he actually liked me.* Flying at sixty miles an hour with tear-streaked vision seemed like a bad idea, so she dropped down into a copse of trees, sat on a rock, and sobbed into her hands.

* * *

Chloe entered the dorm and peeked into the lounge. Lindsay and Izzy sat at the table together, huddled over math homework, and Jacob sprawled on a couch, reading and bobbing his head to the beat of whatever music played through ear buds.

Lindsay looked up and concern flashed across her face. "Where have you been? I thought you'd be out here."

"What's wrong?" Izzy asked, seeing Chloe's red, splotchy face.

"Girls' meeting, our room, now." A glance down the hall confirmed Zayden's door was shut. "Get Rhiannon. Ava, too, if she'll come."

Lindsay and Izzy got up and gathered their stuff as Chloe went to her room. She grabbed a protein bar and an energy drink and sat down with her back against the headboard, a pillow behind her back to cushion her tired wings.

A minute or so later, the other four freshman girls came in. Lindsay and Izzy sat on the other bed. Rhiannon sat cross-legged at the end of Chloe's. Ava hovered inside the closed door until Chloe asked her to please sit down, and then she grabbed a desk chair and perched on the edge, ready to bolt.

Chloe swallowed the last of the protein bar and washed it down with a long drink.

"I have something to tell you guys. Some of it will probably sound crazy, but I swear it's all true."

After crying in the woods, she'd thought over how best to tell them about what had happened in Zayden's room. She realized it wouldn't make sense unless she included the dreams and flashes she'd been getting, so she started at the beginning and told them everything—the early dreams, remembering them when he touched her hand, him emerging from the burning building, then the way he'd acted after closing the door.

"I was so angry and scared and confused, I just flew, as hard and fast as I could, until I got it all sorted out. I wanted to make sure you guys all knew so you could be careful around him."

They sat in silence for a moment, all of them looking stunned and scared.

"Don't you think you could be over-reacting?" Izzy said, sounding apologetic. "I mean, when you add in the weird flashes, yeah, sure it was scary. But he was probably just nervous."

"Do you really think he would've, like, forced you?" Lindsay asked.

Chloe took a shaky breath. "I don't know. Maybe you're right, Izzy. I want to think he was just confused. You know, awkward situation, nervous . . . Something about the way he looked at me when he blocked my path, though. Calculating, like, figuring out what he could get away with, maybe."

Lindsay came over and hugged her around the neck. "I'm so glad you got out of there okay."

Chloe hugged her back and forced away tears she was surprised to still have. "So, I need to talk to him and tell him it's over, and I want to see what he has to say for himself."

Izzy sighed. "If you want to break up with him, that's your business, but really, you should keep an open mind when you talk."

"I will. I'm not gonna tell him about the flashes, or memories, or whatever they are. I'm wondering if I should tell someone he might be telepathic, too."

"I don't think he is, though," Rhiannon said.

"What do you mean?" Chloe asked.

She shrugged. "Think about it for a minute. You said you saw him coming out of the burning building, right? And you somehow watched it from a bed, staring at the ceiling, attached to machines? If you were somewhere else watching Zayden, you weren't seeing *his* memory. You were seeing someone else's."

"Oh, my gosh, you're right." Chloe couldn't believe she hadn't realized that. "So whose was it?"

Rhiannon shrugged.

"His brother," Ava said. "The one in the hospital. What's his name, Jackson or something? Isn't he telepathic?"

* * *

"Jacob," Lindsay said for the third time, shaking him by the shoulder. He'd fallen asleep on his history book.

He jerked awake. "Is it time for dinner?"

"Not quite, but we need you to go to your room, okay?"

"Why?" he asked.

Lindsay sighed. "We'll fill you in later."

He sat up and snapped the book closed. "Fine. Come get me when it's time to eat."

Chloe sat at the table. Izzy stood inside the open door to the girls' bathroom while Rhiannon and Ava took up positions across the hall in their doorway. Lindsay marched down the hall and knocked on Zayden's door. He opened it and looked disappointed that it was her.

"Chloe wants to talk to you," she said, arms crossed. "In the lounge."

"Oh. Okay." He looked wary but headed down the hall. Lindsay followed, but stayed just inside the boys' hallway.

Zayden sat down across from her. "Lindsay said you wanted to talk to me."

Chloe took a deep breath and steeled herself. "I think it's best if we end . . . everything."

"Chloe, don't." Zayden looked stunned and hurt. "I really like you, and I'm sorry about earlier. I thought you wanted me to kiss you—"

"Look, I know it was probably just a misunderstanding, or nerves, or whatever. I get that. I just think you're ready for stuff that I'm not and it's better if we just . . . stop."

He stood up, shoulders slumped, and put his hands in his pockets. "Okay, yeah. I was a jerk and I'm sorry. Can we still be friends?"

She gave him a weak smile. "Yeah, sure."

He nodded and an awkward silence stretched on for several seconds before he slunk to his room. Once the door closed behind him, the girls all gathered in Rhiannon and Ava's room.

Chloe let out a sigh. "So I guess he took it pretty well."

"I don't know," Lindsay said. "When he passed me, on the way back to his room, just at the last second he shot this nasty look at me. Seriously, my blood went cold. I always thought that was just an expression, but now I get it." She rubbed her upper arms.

Izzy shook her head. "You guys are making this into such a huge *thing*."

Chloe's stomach growled loud enough for them all to hear. She let out a strained laugh. "I don't really feel like eating, but apparently I need to."

Rhiannon glanced at her phone. "The dining hall opens in three minutes. Want to head over?"

Chloe stood. "Yeah, I guess."

"Wait a second," Ava said. All eyes turned toward her. "I just wanted to say . . . thanks for including me in this. I know I can come off bitchy but I don't mean to. My mom says I have no filter. So, can we try to be friends?"

Chloe looked from Ava to Lindsay, who sighed and gave a little nod. "You need to apologize to Lindsay, but yeah. We'll give it a shot."

"I really am sorry! I didn't think about what I was saying, and when you got upset, I was defensive and rude and bitchy. Plus, I totally shouldn't have called you out in Combat Training. I was just hurt that you guys wouldn't talk to me."

Lindsay didn't meet Ava's eye and didn't respond right away.

Ava sighed. "Rhiannon told me to apologize, like a million times, and I wanted to, but, I don't know, I guess I'm stubborn."

Lindsay relented. "Thank you for the apology. I can't say we'll be best friends tomorrow, but I'll try, okay?"

Ava nodded and looked like she might burst into tears.

"Yay! Group hug," Rhiannon said, and the five girls crowded in to put their arms around each other.

CHAPTER TWENTY

Tuesday, Sept. 6, 2016
Denver, Colorado

"You may have noticed extra security guards on campus this morning," Mr. Kirby said in Criminal Law, the freshmen's first class in the morning. "More cameras are going up today and tomorrow, as well."

"Is that because of the fires?" Lindsay asked.

Mr. Kirby nodded. "Mr. Jordan has asked us to let you all know the school is investigating and to report anything strange—anything at all—that might be related to them. Fire is never a joke or a prank." He unbuttoned his shirt cuff and rolled up the sleeve. The dark brown skin over much of his forearm looked mottled, stretched tight, and puckered. Lindsay flinched and looked away. "Who's heard of the villian Napalm? Lindsay, I'm guessing you have." Napalm had died during the Deep Six prison break Katie Malone had brought to an end. Lindsay nodded and a few others raised their hand. "I came up against him about fifteen years ago, when I was working solo, and I'll always have these scars to remind me. Not that you ever forget the pain of being burned."

"So, is that what they think it is? Someone pulling a prank?" Ava asked.

"I don't know the details of the investigation, and I couldn't discuss them with you if I did," he said. "I just wanted to impress upon you how seriously you should take this. You know how it is—if you don't think someone's really intending harm, you don't want to get them in trouble. But then someone gets hurt and you realize you should've done something before things went too far. Don't put yourself in that position."

Chloe couldn't help glancing at Zayden. Is that what she was doing? She'd taken it seriously enough to tell the other girls, but what about going to a teacher, or Mr. Jordan? She didn't know, and she didn't want to disrupt everything just after they'd resolved the conflict with Ava. She decided to keep an eye on Zayden and report it if anything else happened, but she felt pretty sure that it wouldn't—he was a nice guy who made a mistake. It made her uncomfortable with him, but she didn't think he'd do it again.

She did want to make sense of the visions she'd been having, though. She needed to talk to a telepath, but she didn't know any other than Solomon, and she wasn't crazy about him.

After Spanish, she headed off to the stadium for Flight Training—or, in her opinion, the best class ever.

"Chloe, wait up."

She stiffened at the sound of Zayden's voice and turned around, her brow furrowed. "Yeah?"

"You have Flight Training now, right?" he asked. "Can I walk you to the stadium?"

She hesitated, wanting to say no but feeling like she shouldn't. "Um, yeah, I guess." She wondered if maybe he wanted to apologize again.

"You asked me to help get Lindsay and Ava talking to each other again, so I was really surprised to see her hanging out with you guys later. Seems like things are fine now."

"Yeah, Ava apologized, so things are mostly better." He'd edged so close that their arms almost brushed. His presence looming beside her made her feel uncomfortable, and she increased the distance and spread her wings to keep him away. "Gotta stretch out before flying."

He looked at her wings with admiration. "I wish I had wings. They're so cool."

Yeah, until some jerk smashes them against your back, she thought. "So, is that all you wanted to talk to me about?" She was glad they'd almost reached the stadium.

"No, not exactly." He stopped.

After a few steps, she stopped, sighed, and turned around. Then she just stared at him and waited.

"I still really like you." Zayden looked at the ground. "I was crazy nervous when you were in my room and I couldn't think straight, 'cause you're so pretty, and I get so anxious around you. I guess I'm hoping you'll give me another chance."

Chloe expected a pleading expression when he at last looked her in the eye. Instead, it felt more a doctor trying to figure something out. Detached. Cold. Goosebumps rose despite the 92-degree weather. *Something's just not right about him,* a little voice said. She studied him back, apparently long enough for him to realize it, because all of a sudden, he gave her his most charming grin. A few days ago, it made her knees weak. Now, it made her stomach churn.

NO! NOT REAL!

She jumped as someone screamed in her brain.

Zayden's eyes narrowed. "What's wrong?"

"N-nothing," she stammered. "Just a little cramp in my flying muscles. They've been sore all day." She realized she was backing away from him. *Way to sell that nothing's wrong,* she thought.

Zayden closed the distance between them, blue eyes icy. "Why do you jump and tense whenever I'm close to you? Do you think I'm going to hurt you?"

"No, of course not." She resisted the urge to back up again.

"Tell me about the burning building you saw after the mower blew up." It sounded more like a demand than a request.

Goosebumps flared again. "I have to go. I'm gonna be late and so are you." A shadow passed over them and they both looked up to see Charlie's moth wings silhouetted against the sun. He dropped down and landed beside her.

"Hey, Chloe." He gave Zayden a disapproving look. "What's your name again?"

"I'm Zayden."

"Well, Zayd, I don't see wings on you, so unless you can fly without them, you'd better go find your own class." He turned to Chloe. "C'mon, let's make an entrance. Up and over?" He gestured up to the top of the stadium wall and they turned their backs to Zayden.

"Sounds good to me." Chloe buzzed her wings harder than necessary so Zayden would take the full force of the wind. Charlie flapped his wings with a *whoomp* and they both lifted off without so much as a glance at the boy on the ground. Moments later, they touched down on the wall.

"Hope I read things right. You wanted to get rid of him, didn't you?"

Chloe, a little shaken, took a deep breath and let it out in a rush. "Yeah. Thanks."

The bell rang and Ms. Donovan waved them down.

"Wait," Charlie said as she prepared to take off. "I know it's none of my business, but if you want to talk, I'm a pretty good listener."

She gave him a grateful smile before flying down to the stadium floor.

* * *

"They definitely think it was a pyro who started the fires," Lindsay told Chloe, Charlie, and her two fellow fire-shapers, Austin and Kaci, over dinner. Lindsay had messaged the pyros on Parable about wanting to meet with them and Charlie had joined them while walking over from the dorm. He'd been sitting outside in the rain, wearing an Army-green rain poncho over each wing. The way he hopped up when they approached gave Chloe the impression he'd been waiting for her. Or maybe Austin, since they were friends. Yeah, probably Austin, she decided.

"How'd you find out?" Kaci asked. "Mr. Jordan wouldn't tell me anything."

Lindsay glanced around. They all huddled close around a table on the fringes of the dining hall, making sure no one could hear them. "My mom knows someone, she wouldn't say who. But yeah, they didn't find accelerant or anything at either scene, and security video shows it bursting into flames with no one near it." She rolled her eyes and looked sulky. "Of course, I was the last one to walk past."

Lindsay had been called away from Fire Training for tests of her abilities, and so far, they'd found no sign she could light fires by accident. Her mom and middle school had confirmed that there'd been no fires, mysterious or otherwise, around her. Since her ability had come on early, at just five, they thought it unlikely she'd start having accidents now.

"I'm just glad I wasn't anywhere near it," Austin said, and Kaci nodded in agreement.

"I don't mean any offense," Charlie said, "just looking at what-ifs—but is it at all possible that you did start them?"

Lindsay flushed red, but she looked sheepish rather than angry. "No, I'm positive. When the mower blew, I tried to wipe out the flames like I do with my own, just in case. It didn't work."

"Did you really think it could've been you?" Chloe asked, stunned Lindsay hadn't mentioned it to her before.

Lindsay shook her head. "I just wanted to be like, a hundred percent sure. Now I am."

"That was really smart." Charlie looked impressed. "Where does that leave us, though? If it had to be a pyro but not one of you, that must mean . . ."

"There's another pyro," Chloe finished.

"Whoever it is," Lindsay said, "they must be pissed that Zayden keeps putting their fires out."

The others kept talking while Chloe got lost in thought about Zayden. *How could he be such a hero and still a jerk?* It was hard to reconcile. The image of him emerging from the building flashed through her mind, and she remembered a rescue from a fiery car wreck, too. Plus the visions that started when he touched her hand all involved smoke and fire. "Guys, you're gonna think I'm crazy, but could the other pyro *be* Zayden?"

They all stared at her, confused.

"Why would you think that?" Lindsay asked.

"Think about it. Like you just said, Zayden put them both out. Or, at least, he put out the second one and helped with the first, using a water bottle. Have you seen him carry a water bottle since then?" Chloe asked. "Because I've paid a lot of attention to him, and I'd swear he never had it with him again."

"And your . . ." Lindsay almost mentioned Chloe's vision but stopped herself in time, to Chloe's relief. "And you said he rescued people from a burning building once?"

"Plus a car crash. Where an engine burst into flame." She looked around the table. "Have you ever heard of that happening outside of a movie? I mean, it just doesn't happen very often in real life."

"Didn't his brother make those cars crash or something?" Kaci asked.

Chloe picked at her bottom lip, remembering how she'd breathed in heat to diminish the fire in what seemed to be Dax's memories. "He got blamed for it, but they're both telekinetic—what if Zayden did it so he could play hero? His brother can't talk to defend himself. It'd be easy to set him up."

"If that's his M.O.," Austin said, "maybe he's setting you up now, Lindsay. He just waits for you to get mad and, boom."

Lindsay's face went pale, freckles standing out even more than usual. "You guys, whoever blew up the lawn mower could've killed that groundskeeper."

Chloe swallowed hard. "A couple of people got hurt really bad in the building fire, too. If it is Zayden . . ."

Charlie whistled through his teeth. "So we could be looking at not just a pyro, but a frigging sociopath."

"Unless I'm totally wrong and just mad at him for being a serious jerk-face," Chloe said.

"Either way, we need to tell the guys about his jerk-faciness so they can keep an eye on him, too." Lindsay nodded toward their classmates. "Do we tell a teacher, or Mr. Jordan?"

Chloe thought for a minute. "I don't know. If I'm wrong, it could land an innocent—well, *relatively* innocent—person in hot water and make me look like an idiot."

"For the record, I think you should. They need to know if one of the students might be a . . . a supervillain," Charlie said. "Either way, you need to watch out for him. He put off some serious anger vibes outside the stadium."

"I'll be careful." Chloe wondered how he'd react if she told him what happened in Zayden's room.

"And I'll watch your back," Lindsay added.

Charlie nodded. "I will too, whenever I can."

Chloe and Lindsay finished eating and headed back out into the drizzle. Half way there, Kaci caught up with them. She looked fragile and a little green.

"Hey, Chloe, I didn't want to say anything in front of the guys," Kaci said, "but I don't think you should wait to report Zayden—and I'm not even talking about the pyro thing."

"What do you mean?" Chloe asked.

Kaci's eyes darted around. "So, you were going out with him, right?"

"Yeah, kind of." Chloe shrugged. "But only for like a week."

"Why so short? If you don't want to tell me, that's cool, but if he did something . . . something aggressive, maybe, that made you break up with him . . . please let someone know." Kaci swallowed hard. "I didn't, when my boyfriend got violent, and I'll regret it for the rest of my life." The blood drained from Chloe's face. Kaci hugged her. "It's not a group you want to be part of. Do something, okay?"

Chloe nodded, mouth dry. "Yeah, okay. Thanks."

Kaci gave her a wan smile and jogged back to the dining hall.

The roommates stood there silent for a while before Lindsay spoke. "So, what do you want to do?"

Chloe sighed. "Who should I tell? Mr. Jordan? Mrs. Jordan?"

Lindsay glanced at Heroes Hall. "They're probably long gone. Want to see if any teachers are hanging around?"

She considered Mr. Rodriguez, then had a better idea. "Let's check the gym."

* * *

Mustang Sally sat back, brow pinched and lips pressed into a thin line. "First, thank you, girls, for saying something. Second, Chloe, how are you holding up?"

Chloe took a deep breath. Her hands shook. "I'm okay. A little rattled, I guess, but I've faced him twice and I know I can handle it."

"If you ever aren't okay, you can always come to me. Mr. and Mrs. Jordan are great options, too, and so is Mr. Rodriguez." Sally leaned forward. "These are really serious matters and I have an obligation to take this to Mr. Jordan right away. I'm certain he'll want to talk to you, as well. Want me to come with you for that?"

"Would it just be me and him?" she asked, not sure how comfortable she'd be talking about this with a man she'd barely exchanged two words with, and someone she'd grown up seeing in calendars, too.

"For something like this, I'm sure Ingrid will be there, as well," Sally said.

"That'd be okay then. Thanks for the offer, though."

Sally gave her a warm smile. "Not a problem. As far as your suspicions related to the fires, I'm sure you realize it's a lot of circumstantial evidence and what-ifs. That doesn't mean we won't take it seriously—we've all seen hunches pan out—but I just want you to keep some perspective, all right? Please let the investigators handle it and don't spread this all over the dorm or Parable or anything."

The girls nodded in agreement.

"Do you know where Zayden is now?" Sally asked.

"He left the dining hall before we did, so probably back in his room," Lindsay told her.

Sally thought for a moment. "Step out into the gym for a minute. I'm not comfortable with you going back to the dorms just yet."

The went out and sat on a bench.

"I feel like a complete jerk," Chloe said.

Lindsay gaped. "Why? You haven't done anything wrong, Chloe!"

"Am I making too big a deal out of everything?" she asked.

"Remember what Kaci said? Plus, if someone does something wrong, it's not your fault if they get in trouble for it." Lindsay put a hand on her shoulder. "The bad guys are supposed to get in trouble, and someday it'll be our job to make sure they do."

Sally emerged from the office a few minutes later. "I briefed Mr. Jordan and had campus security go to the dorm. Zayden's not there. The guard will stay nearby for when he returns. Mr. Jordan wants to talk to him tonight. You too. He's on his way in now." She hugged both girls. "Thank you again for coming to me. And Lindsay, thanks for being a good friend to Chloe." The door opened and a security guard stepped in. "Please take these two to Mr. Jordan's office and wait there until he arrives. They're not in trouble—they're witnesses." Sally turned back to them. "I'll see you tomorrow, girls."

A few minutes later, they sat in cushy leather chairs facing Mr. Jordan's desk. When he and his wife entered the office, it was hard for Chloe not to think of them as MetalBlade and Icebreaker, even when they wore civilian clothes and hadn't been Just Cause heroes for years. Mr. Jordan apologized for making them wait as he sat down behind the desk. Mrs. Jordan pulled a chair up next to Chloe's. Mr. Jordan asked for Chloe to start at the beginning and tell him everything. Chin rested on steepled hands, he listened with an intense focus.

"Our top priority here is always keeping our students safe," he said after she finished. "As soon as Zayden comes back to the dorm, he'll be brought to us. By the time he leaves, at the very least he'll know the way he's behaved toward you is unacceptable. We'll consider your suspicions as we move forward in the fire investigations as well, I can assure you."

Mrs. Jordan leaned forward and put a chilly hand on Chloe's. "If you're uncomfortable with the living situation, we do have some alternatives we can explore. Is that something you'd like to talk about?"

Chloe shook her head. "Not right now, but it's good to know there are options in case things get worse."

"Let me be clear on this," the principal said, deep voice filling the room. "If things escalate at all, he will cease to be a problem for you or anyone else at this school. If he wants to stay here under my watch, his behavior better improve."

Chloe let out a sigh of relief. "Thank you. I'm sorry you had to come back after hours for this."

"Nonsense," Icebreaker said. "It's what we're here for. I'm really proud of you girls for coming forward. I know Keith is, too." She glanced over at her husband.

He nodded. "Absolutely. I'm looking forward to seeing what kind of heroes you'll make—you're brave, intelligent, and observant. Those words describe the best of us." Both girls flushed. Mr. Jordan gestured to the guard. "Nadeem will walk you back to your room. Do you have the number for campus security on your phones?" Chloe shook her head and pulled out her phone. Lindsay followed suit. Mr. Jordan rattled off the number and they both punched it in. "You can summon them from Parable, too. Don't hesitate to call if you ever feel threatened."

They thanked the Jordans and left, following Nadeem. He was short but so broad and muscle-bound he could only be a brick—and one of those like Sally mentioned to Ava, who worked out all the time to enhance his super strength. They went inside after him.

"Have a good evening, girls," he said with a thick Middle Eastern accent, then stopped to talk to Glenn, the security guard at the desk.

Just as Lindsay opened the door to their room, their phones both dinged. They checked the alerts and saw Zayden had posted on Parable—his dad had come for a visit and Zayden was staying the night at his hotel.

"We need to call a meeting," Lindsay said. "You check the lounge and I'll start knocking on doors."

First, Chloe showed the guards Zayden's post. Glenn's brow furrowed. "He didn't sign out. I'll contact Mr. Jordan."

Then she went down to the lounge, where she found L.J. at the table, tinkering with an intricate mechanical model. On the couch, Miguel coached Jacob on the proper pronunciation of Spanish swear words.

"Have you guys heard from Zayden at all?" she asked.

"No, nothing. And the guard told us not to contact him. Any idea what's up with that?" L.J. muttered without looking up.

"I know exactly what's up," she told them. "Meeting in my room, right away. For everyone."

L.J. glanced at her, annoyed. "I'm kinda in the middle of something."

"It's important. You can bring your . . . thingamajig, just please come." She went down the hall and to her room with the three guys lagging behind. L.J., the last one in, sat at her desk and kept tinkering. Once they'd all crammed in, she shut the door and locked it.

"Has everyone heard what Zayden did the other day, when I was in his room?" she asked.

Miguel nodded. "Izzy told me."

"Miguel told me," Jacob added.

L.J.'s eyebrows rose up under his beanie. "Uh, I'm the only one who doesn't know, apparently."

"Sorry, L.J., it totally wasn't intentional." She went over the attempts to kiss her, the wing smashing, and him grabbing her wrists. "The worst part was, when I told him to let go, he said, 'What if I don't?' So I shoved him out of the way and got out of there."

"Dude, that's eff'ed up," L.J. said.

She went on, telling them about her visions and why they thought they came from his brother, and their suspicions regarding the fires. "But that's not all. Today, he followed me down to the stadium and acted really weird and aggro over the burning building I saw, so I have to wonder if he thinks I suspect him. I'm getting scared, you guys." She felt emotionally drained from going through it three times.

"So what are we gonna do?" Jacob asked. "Do we report him?"

Lindsay, reading the emotion on Chloe's face, jumped in to answer. "That's why the guard is here. We went to Sally after dinner, and she called Mr. And Mrs. Jordan back so Chloe could tell them everything, too."

"Does anyone believe his dad came to visit?" Rhiannon asked. "'Cause the timing seems kinda fishy to me."

"Wow, guys," Izzy said, "I can't believe how ready you are to convict him without a trial. Don't you think we should let the investigators figure things out first? Or at least hear Zayden's side of it?"

Lindsay's face went red and her eyes sparked. "His side of practically attacking Chloe and then harassing her? Really, like he could say anything to justify that?"

Izzy squirmed. "Well, no, but with the other stuff. There's no evidence whatsoever that he's a pyro, and you're ready to throw him in Deep Six."

"We are not." Chloe's voice sounded listless and flat. "It's just . . . weird stuff is happening, and he disappears all the time. We're just trying to piece it together."

"Yeah, well, that's not your job, and it's a good thing, considering all the conclusions you're jumping to. I'm not gonna be part of the lynch mob." Izzy got up and stormed out.

"She does kinda have a point," Miguel said. "Look how you felt, Lindsay, when Ava jumped to conclusions about you."

"Look, I know what he did, and I know what I'm seeing in the dreams and visions and stuff. If you can come up with another explanation, I'll listen." Chloe sighed. "Some actual investigators are looking into it now —I'm sure they'll figure it out soon enough. For now, I'm really freaking tired and I just want to go to sleep."

Lindsay stood up and motioned everyone toward the door. "Okay, guys, let's give Chloe some space."

CHAPTER TWENTY-ONE

Wednesday, Sept. 7, 2016
Denver, Colorado

Chloe and Lindsay had just gotten up when Rhiannon knocked on their door.

"What's up?" Lindsay asked once Rhiannon came in and shut the door behind her.

"Zayden showed up a few minutes ago and the guard took him away before he even went in his room."

They all eyed each other anxiously. "Did he say where he spent last night?" Lindsay asked.

Rhiannon shook her head. "The guard said 'come with me,' Zayden asked why, and the guard said Mr. Jordan would tell him. That was it."

They threw on clothes and went to breakfast. Just as they finished eating, Rhiannon's phone buzzed. As she checked a message, her brow furrowed. "It's from Bridger. He says to come to his room—and bring Chloe."

"Why me?" Chloe asked. Rhiannon shrugged.

"Wait," Lindsay said. "Doesn't he have super hearing?"

Rhiannon's eyes fell closed. "OMG. I'll bet he listened in on the questioning."

Chloe's jaw dropped. "Would he do something like that?"

Rhiannon snorted. "Oh, yeah. He totally would. Let's go."

Back at the dorm, they climbed to the third floor. Bridger motioned them in through the open door. He sat at his desk, and Sol lounged on the bed across from him.

"What's up, bro?" Rhiannon hesitated inside the door. "Should I shut it?"

Bridger gave them a mischievous grin and nodded. "I thought you'd want to know how things went with everyone's favorite hero this morning," he said after it was closed.

"Called it," Lindsay said.

"Dude, I'd say I can't believe how stupid that was, but because it's you two, I can so totally believe it." Rhiannon plopped onto her brother's bed.

Chloe's hands shook. She knew Bridger shouldn't have listened in, but she had to know what Zayden said. "So, what happened?"

"Pull that chair over," Bridger motioned to Sol's chair, "and I'll show you. I can't type for crap, so Sol tapped into my brain and took notes." He opened his laptop and scooted back to let Chloe see better. Lindsay read over her shoulder and Rhiannon leaned in from the foot of the bed.

Mrs J there plus Mr Rodriguez and Sally. Asking what happened when C was in his room.

Z said thought she liked me, thought she wanted me to kiss her, knows he shouldn't have closed the door but wasn't thinking straight. She tripped and I caught her, didn't mean to crush her wings, total misunderstanding. Didn't grab her wrist just tried to take her hand to comfort her, tried to apologize.

"Lying jerk," Chloe muttered.

Asking about outside stadium.

Z said concerned she was seeing visions, paranoid about telepaths because of his brother, wanted to make sure no one was messing with her head like the rude guy who had dinner with them the other night.

Hey, he's talking about me! I'll show him how I mess with heads!

Mr J telling him why behavior was inappropriate, asking if he understands.

Chloe's phone chimed with a Parable alert and she ignored it.

Z said feels bad, didn't mean to hurt her, tried to apologize. Will stay away from her, make sure not to scare or bother her again.

Simpering little shit lays it on thick. I don't trust him.

Mrs J says no tolerance to sexual assault or any form of harassment, he needs to think before he acts. Mr R says he can help him learn appropriate boundaries if that's a problem. Z says he understands where he messed up and it won't happen again.

Mr J asking about fires now, if Z saw anything, knows anything. Z says no. Mr J-you've saved people from fires a few times, is there any possibility you have fire-based powers?

Z-no, no way.

J-some witnesses wonder why you've been prepared to put them out both times.

Z-just had ideas right away I guess. Probably from growing up with his brother.

J says they want to do some tests and have to get permission from his parents. Says don't leave campus, be sure to let someone know where he is any time he's not with friends or classmates. Dismissing him.

Z gone. J asking Mr R what Z was feeling. R says hard to get a read on him, maybe good at blocking because of growing up with a telepathic brother.

Ha! Knew I was right about that!

S and Mrs J agree Z's story is reasonably consistent with C's. Mrs J will call parents about testing and will see whether his dad was really in town. Meeting breaking up. Mrs J staying behind and

SO DIDN'T NEED TO HEAR THAT! GAH!

Need mental bleach. Stat

Rhiannon giggled when she got to the end. "I'm guessing the Jordans have a decent love life."

"Um, yeah," Lindsay said. "He's only one of the hottest heroes ever, even though he's old. And so is she."

"So what do you guys think?" Chloe asked. "About the questioning, not the Jordans' sex life."

Lindsay sighed. "I think Zayden said all the right things. Not that I believe him, but who knows. Maybe they bought it."

"They've interrogated way smarter people than him. I'm sure they can tell he's lying," Rhiannon said.

"I sure hope so." Chloe felt guilty about the eavesdropping and nauseous over what Zayden had said.

"So this probably goes without saying, but you guys have to promise not to tell a soul about this." Bridger looked them each in the eye. "We'd be expelled in a heartbeat if Jordan ever found out."

Rhiannon crossed her heart. Lindsay nodded.

"Yeah, sure." Chloe wished they hadn't done it in the first place, but there was no putting that genie back in the bottle.

* * *

Wednesday, Sept. 7, 2016
Kansas City, Missouri

"Anna, it's good to see you." Dr. Huxley crossed the office to shake her hand. "This is my research assistant, Misteya Michaels."

Misty shifted a clipboard to her left arm while trying not to spill her coffee and shook Anna Lord's hand, which felt like a chilled butterfly. She was pretty, but Misty could tell the worry lines around her eyes and the corners of her mouth were nothing new. *Stay professional,* she told herself. *The last thing she needs is pitying looks.* Misty knew plenty about those. Well-intentioned poison.

"They said at Reception you wanted to see me before I went to Daxie's room." Anna managed a shaky smile that came nowhere near her eyes. "Is he all right?"

Dr. Huxley took her elbow and guided her out of the room as he spoke. "He is, certainly. But Anna, we've had to put him on a few more machines. They're purely for observation, but I wanted you to be prepared for that before you saw him—it can be upsetting."

She gave a hesitant nod. "Have you figured out why he's getting weaker?"

"Misteya has an interesting hypothesis, based on a case report of a remote viewer," he told her. "'Remote viewing' is exactly what you'd expect, based on the name—someone who can view things happening great distances away."

Misty cut in, resisting an eye roll at his characteristic over-explanation. "Your son's brain activity is similar to one of the more powerful viewers who's been studied, although Dax has more activity, and it only quiets down when he's asleep. Even then, it seems to operate at half-power."

"You think he's viewing something . . . all the time?" Anna asked.

Dr. Huxley nodded. "We're working under that assumption. Do you have any idea about what could be holding his interest?" They reached the door to Dax's room and he paused with a hand on the knob, waiting for her answer.

Anna chewed her bottom lip and stared at the door. "Would the amount of distance change how much effort it takes?"

"It's possible, but most likely not to the degree we've observed."

"Because I just wondered, maybe it's because Zayden left home. He's at the Hero Academy now."

"What date did he leave home?" Dr. Huxley asked, nodding to the folder on Misty's clipboard.

Wishing she'd left her coffee in the office, she stuck it between her side and an elbow so she could thumb through the records to find the date Dax's heightened activity began.

"Two weeks ago. The sixteenth, I think."

Misty shook her head, not needing the exact date to know it didn't line up. "That's too recent. I was already studying the case by then."

Anna looked near tears. "Please, Dr. Huxley, can I see him?"

"Of course, of course." He at last turned the knob and swung the door open.

Misty followed Anna in and set her cup down on the small end table between two stiff chairs just inside. She stayed a few steps behind as Anna approached her child's bed. New electrodes and cables attached to his head lead to a monitor displaying several jagged lines jumping up and down. Anna put a shaking hand on Dax's cheek and made a pained noise, then took his hand in both of hers. "Mommy's here, Daxie," she whispered, as if afraid to disturb him. The heart monitor beeped along at a steady pace. She turned to Dr. Huxley, who now stood at Misty's left elbow. "No response. Does that mean he doesn't know I'm here this time?"

The Doctor nodded. "I'm afraid it probably does. Other than perhaps a general soothing when he hears music, we've had no sign that Dax is aware of what's going on around him anymore. I don't think his condition is worsening, though. I think he's simply distracted, mentally elsewhere." He put a hand on Anna's shoulder. "However, that's just my best guess. It's hard to be certain of anything with him, as you know."

Anna closed her eyes, chin trembling. Dr. Huxley pulled out a tissue and offered it to her. She took it, mumbling a thank you, and dabbed under her eyes.

* * *

"There he is," Lindsay said under her breath when Zayden walked into the dining hall for lunch. He hadn't come back to the dorm after being questioned.

They sat as far from the door and the food line as possible, Chloe's back to the entrance. "Does he look mad?"

"No, he looks totally normal." Lindsay's brow creased. "Oddly normal, in fact."

"I'm starting to think he's a really good actor," Chloe said.

Rhiannon nodded. "Me too, 'cause yeah, he looks like nothing at all is wrong."

Chloe started to turn but stopped herself. "Is everyone with him?"

"No, he's alone," Lindsay said. A few minutes later, the rest of the freshmen came in. Izzy looked around and spotted them, a questioning look on her face. "There's everyone. I think Izzy's annoyed we didn't wait for them."

"Zayden just sat at a table with a bunch of juniors. I think one of them's a 'kinetic," Rhiannon reported.

Izzy's eyes landed on him and narrowed. She glanced back at the girls and whispered something to Miguel. Once they made it through the line, the twins came over and sat down.

"Okay, what the what?" Izzy asked.

Keeping their voices low, they filled the others in on the morning's events.

"Gee, thanks for letting us know." Ava took a big bite of oatmeal.

"Sorry." Rhiannon looked sheepish. "Bridger and Sol could really get in trouble, and we didn't want anything to get back to Zayden before they questioned him."

Izzy sighed. "We're supposed to be a team. I think we should all be in the loop on stuff like this."

"I don't know," L.J. said. "Isn't there some saying about three people only keeping a secret if two of them are dead? It doesn't hurt to lower the odds someone will slip up."

"Or say something intentionally," Jacob added.

Izzy's head flipped around. "What's that supposed to mean? You think one of us would betray the group?"

The speedster shrugged, face scrunched up. "No, just . . . I mean, if someone felt bad for him, or disagreed with what was happening . . ."

"Please, guys, let's not fight." Chloe said. "I'm sorry we kept it a secret. I think after trusting Zayden when I shouldn't have, and trusting my gymnastics team when

I shouldn't have . . . I don't know. Am I getting paranoid or smart? I just don't know what to even think anymore."

Silence descended and tension hung thick as they all ate. Lindsay tried to break the silence a few times, but it would just descend again, more awkward than before. Eventually, they all got up and went to class. Zayden didn't give any sign he noticed them walk by.

They all got settled into their places in history and Zayden slipped in just as the bell rang, not meeting anyone's eye. L.J. and Miguel pulled Javelin's tech from large sheets of construction paper, and Chloe remembered, with a jolt, that they had to do their presentation. She pulled out her notes, grateful now to be working with the guys. She was also glad she'd finished her part early.

Mr. Halabi had her group go first. Chloe's heart pounded as she walked up to the front. She didn't know if she imagined it or Zayden really tried to burn holes in her with his eyes. After several stumbles, she shot L.J. a panicked look. He took her notes and bluffed his way through the informational portion and then moved on to the tech. She slipped behind him to block Zayden's view of her and tried to take deep breaths to calm down. She didn't know how she'd get through a whole day of classes with him there.

When the bell rang, Mr. Halabi asked Chloe to stay behind for a moment.

"What happened to you during the presentation?" he asked once everyone else had filed out.

"I guess I just kinda froze. I had a rough night and forgot it was today, so I wasn't as prepared as I should've been."

"Mrs. Jordan sent out an email about some problems you've had. Does it have anything to do with that?"

She nodded. "It's no excuse, though. I should've been more on top of it."

He gave her a kind smile. "I'll forgive it this time, but yes, next time I will expect you to be more prepared. I know you're a bright and ambitious student, so I set a high bar for you." He grinned and seemed expectant, and she knew she'd missed something. "What, no appreciation for my gymnastics pun? High bar?"

It was such a bad joke she couldn't help but laugh, which made her feel a lot better. "Nice one, Mr. Halabi. I should've caught that."

"You'd better move along so you're not late," he said.

Her improved mood didn't last long. As soon as she stepped out into the hallway and saw more than a dozen people clustered around the site of the garbage can fire, a sense of foreboding descended.

"What's going on?" she asked Lindsay, unable to see over the taller students in front of them.

She swallowed hard. "I think someone's taking responsibility for the fire."

Confused and concerned, Chloe pushed through a knot of girls and saw a word—or name—scrawled on the wall in red letters:

Blayze.

"Who in the hell is Blayze?" she asked of no one in particular.

She startled as she heard an answer in her mind. *It seems our mystery pyro is revealing himself.* Chloe whipped around to see Solomon standing there.

"Can you at least say 'hi' first?" Chloe muttered to him. "It'd be a heck of a lot less creepy."

One corner of his mouth turned up. "Where's the fun in that?"

Chloe couldn't decide whether he was entertaining or a total jerk. She supposed both wasn't impossible.

"Something's going on outside, too," an older girl called from down the hall. The crowd moved that way. Zayden followed along, his expression blank.

Sure enough, a group clustered on the quad, staring at the ground right where the mower had exploded.

Charlie, Justin, and two non-winged fliers hovered in the air above it. Charlie waved her up. She zipped to him in a flash and saw, in the middle of the manicured green lawn, lines of bare, reddish-brown soil standing out in stark contrast. They, too, spelled out *Blayze*.

She told Charlie about the writing on the wall and he agreed someone was taking credit for the fires. "I wonder why he spelled it that way."

Chloe thought she just might know.

* * *

"That poor woman!" Misty fell backward onto the bed. "I wish I could tell her he did know she was there, and that he's desperately trying to communicate something."

Joe, sitting at the tiny desk they shared in the studio apartment, swiveled around in the task chair to look at her. "Honey, I think it's time you came clean with Dr. Huxley. He specializes in paras—he'd probably see your powers as a huge bonus. Plus, isn't it unethical or something to have information on a patient and not use it?"

She sighed. "If I thought it would change anything about his condition, I would. I mean, it'd be nice to comfort his mother, but to be honest, I think she's beyond comfort at this point. Her baby boy is essentially lost, and her older kid is away at school now. She's all alone and stressed about to the breaking point. I can feel it coming off of her in waves."

"Have you tried communicating with Dax about his brother? To see if you're on to something?" Joe asked.

She rolled onto her side. "Yeah, I just saw someone filling the propane tank on a barbecue. I don't know, maybe Zayden likes to grill. Maybe it was something else entirely." She sighed. "I don't want to talk about the Lords anymore—too depressing. What did you do last night?"

"Ha! You don't want depressing and yet you ask me that."

"Yeah, I may not have the best judgment."

Joe worked a few nights a week as a paramedic and went to med school during the day. She didn't know how he functioned on so little sleep and teased him about that being his parahuman power. Misty would feel better if he did have abilities. She'd never wanted to be different in yet another way.

She had fair enough skin that people didn't automatically identify her as black. While she didn't attract much racism herself, though, she'd experienced far too much when with her mother. However, Misty did get the ignorant questions and comments from people perplexed by her racial ambiguity. *"What are you? Are you some kind of mix? You can't be black, you have normal hair."*

In fifth grade, her para powers came on and she'd always pushed them away, hidden them. People expected too much of parahumans, especially young ones. *And now here you are pressuring a disabled little boy for information,* she thought. Then again, he did seem rather anxious for someone to receive his message.

Joe went back to homework. Misty put in ear buds and pulled up the Lords TV show on her tablet. Seeing Zayden's face gave her chills, it never failed. From the first time she'd seen him, sitting next to Dax's bed holding his hand, she'd distrusted that kid. Something was just . . . off about him. At the same time, Dax seemed sweet and earnest. It didn't jibe with what she knew of their lives—unless Dax really just didn't understand the things he did.

He must understand more than they think, though, she thought. *Why else would he be working so hard to communicate something?*

As she re-watched the *Heroes Among Us* episode about him for what must have been at least the twentieth time, she wished she'd known Dax before the accident that turned his eyes white and landed him in the hospital. She watched Dax with more interest than usual, trying to pick up clues as to what he'd been like.

When it showed Zayden's TV news interview, with Anna holding Dax in the background, she sat up straight on the bed and rewound, closing her eyes to listen to something she hadn't noticed before. *How did I miss that? How did anyone miss that?*

* * *

One by one, each freshman went to Mr. Jordan's office for questioning. Zayden went first, leaving Psych for thirty minutes. He returned, cool and unruffled. Chloe went next and flew to Heroes Hall to burn off some nervous energy.

"Chloe, how are you doing today?" Mrs. Jordan asked when she arrived.

She tried to smile. "A little shaky, to be honest, but not too bad."

Mr. Jordan flashed his famous smile, which didn't help her knees feel any more stable. "Good. Sit down, please. This shouldn't take long."

She sat, wishing she had a drink because her mouth and throat went bone dry.

"So, I'm assuming you saw the name on the wall and in the grass."

"Yeah, like someone's claiming responsibility, right?"

He nodded. "That's right. It's common enough for terrorists and criminals who want notoriety. Do you have any idea who could have put them there?"

She paused. "It's hard to say. I mean, they weren't there when we went to class, and Zayden came in a couple minutes behind the rest of us, but there's no way he had time to do that. Plus, before class, there are people everywhere. Someone would've seen."

He raised an eyebrow. "I'm sensing a 'but.'"

"But," she continued, "the way it's spelled, I can't help but think Zayden chose it so I'd know it was him."

The Jordans looked at each other, confused.

"Why is that, Chloe?" Mrs. Jordan asked.

"He liked how I used my last name as part of my codename, keeping the 'Y.'" She looked from her to him and could tell they hadn't caught on yet. "So when I saw Blayze, it struck me that it has a 'Y,' just like 'Wyld.'"

"Interesting observation." Mrs. Jordan didn't sound convinced in the least.

Mr. Jordan looked thoughtful for a moment. "I appreciate you mentioning it, Chloe, but it feels like you're reaching. That's understandable, with how you feel about Zayden, but do you think maybe you're trying to force the evidence to fit your theory, instead of the other way around?"

She wanted to crawl under the desk and hide. "Yeah, I guess I could be."

"Thank you, Chloe, you can return to class now."

She stood, then hesitated. "Um, there's surveillance video all around campus, right? Extra cameras, even, since the fire?"

"That's right," he said.

"So, can I ask what it shows?"

They eyed each other again and Mr. Jordan seemed to give a slight nod.

"I suppose it's better to have the truth out there rather than speculation," Ingrid Jordan said. "The video shows a marker writing on the wall with no one around. The grass took more effort—some chemical appears to have been spread on the lawn early this morning, before the sun came up, but again, the video showed an empty quad. The water came on as scheduled during first period and activated the chemical, which burned away the grass."

"So it had to be a telekinetic." Chloe knew in her heart it was Zayden. *They have to know that, too, don't they?* she thought.

"Zayden wasn't even on campus when the chemical was laid down," Mr. Jordan said. "He's simply not powerful enough to have done it from so far away, and it would've been obvious if he'd written on the wall during class. Mr. Halabi knew to keep an eye on him, and he says Zayden didn't appear to be especially focused."

Mrs. Jordan leaned toward her, radiating her natural cooling. "Also, while it could've been done with telekinesis, it also could've been done with invisibility, super speed, control over the air or even the materials in the pen, or any of half a dozen other known para abilities."

Chloe's shoulders slumped. They were right—every time she'd seen Zayden use his abilities, it was obvious. With new para powers surfacing all the time, who could say for sure which one was used?

As she walked back to class, though, she couldn't help but think of different ways Zayden could've accomplished it—although she had to admit it would be difficult without help.

* * *

"Joe, do you have a minute?" Misty's heart raced.

He looked over his shoulder. "Sure, as long as you quiz me on the bones of the foot later."

"Ugh, the foot? Can't we do something easy like brain regions or neurotransmitters?"

He blinked. "Yeah, no. It's the foot or nothing, babe, that's the deal."

She gave him a mock sigh. "Fine, if I have to."

He sat down on the bed. "That show again. Maybe I should renege."

"Here, during Zayden's interview, Dax is making noises in the background. The first time, I heard 'nausea,' which I knew wasn't really what he was saying, but I never thought beyond that. Listen to it, though, and tell me what you think he's saying." She tapped play and watched his face as the scene rolled.

His eyes narrowed. "Wait—is he trying to say Zayden, do you think?" He tapped the screen to go back and listen again.

"Nah-Zay. You hear it, too."

Joe nodded. "What do you make of it, just to see if we're on the same page here?"

Misty swallowed. "Zayden says he just wants to help and Dax says 'Nah-Zay.'"

"Not Zayden," they said together.

Misty snorted. "I knew I didn't trust that creepy little shit."

CHAPTER TWENTY-TWO

Thursday, Sept. 8, 2016
Denver, Colorado

Chloe woke up smelling smoke and tried to dismiss it as a dream, but something refused to let her drift back off to sleep. Then she realized her lungs hurt and snapped to attention. Lindsay's closet door stood open a crack, and light from inside it flickered on the wall as smoke poured out.

"Lindsay!" she yelled as she leapt from bed. "Wake up!"

Her roommate didn't move. Chloe shook her. She got no response and panic set in. "Lindsay!" she yelled. Nothing. Smoke grew thicker and the closet door caught flame with a sudden *whomph*, blocking the door to the hallway.

Chloe unlocked the window and tried to open it, but it wouldn't budge. She yelled Lindsay's name until she started to choke and cough. Intending to smash the window, she grabbed the stool from her desk, but as she raised it, a hard coughing fit seized her. She stumbled sideways into her bed and the stool smacked the side of her head. She reeled at the sudden headache. Her eyes burned and teared. She managed to stand up again but was too disoriented to know where the chair had landed. Thinking maybe she could throw a heavy text book through the window, she took two steps toward her desk and tripped over a stool leg. She sprawled face first into the floor, gasping for air between coughing fits, trying to breathe but finding no air.

As she slipped from consciousness, she heard a hissing sound and, dimly, her name.

* * *

Chloe awoke to a strange pressure on her face. Her lungs ached, but each breath came easier than the last. Her stomach growled and she felt drained, sure signs her body worked hard to heal itself.

Struggling to open her eyes, she first saw stars in the night sky and dimly wondered why she was sleeping outside.

"She's awake!" A woman leaned into view and Chloe realized the pressure came from an oxygen mask.

"Hey there, Chloe," the woman said. "They say you have super healing. Do you think you can breathe on your own?"

Chloe nodded and the woman—a paramedic— removed the mask.

Taking a deep breath, Chloe smelled smoke. Everything flooded back—the fire, the stuck window. Lindsay, not waking up.

Adrenaline shot through her and she sat up, whipping her head around. Two paramedics wheeled a gurney toward an ambulance, and black hair spilled over the side.

"Lindsay!" She tried to yell, but it came out a croak. "Is she okay?"

"Don't worry about her, hon. Just lie down and rest." The paramedic, whose name tag said "Brenna," eased her back onto the gurney.

A firetruck stood between her and the building, blocking her room, but she didn't see smoke or flames.

On her other side, Zayden sat on the lawn as a single paramedic tended to him. Their eyes met and he gave her an angelic grin that made her blood boil. Chloe glared at him. His face went blank.

"Chloe's awake!" Rhiannon yelled from the quad. Students in pajamas and bathrobes had gathered to watch. Charlie's wings, visible above the crowd, moved toward her, but a security guard told him to stay back.

"How are you feeling?" Brenna asked.

"Tired. Throat hurts," she managed.

"That's normal," the paramedic assured her. "We're going to re-check your vital signs now. Just try to breathe and stay calm."

The male paramedic slipped a blood pressure cuff on her arm while Brenna put a stethoscope to her chest. After listening for several seconds, she smiled. "You're doing really well considering how much smoke you must've inhaled."

"I need a Power Bar." Her voice already sounded stronger.

The guy laughed. "You what?"

"When I heal, it takes a lot of energy. I need to eat, like, now."

"Let's start an IV," Brenna told her partner.

He shrugged. "Might as well. She's probably dehydrated anyway."

Brenna looked her in the eyes. "That'll give your body some sugar to burn, okay? Lie down and rest—don't expend any extra energy."

Chloe nodded and lay back, then grimaced as a needle went into her hand. She fell asleep, her body demanding all of its resources.

* * *

Chloe woke up again as they wheeled her into the hospital. She felt almost well.

"Hey, Chloe," Brenna said. "We brought you in just to make sure everything's good, okay? You're going to have some tests and a doctor will look you over, but everything looks good so far."

"How's Lindsay?" she asked.

Brenna shook her head. "Sorry, hon. I don't know. I'm sure someone from the school will be along soon. Maybe they'll be able to tell you something."

They took her to a curtained-off room in the ER and transferred her to a bed. Brenna helped her into a hospital gown. She still had the IV in and wore a little nose mask for oxygen. The paramedic told her someone would be in soon, and left. A few minutes later, a sour-faced man with gray hair came in and drew blood.

"Have you seen the other girl who came in from the fire? My age, black hair?" Chloe asked.

"Is she your sister?" the phlebotomist asked.

"No, she's my roommate."

He shook his head. "I'm sorry, I can't tell you anything if you're not family."

A while later, a red-cheeked white guy who looked around twenty came in and wheeled her down the hall for a chest X-ray. She asked him about Lindsay as well.

"I'm really not supposed to say anything." He glanced around. "But I just took her back to her room and I'm sure she'll be okay. She was a little groggy, but she asked how you were doing."

She thanked him, letting out a breath she didn't realize she'd been holding.

When she got back to her room, Mrs. Jordan and Sally waited there. Sally hugged her. "I'm so glad you're all right! Gotta love that rapid healing."

"Yeah, I'm fine. How's Lindsay?"

"Worse off than you, but she'll be fine in a few days." Mrs. Jordan hesitated. "I hate to ask this while you're recovering, but did you notice anything strange before you went to bed? Or before you passed out from the smoke?"

Chloe thought back. "Nothing from earlier, but I couldn't wake Lindsay up, and she's usually not that hard a sleeper. Plus, the window wouldn't open."

"Are you sure it was unlocked?" Mrs. Jordan asked. "Sometimes when we're panicked, it's easy to forget things like that."

Chloe shook her head. "No, I remember flipping the latch. It was stuck, but it's always opened easy enough before."

The Dean of Students looked concerned. "Excuse me for a moment," she said, and slipped out of the room.

Sally sat down on the doctor's wheeled stool. "Mr. Jordan called your parents, and Lindsay's too, of course. They're going to fly in as soon as they can."

Tears sprang to Chloe's eyes. She didn't remember the last time she'd wanted to see them so badly. "They must be freaking out, them and Mrs. Malone. At least my parents know I'll get better fast."

Sally looked grim and put a hand on her arm. "You should know, Chloe, that Zayden rescued you. Another few minutes and your body may not have had a chance to start healing."

"I think I remember hearing something—a fire extinguisher, maybe? I knew someone was there, but then I passed out." She thought for a moment. "That's the third time Zayden's been there to save the day when fire breaks out."

"That's true," Sally said, "but he also breathed in a lot of smoke. He had to come in and get checked out, too."

"It's so hard to know what to think." Chloe sighed. "Even if he set the fire, running into a burning room . . ."

Sally rubbed her arm. "Don't try to figure it out right now. We'll piece it together. This 'Blayze' person's got nothing on the super villains we've gone up against, remember that."

Chloe smiled and nodded, feeling safer thanks to the reminder about who was on the case.

Mrs. Jordan poked her head in through the curtains. "Sally, can you step out here for a moment?"

"I'll be back when I can," Sally said as she left.

Chloe wished she had her phone so she could text her parents and check Parable. She realized she didn't know how bad the damage was. Did she even still have a phone or was it a melted lump? What about her gymnastics medals? The homework she'd put so much time into?

The heart monitor next to her bed beeped faster. A nurse rushed in to check on her. She determined Chloe was fine and asked if she wanted to see her friends.

Chloe's heart leapt. "Yes, please!"

The nurse left and a minute later, in came Rhiannon, Ava, L.J., Charlie, and Bridger. The two girls gave her big hugs while the boys stood back looking awkward. Everyone wore pajamas except for Charlie, who was in jeans and a t-shirt.

"I'm so glad you guys are here!" Chloe said. "Were you out there this whole time?"

"Yeah," Rhiannon said, "we pretty much insisted on coming with Sally and Mrs. Jordan, so they had to bring a school van."

Chloe laughed. "You guys are awesome. Where's everyone else? Could they go back in the dorm?"

Charlie shook his head. "They hadn't by the time we left, but I saw on Parable that the fire department cleared everything above the second floor."

"So where's everyone sleeping?" she asked.

"They moved everyone up to empty rooms on the other floors, freshmen on the fifth floor with the post-grads, sophomores on the third and fourth."

She asked about the damage to her room, but they didn't know the extent of it—they'd left before being allowed anywhere near it.

"I tried to see the damage from the air, but I couldn't get a good line of sight on it with the fire trucks blocking the building," Charlie said.

Chloe sighed. "So, Sally told me Zayden pretty much saved our lives."

They all gave each other uneasy glances.

"What's going on, guys?" Chloe asked.

Rhiannon sat on the stool next to the bed and leaned in to whisper. "Zayden's gone. No one knows where he is."

Chloe looked at her, confused. "Sally said he came here to get checked out. You guys didn't know?"

"We did know," Bridger said, "but I listened in to see how you guys were doing, and after Mrs. Jordan pulled Sally out, she told her Zayden had disappeared from the hospital. Campus security hasn't seen him. They're checking security video now, and I messaged Sol—he hasn't come back to the dorm."

Chloe's eyes went wide. "Okay, disappearing from the hospital? That's not something an innocent person does."

"No, it's not," Rhiannon said.

"Plus, Zayden wasn't in our room until right before the fire started," L.J. told her. "He seriously came in like three minutes before I smelled smoke, and the second I mentioned it, he rushed down to the lounge. And for some reason, the smoke alarms didn't go off, or the sprinklers."

Chloe told them about the stuck window and Lindsay not waking up. Everyone looked pale and scared.

Chloe took a deep breath. "We have to do something. I'd thought about it before, but now I have to do it—I'm gonna tell his mom everything."

L.J. snorted. "Tell her that her little hero is an arsonist and a creeper? She thinks he's perfect."

"Yeah, but putting his little brother in the mental hospital pretty much crushed her and ruined her marriage," Chloe said. "If I tell her Dax is innocent, I know she'll listen."

"Are you serious?" Ava gaped. "I mean, what do you really know for sure? There's been fires and you've had weird dreams. That's it."

Charlie looked sympathetic. "I know there's a lot of circumstantial evidence pointing at him, but that's a lot to drop on this poor woman if you're wrong. I know I wouldn't want to make that phone call."

Chloe shook her head. "Guys, I know what I know. I'm not calling, either—it'd be too easy for her to just hang up. She only lives a few hours away. I'm gonna fly there." Then she remembered her parents and Lindsay's mom were on their way. "Unless she's already headed here."

Bridger shook his head. "I listened in on Mr. Jordan's phone calls before we left. She was too upset to drive and Zayden's dad was drunk, so he wouldn't be able to pick her up until sometime this afternoon."

"What time is it now?" Chloe had no idea what time the fire had even happened.

Ava checked her phone. "Just after four a.m."

"Let me see that." Chloe reached for the phone and Ava handed it to her. She search for Anna Lord in Hays, Kansas and a street address came right up. She hit the button to map it from her current location. "It's 328 miles along the freeway, but shorter in a straight line. If I leave now, I can be there in . . ." She pulled up the calculator and punched in some numbers. "Five or six hours. Even with breaks, I should be there before noon, hopefully before she leaves. Ava, I'll need to keep your phone."

Ava groaned and then sighed. "Yeah, okay." Everyone else looked stunned.

"Chloe, you can't fly there now," Charlie said. "You're in the freaking hospital after almost dying in a fire."

"Yeah, but I'm fine," she told him. "The school will freak, and so will my parents, but I have to do this. I'll text my mom that I'll be back sometime this evening." She took the nose tube off over her head. Looking at the IV needle, and the tape holding it in place, she grimaced. "This is gonna hurt."

"You can't just do that yourself!" Rhiannon sounded hysterical. "You're gonna get us all in trouble."

Chloe looked at each of them, knowing they could see her determination. "You can watch me do this, or you can go back out to the waiting room and say you didn't know anything. Your choice." She pried up a corner of the tape and ripped it off, stifling the yelp of pain.

Everyone but Charlie scrambled out. He gripped the bed's side rail. "I'll come with you, just to make sure you're safe."

"Sorry, Charlie." She grasped the IV and pulled the needle out, not flinching even though she thought she might throw up. "I really, really appreciate the offer. You have no idea how much, actually, but you'd slow me down too much. That's the only reason I'm saying no, and that's the truth." She smiled at him. "Do you have any money I can borrow? This trip is gonna take a ton of calories."

* * *

Thurs., September 8, 2016
Text exchange on burner phones

I gotta disappear. C suspects, I saw it in her face
Where you going?
Think about it. You know.
Are you calling things off?
No way.
I want to come with you
No, stay there. Act natural and follow the plan. Tell the others. FOLLOW THE PLAN

* * *

Chloe had never flown for anywhere near that long. She took a few breaks to rest and slam down protein bars and energy drinks she'd bought at a convenience store—along with some cheap sunglasses, since she didn't have any goggles.

If she dwelt on the muggy heat, she'd never be able to get through it. The scenery consisted of the interstate, corn fields, and little else, so she tried to stay focused on the puzzle in her mind and what the various pieces meant. The change on Zayden's face when she glared at him kept playing over and over in her mind. *He knew,* she thought. *He knew I'd figured it out, that he couldn't fool me anymore.* She wondered if that's why he disappeared from the hospital.

She also found herself wishing she'd allowed Charlie to come with her after all, even though she'd have to cut her flight speed back so he could keep up with her. He was so nice, always looking out for her, even lending her money for the trip. She thought back over the time she'd spent with him, especially at the lake when he'd asked if she and Zayden were going out. *Wait, maybe he really does like me.* The thought made her feel warm inside, and that surprised her. *Do I like him?* She wasn't sure. Maybe.

In just over six-and-a-half hours, she hovered over Anna Lord's back yard, comparing it to the satellite images on Ava's phone to make sure she had the right place.

She touched down on the grass beside a small patio, relieved to be on solid ground. Her wings and back muscles ached like crazy. Even her abs and thighs hurt from staying stiff for so long, and she realized it might have been an unrealistic expectation for her to think she could fly there and back in one day.

She hoped Anna Lord was home. She didn't know where the woman worked, or for that matter if she even had a job. Nevertheless, Chloe smoothed back the ruffled hairs around her face and slipped around to the front of the new-but-small house. "Here goes nothing," she muttered as she knocked on the door. It opened to reveal Anna, dark circles under her eyes, looking even thinner and more frail than at orientation.

"Can I help you?" She gave Chloe a puzzled look. "Wait. You're at the Academy with Zayden, aren't you? Do you know where he is? Is he with you?"

"No, I don't know where he is, Mrs. Lord, but I do really need to talk to you. It's about Zayden. And Dax."

Her brow furrowed. "Come in. What's your name?"

"I'm Chloe. Did Zayden ever mention me?"

Anna led her through a small but tasteful great room and kitchen to a little breakfast nook, where a single bowl and glass sat on a bistro table with two chairs. "I don't think he did. How did you get here, Chloe?"

"Oh, I flew."

"All that way?" Anna's voice sounded surprised but her face didn't seem to have the energy to change expressions. "That must've taken a while."

Chloe shrugged. "I can move pretty fast."

"I was just sitting down to lunch. Would you like something to eat?"

"I am kinda hungry, if it's not too much trouble. If you don't have enough, I've got protein bars."

"I still cook as if I have a family of four, I can't break the habit, so there's more than enough." Anna dished her up some stew, then sat and stirred her own but didn't take a bite. "All right, tell me what's important enough to make you fly all this way."

Chloe swallowed a bite and took a deep breath, trying to sort out her thoughts. *Might as well just jump in,* she thought. "First, I have to ask if you know whether Dax can see things that are far away."

Anna looked taken aback. "Well, yes, but his doctor has only just figured that out."

Chloe nodded. "It all fits then. Mrs. Lord, I'm not telepathic or anything, but I've been having these weird dreams and visions since getting to know Zayden. It's mostly when I'm near him or like, if he touches my hand, and I'm pretty sure they're Dax's memories." She told Anna in detail what she'd seen, leaving out the parts that made Dax look innocent and incriminated his brother. She'd get to that soon enough.

Anna's hand fluttered to her mouth. "Oh, my God. You describe it perfectly—the fire, and Dax's hospital room. When I visited him just the other day, the doctor said Daxie seems to be transmitting telepathically, but we couldn't think why. I guess now we know who he's been contacting, even if we don't know the reason."

"I have an idea about that, actually." Chloe's heart pounded. "See, Dax tried to put out the fire. I could feel him breathing in heat and smoke, and when he did it, the flames would shrink. He was worried that . . . *someone else* would get his way this time and people would get hurt."

Anna's eyes lost their dull cast for the first time. "Someone else? Wait, are you trying to say that Daxie is innocent? That someone else did the things he's accused of?"

Chloe nodded, expression solemn. "Mrs. Lord, Zayden has saved a lot of people from fires. We've had three fires on campus since school started, and not only was he there every time, he was prepared to put it out every time."

Tears welled up and spilled down Anna's cheeks. "No, no it can't be Zayden! He's always worked so hard to help people, putting himself at risk . . ."

"The *Heroes Among Us* episode said after Mr. Lord got hurt, police questioned why your family seemed to be there for so many accidents." Chloe swallowed hard. "Please don't hate me for saying this, Mrs. Lord, but I think Zayden's been behind them all along, and taking credit for the rescues. I think Dax tried to stop him, and I have to wonder if he's still trying to stop him."

Anna buried her face in her hands. "I didn't want to believe it of him . . . how could I?"

"I'm sure it was hard, with Dax not being able to talk."

Anna looked at Chloe with haunted eyes and shook her head. "I don't mean Dax."

Chloe didn't understand what she meant at first, but they sat in silence for several seconds and it sank in. "Mrs. Lord, what has Zayden been doing?"

Anna stood up and paced, trembling all over. "I should've known. I'm their mother! How could I let this happen?"

She went on, Chloe sitting at the table not knowing what to do. She wanted to comfort the poor woman, but she didn't know how.

"I . . . I'll be back in a few minutes," Anna said at last. "Please, just wait here."

Her footsteps retreated down a hallway and a door shut. Chloe didn't know what else to do, so she finished her stew and washed the bowl, then sat down and waited.

* * *

"I honestly thought I was losing my mind." Anna had been in the bathroom for around twenty minutes, then came out seeming much calmer. They now sat in the living room, Chloe on the couch and Anna in a chair across from her. "I suppose I should start at the beginning."

She went on to tell Chloe how she'd had a rash of disturbing dreams a few months before. "They were mostly confusing, just smoke and flames and heat, but I also remembered seeing Zayden's face and being so afraid."

"Did you tell Zayden about them?" Chloe asked.

"Not at first, but then I started hearing Daxie's voice." Anna paused to blow her nose. "He kept telling me Zayden wanted to hurt people. It all seemed so real. So I asked Zayden if Dax ever sent him dreams and he looked like something inside him turned off. He went from being my sweet, loving boy to . . ."

"Cold and calculating?"

Her chin quivering, Anna nodded. "He told me Dax had tormented him in dreams and he'd learned to block them, and I needed to learn how. He said Dax wanted to turn me against him. That's when . . . odd things began to happen."

Chloe didn't want to push—Anna seemed so fragile —but she knew the woman could have important pieces of the puzzle. "What started to happen, Mrs. Lord?"

"First, I couldn't seem to cook anything without it burning. Then, I'd go to grab something and it would be hot enough to scald me. My flatiron burned off a chunk of hair, and I didn't even think it could get that hot." Chloe remembered seeing that missing hair at orientation. Anna sighed, shaking her head. "Zayden said he was worried about me, that Dax's manipulation was making me fall apart. I really thought I was crazy— when something would burn my hand, Zayden would touch it and say it wasn't hot at all."

"Why would Zayden do all that, do you think?" Chloe asked.

"I wish I knew. He got some counseling after the divorce—I thought it was best after all he'd been through—and he urged me to see the same doctor. I guess they'd talked about Dax sending him dreams, and the counselor said a sedative might help stop it, or at least keep him from remembering."

Chloe remembered how Lindsay wouldn't wake up during the fire and something clicked. "Did you start taking the sedative?"

"I did, but I didn't like taking it, so I didn't use it often. Zayden . . . he seemed obsessed with it. He checked with me every day to see if I'd taken it, and when I said no, things would . . . happen." She broke down in tears.

"More fires and burns?"

"That, yes. Plus, I kept tripping over things I'd swear hadn't been there a moment before, and he'd bring up conversations I didn't remember, tell me I'd done things I had no memory of . . ."

Chloe went to the couch and sat down next to Anna. "I'm so sorry, Mrs. Lord." Not knowing what else to do, she gave the woman a long hug.

* * *

I feel so bad for her, Zayden's been basically torturing her, Chloe texted Lindsay from Anna's couch. Lindsay had sent a message to Ava's phone hours ago, before Chloe arrived, but she hadn't seen it until after her talk with Anna and a shower to wash off the bugs and grit from flying. She now wore Anna's bathrobe—backward, to accommodate her wings—while her clothes were in the wash.

Chloe'd almost cried to know her roomie was okay. They texted rather than use Parable so the school couldn't peek in on them. *Anna said she was calling the hospital but I think she needed some time alone. Oh, and she called Zayden's dad to say not to pick her up, but he was too hungover to come anyway. Great dad, eh?*

Ya, awesome, Lindsay sent back. *So they're saying I was drugged. A sleep med and something called diralipam that's used for anxiety.*

OMG, that's so scary! How would he have drugged you? Chloe slipped down to the bathroom.

I guess it's a liquid, so he must have put it in my soda somehow.

How? He wasn't around at dinner or in the lounge last night. She opened the medicine cabinet and there it stood—a brown prescription bottle with DIRALIPAM on the label, right next to Anna's sedatives. She snapped a picture of them and sent it to Lindsay.

Doesn't that just figure, Lindsay replied. *He must've stolen some. I'm guessing he drugged me the same way he poured chemicals on the lawn. Btw no one has seen him. He wasn't at lunch and there's no sign he's been back to his room. They let us into our rooms to get some things and LJ found Zayden's phone on his desk.*

How's our room? Chloe asked, heart in her throat.

Pretty bad. Everything in my closet is gone, all the paper, most of the stuff on my wall.

What about my phone? My medals? She held her breath.

Medals are fine. Letting the phone dry before I turn it on.

Chloe breathed out, head slumping to her chest. *Ok, good. How's your mom?*

A wreck. Your parents too, even with your text. We're all trying not to say anything but it's hard.

Sorry. My wings are killing me so I'm not sure I can make it back tonight. I'll text my mom again.

Ugh. K.

Sorry again. Gotta go. Chloe hit send as Anna came out of her bedroom, puffy eyed and red faced. She sat next to Chloe on the couch.

"Dr. Huxley is out of town, but he's catching the first flight back and would like us to come to the hospital tomorrow morning. I was thinking we could drive to Kansas City tonight and stay in a hotel. The Academy has canceled classes for tomorrow, so you won't be missing anything."

"Okay. We can go once my clothes are dry. I don't have any others."

"I'm sure not, taking off from the hospital the way you did." Anna raised an eyebrow in true mom fashion.

Chloe looked sheepish. "You know about that?"

"Of course. I let the school know you'd come here when I called to tell them I wouldn't be coming right away. They were both surprised and relieved."

"I guess I'll let my roommate know they don't have to keep my secret anymore." She turned on the phone again and texted Lindsay: *Z's mom called school, they know I'm here.* Next, she messaged her mom. *You probly know I'm with Zayden's mom. Heading to Kansas City with her tonight. Sorry to scare you but I have to do this.*

Anna looked Chloe up and down. "You can borrow some of my clothes, you're not that much sho—" she broke off as her eyes fell on Chloe's wings. "Oh, never mind. I suppose we'll have to wait for your clothes."

"Yeah, my mom came up with some great designs with clips and Velcro, like the harness-back on the shirt I wore here, or ties on dressier stuff."

Anna sighed and looked at her. "Do you miss your mom, Chloe?"

The question took her by surprise. "I guess. I mean, school's been really busy and exciting so there's not a lot of time to think about it. But yeah. I'm glad I get to see them soon."

"They must be so worried . . ." Anna's voice broke. "There's nothing in the world like a parent's love. I can't believe Zayden is intentionally putting people in danger. The only way I'll believe that is if I see it for myself, or if Dax can somehow tell me. My baby boy doesn't have the capacity to lie, especially if he's sharing memories. I've always known he's a good boy." Her voice died away to a whisper and tears spilled down her cheeks again. "Since we can't leave yet, I think I'll lie down for a while. Make yourself comfortable." Anna went back into her room and shut the door. Chloe could hear her sobbing and felt awful.

She knew how to pass the time, though—she'd been itching to take a peek at Zayden's bedroom. She figured it had to be the one across from the bathroom, with the closed door. She slipped down the hall and let herself in.

The room comfortably held a double bed, dresser, and desk. The space said nothing about the boy who lived there, though. The pale blue walls didn't hold a single poster of a band or sports figure or anything. A navy and white plaid comforter covered the bed. A lamp stood alone on the nightstand. Other than a computer and keyboard, the desk was bare, as well. Chloe at first figured he'd taken everything with him. Then she realized his dorm room didn't have much going on, either. L.J. tacked schematics up all over his side, but she'd describe Zayden's side as tidy and bare, just like this room. She opened the desk drawer and found a few pens and pencils and some blank paper.

The closet rod held some shirts and a suit, but several boxes lined the shelf up above. Too sore to fly, and not wanting Anna to wonder what sounded like an industrial fan in her son's room, Chloe pushed the desk chair over and climbed up, taking down a box and opening it on Zayden's bed. The first one held blankets. She put it back and got down a heavy one next. It held several books plus some school art projects and kids' drawings. She put it back and took down the last one.

It held a stack of comic books. *Hey, finally, an interest!* she thought. Upon further inspection, though, she realized they were pristine—it didn't look like they'd ever been read. Still, they weren't in plastic covers like you'd expect from collectible ones. She assumed someone had bought these for Zayden and he'd never cared enough to read them.

Underneath the comics, she found a scrapbook. Chloe opened it to find colorful, much-decorated pages featuring baby pictures of Zayden, his parents smiling. Pictures of him crawling, walking, smearing cake on his face on his first birthday. Eventually, Dax joined them, too. Zayden looked like a great big brother, holding Dax's hand, always smiling, always close. Dax had bright, sparkling eyes throughout the first few pages, but then, from one picture to the next, his whole demeanor changed. He looked dazed. He sat and stared, instead of being up running around. On his sixth birthday party, which appeared to just include family, yellow balloons were tied to his chair and a bright cake with burning candles sat before him, yet he stared off into the distance. Chloe's heart ached as she imagined what it must've been like for the family to see him go from a normal child to this.

She did a double take on the birthday picture and realized those balloons looked familiar. She couldn't be certain, but she thought maybe she'd seen them in a dream. They made her think of a swimming pool, even though that made no sense at all.

The farther she went through the book, the worse she felt for the family. Dax eyes grew hollow underneath. Haunted. Then several pages held newspaper clippings lauding Zayden's heroics. She turned to the last page and froze. This page held no happy stickers or embellishments. The single low-quality photo was printed on plain paper, and tacked to the page with a single piece of clear tape.

Dax looked straight into the camera. Where his eyes should've been were two neat holes in the paper.

She shuddered. While disturbing, though, it wasn't hard evidence. She put the scrapbook and comics away and sat down at the desk.

The computer took a long time to boot, and when it did, a password screen came up. She sighed and pushed the chair back to stand up, but then had an idea. She typed in "blayze," then remembered he'd probably added the "y" later and tried "blaze." That didn't work, either. Then she tried different combinations of lower case and capital letters, then substituted a one for the L. Nothing. Almost ready to give up, she put in "lordblaze."

Her jaw dropped as the password screen went away. She was in. *He did add the "y" because of me. I knew it!*

She poked through his documents and pictures folders but they didn't contain much and nothing caught her eye. Then she opened his email—the computer remembered the password for that—only to find an empty inbox. She clicked on Sent Items and smiled as the screen filled up with names and subject lines. She skimmed a few exchanges between Zayden and his dad but didn't see anything incriminating. Then she came across a familiar subject line—"Winners Only"—and sucked in a breath. With one click she confirmed it was the same recruiting email she'd gotten twice.

Her head spun as she absorbed the fact that Zayden was behind it all, not just the fires, but the para-supremacist thing, too. She thought back about when she'd received those. The second one arrived the morning after she'd spent the evening studying with Zayden. He'd left campus and sent her a Parable message, too. Then she remembered the first one showed up just after she'd joined ParaFrosh. *That couldn't be related, could it?* She decided it couldn't be— Zayden had never been on ParaFrosh.

Hoping to learn more about what he recruited for, she clicked the link in the email. It went to a forum with a handful of threads. She opened the first one.

Parahumans are more highly evolved than others. We're naturally superior. That's not ego talking, it's truth. It's science. Why else would they call them "super" powers? Meanwhile, humans fear us and try to take our rights away. But that's their biggest mistake. It only makes us their enemies. The way I see it, we have two choices.

1-We let them regulate us and control us like sheep, or

2-We band together and show them what super powers really mean, protecting ourselves and subduing them.

The only thing standing in our way is our lack of clear organization and mobilization against their efforts.

That ends now. The sooner you make the decision to stand with us, and it's really your only viable decision, the sooner we can strike down the politicians who are against us and take on all the enemies of the parahuman race.

"Yeah, that's not scary at all," Chloe muttered. She moved on to the next thread, a conversation between LB and someone with the user name Chupara. Chloe studied the name and decided it must be someone tacking their initials or part of their name onto "para."

The conversation detailed Chupara's experiences with discrimination because of his or her powers. LB, which Chloe assumed stood for Lord Blayze, told Chupara how wrong and horrible "crunchies" were for how they treated paras, and how they needed to accept their inferiority. Chloe grimaced at the casual use of the derogatory term for non-powered humans. It might not have been as offensive as the N-word would be to a black person, but it was still a pretty terrible thing to call someone.

Other threads included LB, Chupara, and a few others—M&M, iGirlie, PowerUp, and Ev0lvd. A few other people showed up for short stints, but a couple called LB a lunatic and said they didn't want to be part of his group, and a few others just seemed to drift away without saying anything.

Chloe got screen grabs of everything and sent them to Lindsay, Mr. Jordan, and Mr. Hutson, along with Zayden's password.

With that taken care of, she decided she could use a nap, too. She didn't feel comfortable using Zayden's bed, so she went back out to the couch.

CHAPTER TWENTY-THREE

Friday, Sept. 9, 2016
Kansas City, Missouri

Anna and Chloe left their Kansas City motel room around seven a.m. and went straight to the hospital.

"Misteya, so good to see you again," Anna said when Misty opened the door to Dr. Huxley's office, "This is Chloe."

"Just Misty, please." The young woman put out her hand. "Good to meet you, Chloe."

Chloe shook her hand and gave her a weak smile. Misty stepped back from the door and motioned them in. Chloe recognized the man who stood up from behind the big desk as the doctor from the *Heroes Among Us* episode. He introduced himself. "I've never seen dragonfly wings before. May I take a look at your back?"

"Uh, sure." Uncomfortable under the weight of his fascination, she turned around and felt cold fingers on her wings and back muscles.

"Misteya, look at this musculature," Dr. Huxley motioned to the intern to join him. "It's more complex than I've seen for other insectoid wings. These must have tremendous power. How fast can you fly, Miss Wyld?"

"I've been clocked at sixty-three in a sprint, but forty-five to fifty is more comfortable for long distances." She felt proud when Misty gasped and the doctor's eyebrows went up. Dr. Huxley thanked her and offered her a seat.

"She flew from Denver to Hays yesterday morning," Anna said as they settled in to the soft leather chairs and Chloe adjusted her lower wings to rest on the arms. Off to the side, Misty shifted metal clipboards in one arm to brush hair from her eyes while clutching a cup of coffee in her other hand.

"How long did that take?" the doctor asked.

"About six-and-a-half hours, but only because I had to take some breaks."

"You made good time. I suspect you'll only get faster as you mature." He sat and leaned forward with his elbows on his desk. "Now, Anna tells me you're the one with whom Dax has been communicating."

Chloe nodded. "A little bit, at least. I've had dreams and visions ever since I got to the Academy." She recounted them for him.

"Extraordinary," he said when she'd finished. "And you say you're not a telepath? Are you certain?"

"I'm sure—a telepath at school even confirmed it."

Dr. Huxley looked perplexed. "How fascinating. I may contact your parents and ask if I can scan your brain."

"So you think Dax is innocent," Misty said, "and Zayden's been starting fires so he can save people from them?"

Chloe shot a sympathetic look toward Anna, who looked shrunken. "Yeah, that's what I think."

"I knew it," Misty muttered to herself.

"What did you say, Misteya?" Dr. Huxley asked, startling her so much she jumped and coffee sloshed over her hand.

"Oh, uh, just thinking that it makes sense. With what we know of Dax."

He scowled at the coffee mess and pulled a napkin from a drawer. "Here, clean yourself up and we can take Chloe down to meet her mental pen pal."

On their way to the room, Misty asked Chloe if she'd had something traumatic happen on the morning of August 23.

"What day of the week was that?" Chloe asked, trying to think back.

"A Wednesday," Misty said.

Chloe stopped in her tracks. "Uh, why do you ask? 'Cause yeah, I had a panic attack in class that morning."

Misty and Dr. Huxley exchanged looks. "Dax had an acute anxiety attack that morning as well," he said. "It seems your connection runs in both directions."

Dr. Huxley initialed the log outside the door and they went into Dax's room.

Chloe stopped as she stepped into the room and looked around. "Whoa, deja vu. I've seen this before." She walked to the bed and looked down at the little boy who lay there motionless, hooked up to all kinds of tubes and wires and monitors. "Hi, Dax. It's Chloe. I think you've been trying to tell me something." She looked over her shoulder at the three adults. "Can he hear me?"

"Possibly. We're not certain how aware he is of his surroundings since he began transmitting," Dr. Huxley said.

Misty stood beside her. "Why don't you touch his hand and see if you can establish some kind of mental link? It might work better with physical contact."

Chloe took his hand. He gripped it with surprising strength. She jumped, and then her eyes rolled back in her head.

* * *

2012
Lee's Summit, Missouri

"It must be so hard, having one child with such extraordinary powers and another who's so developmentally delayed. Six years old and still in preschool! I don't know how Anna does it."

Dax listened, not understanding why sometimes he could see inside his house all the way from school. He scowled as he tried to place a blue block on top of a red one. *There, I did it!* But then his hand brushed the red block and it burned him. He flinched, and the blue block tumbled to the floor. He wished Mommy was in the kitchen, because if she was, her friends would stop *saying*. Mommy didn't let people *say* about Dax.

"She acts like everything's fine, but it's got to be disappointing. Zayden has so much promise, and then there's one that'll be a burden on them for the rest of their lives."

Dax didn't want to be a burn on his parents. A burn hurts you. He knew because of red. Dax didn't feel hot, though, and only hot things burn. He decided lady didn't know what she says.

Mommy walked back in the kitchen then. "I'm so sorry, girls, but Zayden's tests ran long. Nathan needs me to pick Daxton up from school." Mommy looked apologetic and grabbed her purse.

Ladies gave Mommy fake smiles. "That's no problem, Anna," one of them said. "I should go walk Emma from the bus, anyway."

Good, Dax thought. *I like when Mommy gets me.*

"Daxton, I said you need to put your blocks away," teacher told him. "It's almost time to go home. Do you know who's picking you up today?"

Dax stood up and pointed at the lady doll up on the shelf.

"It's Thursday. That usually means your daddy, doesn't it?"

Dax pointed at the lady again, scowling. "Mmm-mm-mm," he insisted. How could teacher not know? Mommy said it just before, Dax heard it fine. Teacher should pay more attention. He pointed to the kitchen to let her know, but the wall was back and he couldn't see his house anymore. Dax didn't know how big walls could be so quiet when they moved around.

* * *

Dax was hungry. He stared at his food, too scared to scoop it up in his spoon.

"Nathan, you know he won't eat out of the red bowl," Mommy said.

"What the hell does it matter? They're all the same."

Mommy took away the hot and put Dax's dinner in the green bowl. "Daxie doesn't like red."

Daddy sighed. "So why do we even keep the red bowl? Zayden's too old for the baby dishes."

Mommy gave him a sharp look. She didn't like Daddy to say Dax is a baby. "I give it to Zayden for snacks in front of the TV, so my good bowls aren't strewn all over the house."

She put the green bowl on the table. Dax clutched his spoon and tried to scoop up some peas and diced ham. He needed to be quick, before the bowl took all the peas for itself. He liked peas and wished Mommy understood that the green bowl stole his vegetables.

"Why is Zayden in such a mood?" Mommy asked.

Daddy sighed again. "He's still struggling to control his powers, I guess. Dr. Huxley says his brain scans show more than what he's able to do."

"Do you think that'll keep him from getting into the Academy?" Mommy looked worried. Dax wanted to hug her.

"He's got four years to work on it, Anna." Daddy shook his head. "With his reputation, I don't see how they could refuse him, even if he was old enough now."

"That's true. He's saved so many people."

Dax banged his spoon on the table. "Nnnnn-nnnn-nnnn! Zay!" *Not Zayden!*

Daddy grabbed his hand and frightened Dax's reflection in the spoon.

"Aww, he wants his brother!" Mommy smiled at him. "As soon as you're done eating, Daxie."

Zayden didn't come out of his room, though, even after Mommy asked and asked. Dax was glad. He sat next to Daddy on the couch and heard her upstairs, whispering in his brother's ear.

"It's okay, my sweet Zayden. You're a hero and everyone knows it. You'll get into the Academy, I know you will."

Dax knew she was wrong. About all of those whispers except for the Academy. And he knew Zayden would do bad things if he went there.

* * *

Dax hoped no one would be at the pool, but they were. Lots of them. Dax was scared.

When Mommy went to the snack bar for ice cream, Zayden got that look on his face. The bad one. "Whatcha gonna do about this?"

Zayden looked at the high dive and Dax's eyes turned orange and crackled. A girl was up there. Tall. Pretty. Yellow swim suit reminded Dax of the six balloons tied to his chair on his last birthday.

She bounced: one, two, three. Went high and arched her body, right above the water. But then she moved backward like a balloon in the wind.

Zayden looked at Dax with devil eyes, thinking Dax couldn't fix it this time. Dax's eyes turned red, and he tugged the balloon string, hard.

The girl's head missed the board, just barely. The girl turned and twisted in the air and then splooshed into the water.

Dax slapped at his eyes. "Owowowowow bnnnnnn."

Mommy ran over, horrified. "No, no, don't hurt my Daxie! Don't hurt those beautiful brown eyes!"

Zayden jumped up, looking confused and frightened. "Mom, what's wrong with Dax? Why is he doing that?"

Shut up, shut up, shut up! You made me burn them!

"I don't know! Did he get splashed or something?" Mommy asked. "Poor sweet Daxie made his eyes all bloodshot."

Zayden shook his head, eyes wide. "No. I didn't see anything, and I was keeping a real close eye on him, just like you said."

"Of course you were." Mommy kissed Zayden on the head. "I can't imagine what got into him. He's never done that before."

Dax had. Zayden knew, but he didn't say. It hurt worse every time Zayden made him turn his eyes red.

Zayden was mad that Mommy made them go home. Dax tried to take a nap but Zayden whispered through the walls and said Dax would be sorry.

* * *

Dax went to bed early. He didn't want to hear Mommy and Daddy talk in his dream but he couldn't help it.

"Anna, you have to face facts," Daddy said. "Dax isn't getting better, he's never going to get better. Sometimes I think he's getting even worse. Since I came back, I've tried . . ."

Mommy laughed, but it didn't sound happy. "Tried? You haven't tried one bit with Dax. You don't know what he likes or what sets him off . . ."

"Because you baby him so much! Sometimes I think all that kid knows is how to manipulate you into getting what he wants. You put all this time into him instead of Zayden, when you know Dax's brain is mush!"

"Stop saying those things! You can't say things like that!" Mommy screamed and cried. Dax could see her thinking about his brain and pictures the doctor showed her of where it was broken.

Daddy stomped out and said he was going to mow the lawn.

* * *

Dax wasn't looking when the car crashed into the pole, but he felt Zayden do it. Daddy ran to the car and the lawnmower snarled on the grass for a few seconds and then was quiet. Mommy ran outside. Dax looked out the window and saw Zayden smile as the car burst into flames.

Dax's eyes still hurt from the pool, but he made them red and tried to suck the heat from the fire. It didn't work and Dax didn't understand. Then he realized—the glass. He pushed his eyes hard against the window and made it shatter.

Zayden glared up at him. Dax sucked. The hot went into his body and turned cool. He blew it out and sucked more. The flames got little.

Daddy opened the car door and pulled a lady out. She was bloody and her flowy skirt was singed, and her hair. Dax saw Zayden look at the pole leaning over the car. It swayed back and forth.

A neighbor lady screamed. "It's going to fall!"

Dax blew out the cold fire and pushed his eyes at the tip of the pole. He pushed and pushed and pushed. It tried hard to pull away from him. His brother was getting stronger. Dax was scared.

Dax ignored the pain and focused hard. He pushed and pushed some more.

Daddy was opening the door to the back seat now. That was good—a little boy was in there. Dax could feel his fear all the way from his room.

"Daxton, no, don't!" Zayden yelled. "Don't hurt Daddy!"

Dax was distracted and looked at his brother. The neighbor lady stood beside him, looking up at Dax. She had big eyes and her hand covered her mouth.

The pole snapped and Dax couldn't grab it before it slammed down and trapped Daddy in the car. Dax sent his eyes there.

"I'll save you, Dad!" Zayden yelled and threw his hands out like the superheroes they saw on the news. Dax's eyes grabbed the pole and started to lift it, and Zayden staggered back like he was pulling.

"Daxie, don't fight me!" Zayden called to him. "Let me save Daddy."

Dax felt Zayden's power holding the pole in place, and then it wasn't anymore. The pole flew off the car and toward the grass.

"Nnnnn-nnnn-nnnn!" Dax yelled at it, shoving it as hard as he could. His head hurt too bad and he thought the whole world was on fire. "Saaa baaaa, huuuuda!" *Stop brother, hurts Dax!*

"Anna, stop your boy," the neighbor lady yelled and pointed at Dax in the window. Mommy looked up and she was scared, too.

"Daxie, no!"

Dax made the pole fall in the street, then collapsed on the floor and clawed at his burning eyes.

* * *

Mommy held Dax and they watched as the red trucks with flashy lights came.

"Mom, I'm tired and my throat hurts from the fire," Zayden said. He was lying and lying was bad. Even Dax knew that. "I know I'm not allowed to have ice cream twice in one day, but please, can I? Just this once?"

"Just this once. You earned it," Mommy said.

The people pulled the little boy out of the car first and then Daddy. Mommy went to see him. "Nathan, are you okay?"

"Tell Zayden I saw what he did. I saw everything. Tell him he's Daddy's hero."

* * *

"I'm sorry, ma'am, but your neighbor said she saw the little boy do it." The policeman's face didn't look sorry to Dax. He came to the waiting room just after the doctor said Daddy needed a surgery on his back.

"Officer, there's just no way," Mommy said. "Daxton is a sweet boy, and he loves his Daddy. He'd never hurt anyone. And we've never seen a hint of super powers in him before."

The officer read from a piece of paper. "'His eyes were bright red and he stared at the pole until it fell, right on the car. Zayden used his super powers to lift it off his father, and then Daxton made it fly right at us. He yelled something strange and then he howled with rage and started having a fit or something, slapping his own face, when Zayden got control of the pole and dropped it in the street.' That's your neighbor's statement, ma'am. We need to talk to your older son and see what he says."

Mommy's hand fluttered to Dax's hair. "Yes, okay."

Zayden sat looking at his hands in his lap. The neighbor lady watched from the hallway, and others, too. They said mean things, and Mommy didn't tell them to stop *saying*.

"It's okay, son," the policeman said. "You can tell me what happened."

Zayden looked up at Mommy, who still held Dax. Mommy said Zayden should say the truth, it would be all right.

Zayden sighed. "I don't think Daxie meant to hurt anybody, I just think sometimes he does things he doesn't understand."

* * *

Dax didn't like the bandage over his eyes. The skin felt red and hot but he didn't know why. His eyes were white now. Mommy told the doctor something about scratching. The doctor wanted Dax to sit up but he couldn't. He just wanted to sleep.

They had to wait for tests on Dax, and they had to wait till Daddy was done with the surgery.

Mommy laid Dax on a hard wood bench in a room with statues and pretty glass. The sun made the room glow and Dax liked it until she laid him in red light. It burned his tummy and he wanted to move away. His brain told his body, but his body wouldn't listen. "Bnnnn," he tried to tell Mommy, but she didn't understand.

Mommy kneeled and said to God inside her head. Dax heard her ask for Daddy to be okay and for Dax to be okay and for Dax not to be a monster. She didn't call him sweet Daxie. Dax wondered why.

* * *

Mommy carried Dax back to the waiting room. She said her arms were tired and put Dax in a chair in the corner, behind a big plant, so he could lean against the wall and wouldn't fall over.

Daddy's doctor came and said Daddy would be all right but it would be a few weeks before he could go home.

Dax thought all the people looked at him funny because of the bandage on his face. Then a man said, "Do you really think he did it?" and one of Mommy's friends said, "Who knows? He's always been so odd. Poor Anna." And the man said, "Poor Nathan. Thank goodness Zayden was there."

Mommy didn't want to talk to the reporter but she did anyway. He asked about all the times Zayden had saved people and if that seemed strange to Mommy. "Does what seem strange? That my son has used his super powers to help people whenever he could?"

"It's the number of rescues that seems . . . implausible. Most people don't witness that many life-or-death incidents in their lifetime, let alone within two years."

Mommy's eyebrows got pinched in the middle. She didn't want to say he was right so she didn't say anything. Zayden put a hand over his mouth like he was upset but Dax knew he was smiling.

"So," the reporter continued, "it seems as if bad luck is following your family. Have you ever wondered if something around you could be *causing* all these incidents?"

Mommy closed her eyes, thinking about pictures a doctor showed her that made her afraid for her Daxie. Of her Daxie. The reporter looked nervous and his eyes went to Dax and then away again. The neighbors peeked from the corners of their eyes.

Dax tried to melt his body into the chair, but it was gray and gray was always stubborn. The red curtain was just a few inches away. If he could use his eyes, he'd pull it down all around him, even though it would burn.

* * *

Dax didn't understand why Mommy was sleeping against the wall outside his room. She woke up when she heard Zayden coming from his room, and Dax was glad she was there because Zayden was coming to hurt him.

"Are you having trouble sleeping, hon?" she asked.

Zayden said "Why are you up so late, Mom? Are you worried about Dad and Daxie?"

Mommy hugged him. "It's been a tough night, hasn't it? What has you up?"

"I wanted to check on my brother. Make sure he's all right."

Mommy rubbed his check. "That's my good boy. You always look out for your little brother, don't you?"

"Will you be mad if I didn't tell you something before?" Zayden asked Mommy in his saying-not-right-things voice.

She put him in her lap. "Of course not, sweetie. What is it?"

He took a deep breath and stared down at his hands. "I think Dax tried to hurt a girl at the pool." He told her about the girl who almost hit her head. "That's when he started slapping his eyes, just like he did after he . . . after Dad got hurt. You don't think Dax would hurt *me*, do you?"

Mommy looked scared, more scared than Dax had ever seen her. She thought she might throw up her dinner.

"Mommy won't let anything bad happen to you, baby," she said. Dax knew she decided to call Dr. Huxley and tell him about Dax. Why did she believe Zayden and think Dax was bad? Those things were wrong.

Light started to come through Dax's windows. He could feel it. Mommy rocked Zayden on her lap. Her eyes were closed and she couldn't see Zayden smile. Dax didn't understand why Zayden's smile looked bad instead of happy.

* * *

Watching made Dax so tired. Always had to watch, always. Dax had to save the people when Zayden was bad.

Dax dreamed the fire all the time. The awful heat and smoke in his lungs, the fear from the people in his head, the pain from the people. He felt like fire burned him all over and never never never *never stopped.*

* * *

Dax didn't like when Zayden held his hand. Zayden told him to look for things and hurt him if he wouldn't, but looking made Dax's eyes burn.

Dax didn't want to see for Zayden but Zayden wouldn't stop asking until Dax showed him the tunnels. Tunnels that went on forever, Dax thought. Dark, scary, down deep where Dax never ever wanted to go.

But Zayden wanted to go. He wanted to go there so he could hurt people. Dax didn't understand how a tunnel could hurt people but Zayden thought it could. Zayden wanted to steal things and hide them there until it was time.

* * *

Dax saw Zayden and Daddy at a baseball game in the mountains. Daddy looked happy and Dax was happy. Zayden looked bored but Dax didn't care. Zayden was always bored when he wasn't planning.

But then Dax saw Daddy go to sleep from drinking and Zayden left him in the room and went to the tunnels. Dax was scared to see Zayden in the tunnels because that meant he was closer to hurting the good people, the ones who helped like Dax tried to. Dax felt bad for showing Zayden a place that could hurt. He had to stop the tunnels from hurting, stop Zayden's plan.

Zayden didn't think Dax could plan, but he could. Dax would find someone who could hear him when he screamed. The nice hospital lady could hear him but not enough. So Dax knew he had to scream louder and louder and louder at everyone who was close to Zayden. Then someone would stop him.

So Dax screamed and screamed and screamed even though his eyes burned all the time.

* * *

Friday, Sept. 9, 2016
Denver, Colorado

Lindsay woke up to Parable alerts on her phone. She'd been discharged from the hospital several hours earlier and went back to her mom's hotel room to rest, figuring it'd be quieter there plus she'd have someone to wait on her. It was after ten—later than she'd expected to sleep, but she sure felt better.

The first message came from Miguel, asking if she'd heard from Izzy. She sent back *No. Why?* He responded: *No one can find her and we're getting srsly worried.*

She opened a group message with all of her classmates who were still on campus, asking for an update. Just as she hit send, she got another notification —this time, from the administration.

Missing Student Alert — If anyone knows the whereabouts of Isabelle (Izzy) Machado, please contact campus security or Mr. Jordan immediately.

Missing Student Update—Zayden Lord remains missing and wanted for questioning. If you see him, do not approach him. Call this number immediately. An 800 number followed. The tone had become more urgent after Chloe had sent the picture of Anna Lord's anxiety and sleep medications.

Lindsay texted Chloe right away.

Just then, her mom came from the bathroom in a towel. "Well, good morning. sleepyhead. I didn't expect you to be awake."

"Mom, now Izzy's missing." Her voice shook. "She kinda had a thing for Zayden and defended him when we all started to think something was up. She's the only one who'd go with him willingly and I'm really scared that he might hurt her."

Katie Malone crossed the room and hugged her daughter, then grabbed her phone off the nightstand. "I'll see what I can find out." She went back in the bathroom and closed the door.

Lindsay's phone buzzed. She expected Chloe, but it was Rhiannon. *Police and campus security are all over. No one's allowed to leave. They're even taking fingerprints from Izzy's door. Have you heard from Chloe today?*

No, just texted her but haven't heard back yet, Lindsay replied.

I talked to her around 6:30, said she was going to the hospital to see Zayden's brother. Nothing since then, no idea when she'll be back. Lucky her, I guess.

Lindsay sighed, realizing how much she missed her roommate and wanted to talk to her. *I don't know. I wish I was there with you guys and I'm sure she does too.*

All the teachers are out searching, Rhiannon sent back. *They canceled classes.*

Her mom came back out. "I found out what they know and it's not much. After the fire, with all the commotion, Izzy slipped away. She hit a dead spot between cameras and poof, she disappeared. They've searched the area, but there's no trail to follow."

"Do they think she's with Zayden?"

Katie shrugged. "No one knows. Do you think maybe she went looking for him?"

"Or maybe he somehow lured her away."

Her mom sat next to her and put a hand on her shoulder. "Don't go making up stuff to be scared about. Focus on what we know, not all the possibilities, or you'll drive yourself nuts."

"Can I go back to the dorm and be with my friends?" Lindsay asked. "I promise I'll take it easy, there's not even any classes."

Katie nodded. "That's probably for the best. Then I can help with the search, too."

On the way to campus, Lindsay mulled over the screen grabs Chloe'd sent from Zayden's computer and something occurred to her. "I was thinking about that user name, Chupara. It kinda sounds like Chupacabra, doesn't it?" She texted Chloe.

* * *

Misty watched Dax grab Chloe's hand and couldn't believe it. He'd never done that to her or his mother, or to Zayden when he used to sit and hold Dax's hand for hours.

Chloe's eyes rolled back in her head and she swayed. Anna screamed. Dr. Huxley yelled, "Catch her!"

Misty grabbed Chloe around the waist the moment she slumped. Her eyes flew wide as a sudden burst of terror bombarded her brain. The doctor hurried over to help get Chloe down to the floor and Misty rushed out for a gurney, calling for a crash cart on her way, just in case.

She got the gurney in the room and they lifted Chloe onto it. Two nurses and an intern arrived with the cart and checked Chloe's vitals. Misty slumped down into a chair, shaken by what she'd sensed while touching the winged girl.

"Misty?" Anna sat in the chair next to her. "What's going on?"

Misty shook her head. "I have no idea why she collapsed, but I'm sure they'll get her revived."

"That's not what I'm talking about. In the office, you said something to yourself—'I knew it.' Then, when Chloe fainted, you appeared totally calm when you caught her, but then something flashed across your face."

She'd been caught at last. Misty stared at her with wide eyes, unable to say anything.

"That 'I knew it' had something to do with my boys, didn't it? Are you able to communicate with Dax somehow? Do you have abilities?" Anna's desperate eyes bored into her.

Misty's eyes fell closed. "I do, yes. I can sense things, not like a telepath, it's just empathy. But I should tell you, I never trusted Zayden, and I know—I don't just believe it, I know—that Dax is innocent. He does know right from wrong and he would never hurt anyone."

Anna's head fell back as tears filled her eyes. "My poor Daxie. My heart told me he was innocent but I didn't want to believe anything bad about Zayden."

Misty put her hand on Anna's, defenses up so should wouldn't experiencing the woman's agony. "When I caught Chloe, I felt what she was feeling. It was sheer terror—Dax's terror—and it's all focused on Zayden. I don't know why, but I know that much for certain."

"I should've known. The dreams . . . the accidents . . ." Anna stared into space.

"Anna, what dreams are you talking about?"

She shook her head, lips pressed tight together as she struggled to contain her sobs.

"Have you had dreams like Chloe's?" Misty asked.

"I have to call the school." A frantic Anna dug in her purse. "I have to warn them."

* * *

Lindsay, carrying bags of clothes her mom had brought from home, found her friends in the fifth floor lounge, along with Charlie, Bridger, Solomon, and the twins' sister, Lucia.

Rhiannon jumped up to hug her. "Have you heard anything from Chloe?"

"I saw her parents in the hotel lobby before they left for Kansas City. I guess Zayden's mom called them and said Chloe touched his little brother's hand and passed out. She's still unconscious."

"Holy crap," L.J. said. "How much weirdness can happen to our class?"

Lindsay sighed as she sat down on a couch. "I guess when you have psycho-secret-pyro in your class, a whole lot."

"My sister told me you guys were ready to convict him." Lucia shook her head. "Looks like Izzy was right, you do all think you know everything. You guys haven't even started investigation training yet—there's serious holes in your logic. Why don't you leave it for the people who know what they're doing?"

"Chloe and I almost died because of him, and he's probably the reason Izzy's missing, too," Lindsay shot back.

Lucia's phone buzzed and she read a message. "Miguel, Mom and Dad are here. Let's go." They both headed out.

"See you later, guys," Miguel said.

"Later, idiots!" Lucia called over her shoulder.

"Anyone else doubt this is all because of Zayden?" Charlie asked. Everyone shook their heads. "Good, because I saw the look on his face outside the stadium, and I know that little creep is dangerous. Lindsay, do you know how to get in touch with Zayden's mom, so we can see how Chloe's doing?"

Lindsay shook her head, looking miserable.

"I do," L.J. said. "I got his number before school started."

* * *

"Can I stay with her until she wakes up?" Misty asked Dr. Huxley. They stood outside Chloe's room on the third floor, where the doctor said she appeared to be stuck in a slow wave sleep state.

"Absolutely not, Misteya. I need you with Dax, in case her state has an impact on him again."

"But if I'm right about what happened between them—"

"What do you think happened? Is there something you haven't told me?"

She sighed, knowing the time had come but terrified to take the step. "There is something I haven't told you, about Dax and Chloe, and about myself."

He regarded her in silence for a long moment, then gestured to chairs in a small waiting area across the hall. "This sounds like a conversation we should sit down for."

"Yeah, fine." She walked over and sat down. He took a seat across the narrow walkway and waited. She took a deep breath. "I'm a parahuman. I've known it for a long time, but I've always kept it hidden. Only my parents and my fiancé know."

"What are your abilities?" he asked, his voice clipped.

"I've got low-level empathy and some electronics manipulation. The times when Dax has seemed soothed, it's when I've sat with him and held his hand and tried to get an idea what's going on inside his head."

"And what have you learned?" He sounded calm but she knew his moods well enough to see anger simmering below the surface.

"Dax's heart is pure. There's no way he could've done the things he's accused of. It's much easier to believe he tried to help while Zayden caused problems. I never trusted that kid, he always felt . . . I don't know, oily or something. When I caught Chloe, I got the impression Dax showed her something that terrifies him, and he passed that terror along to her with a flood of information." She realized she'd been looking at her hands in her lap and forced herself to meet the doctor's eyes. "Her brain is overwhelmed with it right now. I might be able to help calm her emotions so she can process it better and come out of this."

Dr. Huxley tapped his food on the floor in a rapid beat. "Yes, I think that is the best course of action. See what you can do, and I'll contact someone who may be able to help even more."

"A telepath?" she asked as he stood.

"Even better, a psionicist with Just Cause." He turned to walk away.

"Dr. Huxley?" she called after him.

He gave her a cold look over his shoulder. "Yes?"

"Don't you want to know why I didn't tell you?"

He sniffed. "I think we have more important things to worry about right now, don't you, Misty?"

* * *

Anna came into Chloe's room, phone to her ear. "Hold on a moment." She lowered it to her chest. "Misty, Chloe's friends are asking how she's doing. Would you talk to them?"

Misty nodded and took the phone. "Hi, this is Misty. Who am I talking to?"

"Lindsay, Chloe's roommate."

"Hey, Lindsay. Chloe's unconscious but all her vital signs are good. We think when she touched Dax's hand, he flooded her mind with information. She needs time to process it all, but I have some empathy skills and I think I'm helping. She feels calmer, anyway. I'm sure you're familiar with Ment, from Just Cause New York?"

"Wow, yeah!"

The enigmatic Ment was among the most powerful psionicists in parahuman history. He could read and manipulate minds in ways science hadn't even begun to unravel. Like all prominent Just Cause members, he had a certain celebrity status, but he didn't seem to enjoy the spotlight.

"So, was she right?" Lindsay asked. "Was Dax really trying to communicate with her about Zayden?"

"That's what I believe, based on what I felt when I touched her. I understand things have been a little crazy on campus."

"Yeah, super crazy. Will you do me a favor and keep us caught up on things with her?"

"You bet. Let me get your number." Misty got out her phone and entered the number Lindsay rattled off. "I'll text you once Ment gets here."

CHAPTER TWENTY-FOUR

Saturday, Sept. 10, 2016
Kansas City, Missouri

Misty looked up when the door opened. Ment strolled in, wearing his signature black trench coat and an aloof expression. She stood, offered her hand, and opened her mouth to introduce herself.

He sighed and ignored her hand. "Misteya Michaels, intern to Dr. Preston Huxley, low-level empath. You've been able to help the girl sort out some of the emotions but she still needs considerable help processing the data dump from the kid's brain."

Misty crossed her arms, one eyebrow arched. "How much of that did you know before you walked in the room?"

He smirked. "Everything except that you've been able to help her some. Of course I was briefed."

"Is there anything I can do t—"

He waved her away. "Give me the room so I can work."

She raised an eyebrow and snorted. "Fine. Just hit the—"

"I'll hit the call button in the unlikely event that I need anyone." Ment sat on the doctor's stool and wheeled it up beside the head of the bed as Misty walked out.

* * *

"Dr. Huxley, you need to see this!" In the radiology lab, Misty scooted away from the monitor displaying live images of Dax's brain so the doctor could get a look.

"Wait, but that's—that can't be happening." Dr. Huxley tapped the keyboard and scrolled back several seconds, then watched the scan results again. "He's never had activity in that region before, not even before being hospitalized."

"What do you think is causing it?" Misty asked.

"I have no idea."

"I might know," Anna said from the doorway to the MRI room. "Chloe told me she has super healing. Maybe the contact with her did it."

Misty looked from Anna to Dr. Huxley. "Is that possible, do you think?"

He put his hands on his hips and contemplated the image on the monitor. "It's . . . implausible. But then, I'm watching the impossible right now, so implausible doesn't seem far fetched at the moment."

"Doctor, do you think he'll wake up?" Anna's voice trembled.

He shook his head, eyes never leaving the screen. "I can't say, Anna. This is unprecedented."

Misty peered up at the monitor with him. "You know what else, Doctor? He's stopped transmitting."

* * *

Chloe, can you hear me? I'm Ment.

A voice cut through the swirling images and colors that made her cower and wish for darkness. She couldn't see the source but the name sounded familiar.

. . . Just Cause? was the only fragment of thought her mind could piece together.

That's right, Ment from Just Cause, the psionicist. I'm here to help you make some sense of things.

. . . make sense . . . nothing makes sense

What you're experiencing right now is years' worth of Dax's memories all . . . crammed into a Pandora's box and opened up in your mind. His mind is damaged, so his memories—and thoughts and feelings—barely make sense, even to him.

. . . are you?

You can't see me, but I'm right beside you. Chloe, I need you to focus on my voice for a minute, only my voice, do you understand?

. . . your voice . . .

That's right, listen to me, focus on me. You see the red swirl that keeps sweeping through the negative images?

. . . red burns . . .

The red won't burn you, Chloe, that's just Dax's perception of red. That's why it's intruding in the bad memories, he tried to burn them out of his mind so he doesn't have to see them anymore. Chloe, I want you to watch the red. Focus on it. Can you do that?

. . . focus . . . red won't burn . . .

That's good. Now, I want you to imagine the red turning pink. Pink doesn't hurt, does it? Pink is a safe color. A happy color.

. . . happy pink . . . Yes, better

Excellent, Chloe, you're doing great. Now, keep your eyes on that pink and turn it white.

. . . green is coming green will steal the good . . .

Help me build a wall in front of the green so it won't get there. That's right, good, Chloe. Now make the pink white.

. . . white. White is nice and cool.

That's right, nice and cool. Now, make the white fade out to clear. The color is gone and you can see the memories it obscured.

Not Zayden! Not Zayden! Mommy, my eyes burn, mommy. He made me turn them red again and he hurt people, he hurt Daddy and I saved him it wasn't Dax who hurt him, Daxie is a good boy. Zayden doesn't save Zayden hurts. Mommy, the tunnels will hurt people. Why can't you hear me? Chloe, the tunnels. Stop Zayden and the tunnels.

* * *

"That's what Dax needed me to know." Chloe sat up. "How did I get here? Who are—oh, my gosh, you're Ment!"

Ment rolled the stool to the door and opened it. "She's awake, you can come in."

A nurse rushed into the room with Misty right behind her.

Chloe pulled off the tape holding the IV in place. "I have to get back to the school. Everyone's in danger!"

"Chloe, let us check your vital signs before you get up." Misty gently but firmly nudged Ment out of her way to get to the bed as the nurse circled to the other side.

"What do you mean *everyone's in danger*?" Ment asked. "I didn't see anything about that."

"I don't know." Chloe shook her head. "Once Dax's message came out, I just had the knowledge that Zayden's going to do something . . . something huge. But the memory of what it is won't come."

"Either way, this'll be faster than your wings." Ment waggled his phone it back and forth, then dialed a number. "Keith, it's Ment. Chloe's awake and says the school is in danger, but she can't piece together exactly why." He paused, listening to Mr. Jordan. "Yes, sir, we'll be in touch." He turned back toward Chloe. "See, there you go. MetalBlade is informed and he'll do his best to protect everyone."

"Chloe, honey?" Phil Wyld called from the doorway, where he stood with Chloe's mom.

"Dad, Mom, I need to get back to the Academy!" Chloe yelled. "My friends are going to die if we don't do something now!"

"Honey, you need to calm down and be rational," Phil told his daughter as he and Heather rushed to her bedside.

"That's right, Chlo—actual superheroes are combing the campus and everything around it," her mom said. "If there's anything going on, they'll figure it out long before you can get back there. Try to rest."

Chloe's eyes looked wild. Ment snapped his fingers to get her attention and his eyes locked on hers. "The best thing you can do for your friends is stay here, work with me, and try to figure out what it is Zayden is planning."

More settled, Chloe closed her eyes and took a deep breath. "Okay, okay. Fine."

The nurse checked her over, then brought in a doctor who declared her ready to be discharged. Everyone but her mom left as she got back into her clothes.

"Mom, it's so good to see you." Chloe hugged her. "I'm sorry to put you guys through all this."

Heather Wyld kissed her daughter's cheek. "We knew you'd heal yourself, but even so, we we've been terrified." Chloe could tell by the dark circles under her eyes that her mother hadn't slept. She felt awful.

An orderly arrived with a wheelchair but Chloe shook her head at it. "I can't. My wings get in the way. I'll just walk." She and her mom left the room.

Misty smiled. "There's someone who wants to see you. Up on the sixth floor."

"Dr. Huxley?" Chloe asked. "Anna?"

Misty just shook her head and led them up to Dax's room, where she opened the door and motioned for Chloe to go in. Curious but hesitant, Chloe peeked inside and gasped—Dax sat up, his eyes open to reveal nothing but white. It looked creepy until he smiled, his face beaming. Anna stood beside him with tears on her cheeks. Chloe hurried to his side.

"Dax, you're awake!" She almost took his hand but thought better of it. Dax just grinned.

"He woke up a few hours after you collapsed," Anna said.

"We're wondering if the connection you formed somehow allowed him to borrow your healing ability," Misty said. "We're seeing new activity in areas of the brain that were dead."

Chloe's throat tightened. "That's amazing. Dax, thank you so much for contacting me. We're going to stop Zayden, okay? There's a whole bunch of superheroes at the school working on it right now."

Dax's smile vanished and he shook his head, looking worried.

"What is it, Daxie?" Anna asked.

He tried to answer but could only manage a stuttering sound that could've been an *N* or a *D*. Steeling herself, Chloe took his hand and his eyes met hers.

. . . won't find . . .

"Why not, Dax, why won't they find him?" she asked out loud.

. . . no one thought . . .

Dax's eyes rolled back in his head and he swooned. Anna caught him and Misty rushed up to take his vitals.

"He's fine. I think it was just too much for him."

The blood drained from Chloe's face. "I don't think that was it."

"Why not?" the intern asked.

"Because he's transmitting again, and now I'm a lot better at receiving." She broke out in a cold sweat and her body trembled.

Her dad put an arm around her to keep her steady. "What's he showing you, baby?"

"It's jumbled. I . . . I can't work it out yet." She shook her head. "Wait—did you say he woke up a few hours after I collapsed? How long was I out?"

"Overnight and most of the day," Misty said.

Chloe whirled around but didn't see a clock anywhere. "It's the tenth? What time is it?"

Her dad glanced at his watch. "Almost six p.m."

"He's telling me we need to be there in the morning. He's yelling that over and over, so loud I can't make sense of anything else." Near panic, she covered her ears, trying in vain to block him. "We have to get back to Denver, now."

"Easy, Fly Girl," her mom said, "the best place for us is here. You can keep getting information from Dax and giving it to MetalBlade, and they'll stop whatever's happening."

"No, he says I need to be there," Chloe sobbed. "He needs to see through my eyes, through my brain, because I understand things better than he does." She didn't know where the knowledge came from, but she knew it.

Her dad shook his head. "I'm not sending you into danger when trained professionals are there. It's not just the faculty. Just Cause is there, and some of the other heroes who'd planned to be there for the ceremony are helping, too."

Chloe closed her eyes. "The ceremony. That's why he's doing this—he's going to do something big."

"They canceled the ceremony because of all this, so you can relax," her mom said.

She looked from her mom to her dad and could see in their faces that nothing she could say would convince them. "I'm sorry, I have to do this." She took off running for the stairs, barreling past Ment as he approached Dax's room.

Her dad called her name and he and Misty started after her. Chloe flung open the stairwell door and plunged through. As she hoped, the spiraling stairs didn't fill the whole space. Their inner railing created an empty column going straight up where no one could follow her. She buzzed her wings and rose off the ground before her father even reached the door, pushing her speed until the stairs seemed a continuous blur. She slowed as she reached the top and found the door to the roof. A glance confirmed she'd left her dad and Misty several floors down. Still airborne, she burst through the door and took a minute to get her bearings.

The sun hung low over the horizon and she flew toward it, eventually spotting the freeway and following it into Kansas.

* * *

In the hallway outside Dax's room, Misty said good-bye to the Wylds, who left to rent a car and try to find their daughter. She then turned to Ment. "You want to talk to me. What about?"

"I found something in Chloe's brain and I think it explains why Dax could communicate with her."

Misty's eyes widened. "Is she telepathic?"

He shook his head. "Not exactly. Do you know if she was close to Zayden?"

Misty shrugged. "Couldn't you find that out while you were in there?"

"I could, but I try to be as un-intrusive as possible when I'm in someone's head. You know, a little respect for privacy."

"All I know is that she got visions when he touched her hand, among other times, so yeah, maybe they had a little romance going."

Ment nodded. "Whatever. They had some kind of physical contact. And Dax gave her his memories, and borrowed her healing power, when she touched his hand."

"So you think she and Zayden somehow power swapped when they touched?" she asked. "But Zayden's not telepathic."

"No, but I saw in Dax's memories that he can transmit to Zayden, probably because of how much time they've spent together. So—"

"So Zayden touched Chloe, and voila, Dax can transmit to her." Misty thought for a moment. "I've heard of power mimics, but not power swapping. Have you?"

He shook his head. "It's a new one by me."

* * *

Well outside the city, somewhere in Kansas, Chloe landed in a field and opened Parable on Ava's phone. She finally saw Lindsay's text about Chupara sounding like Chupacabra. She remembered seeing a show on that a while ago, but she didn't dwell on it.

Heading back, should be there before dawn, she sent to Lindsay. *Pretty much escaped from my parents and hospital. Getting a better idea what he's planning.* She hesitated, then swiped more in. *If I'm not back by noon, GET OFF CAMPUS and take anyone who will listen.*

She took to the air again without waiting for a reply, wondering how in the world she'd make a ten-hour flight when just getting to Anna's had wiped her out. She didn't have much of Charlie's money left, either.

A few hours later, she touched down at a convenience store and spent a few dollars on an energy drink and power bars. As she leaned against the building and pounded them down, she heard something that gave her an idea.

Taking a quick break in Junction City, Kansas, she sent to Lindsay. *Gonna see if I can manage to land on a train, save myself the effort and move a little faster.* She polished off the first bar, tucked the other one away for later, and took off toward the sound of a train.

It didn't take long for her to find the tracks and she landed beside them. The phone dinged with a message from Lindsay.

Be careful! You don't want to splat on the windshield or anything! Chloe snorted at the joke. Another message popped up. *Sorry if the bug humor is insensitive. But srsly, be careful.*

After a quick search, she sent a gif of a cartoon fly smacking into a windshield and *hahaha. I'll find one stopped or going slow. No splatting, promise!*

Wherever the train was that she'd heard, it was nowhere near here. Before long, she'd need to sleep. She started to regret the spontaneous trip but then remembered Hays, and Anna's house, sat around the mid-point between Kansas City and Denver. She knew she could get there, and she'd noticed Anna didn't lock her door when they left. She pushed herself for another two hours and let herself into the house.

Anna wouldn't come back tonight, would she? Chloe wondered. *No way, not with Dax awake after all these years.* Still, she figured better to know for certain. She texted her parents.

I'm safe, no worries. Where are you guys?

Where are you? her mom sent back right away. *We're driving toward Denver, looking for you.*

Did Anna stay at the hospital?

Yes. Where are you? We're scared to death.

A pang of guilt hit. *If I tell you where I am, will you help me get to campus in the morning?*

We can discuss it. Honey, where are you?

She knew what that meant—she'd plead her case, her parents would pretend to consider it, then they'd tell her no.

Sorry. I'm fine, I promise. At a safe place to sleep for a few hours. Text you when I wake up. She raided the fridge and took a hot shower, ignoring her mother's many texts.

Midnight, the clock told her, twelve hours until the time the ceremony had been scheduled. Something told her the cancellation wouldn't matter, that whatever Zayden had planned would still happen at noon. She just wished she'd figured out more of what Dax put in her head. She set an alarm for four o'clock and put the phone on do not disturb.

* * *

Saturday, Sept. 10, 2016
Denver, Colorado

"Can you believe it's almost time?" Izzy shivered in the cold tunnel, back against an old rock wall. She almost regretted coming down to join Zayden, but, as she'd hoped, the time alone had strengthened their relationship.

Zayden, his face serious, gave her a slow nod. "I've waited so long for this. All the planning—getting Dax to show it all to me, building a team, the scouting trips here with my dad before school started, the late nights putting everything in place—it's coming together perfectly." He sighed. "I still wish Chloe was with us."

Izzy glared. "Why are you so hung up on her? She's not all that."

"You underestimate the value of fliers. Every great team has at least one. Hell, even the pretenders Destroyer and Javelin knew how important it was to fly. Someone on a roof can't see a fraction what Chloe can when she really gets up high. They can't move at sixty miles an hour, drop down on someone unsuspected. If there's one flaw in my preparations, it's that I didn't get her on our side."

"How'd you do all the scouting and stealing stuff when you were here with your dad? Did he just let you take off?" She wanted nothing more than for him to shut up about that stupid, goody-two-shoes bug.

Zayden scoffed. "I could've just waited for him to pass out drunk, but I slipped some of my mom's sedatives in his whiskey—that put him out fast. 'Course, there was that one time I didn't think he'd wake up. Wouldn't have been too big a deal if he hadn't. I knew what I needed to by then."

* * *

"Mm-mm-mm." Dax gave Anna an intense look and Misty could feel the exasperation rolling off him in waves. Just the three of them remained. After the Wylds had gone after Chloe, Dr. Huxley had left with the head of neurology to discuss Dax's recovery over dinner.

"What is it, baby?" Anna asked, taking his hand. "Mommy's here."

His face twisted with concentration, Dax struggled to get his mouth to cooperate. "G-g-g-go."

Anna looked confused and hurt. "You want me to go?"

Dax shook his head. "Nnn-nuh-no! Dah go."

"Where do you want to go, sweetheart?"

"He wants to go with Chloe," Misty said. "He wants to help her stop Zayden."

"Stah Zay! Stah Zay!" Dax yelled. Misty got chills thinking how she'd missed the meaning of Nah-Zay in the TV show so many times. In his presence, though—to her, at least—his meaning couldn't have been more clear.

Anna looked at Misty, perplexed. "He can't leave the hospital."

Misty shrugged. "You're free to discharge him at any time. It's not as if he's been committed or anything, and his life wouldn't be endangered."

"How can you say that?" Anna's wide eyes showed terror. "He had a heart attack last week and passed out less than an hour ago!"

"It was a minor cardiac event, not a heart attack, and his brain isn't over-taxed like it was then. He's not transmitting now, and he's healing." Misty realized her voice had risen and she grasped the metal bar on Dax's bed with white knuckles. She took a deep breath to calm herself. "I'm sorry, Anna. I know it's not my place to push this. It's just that I'm feeling his need to go, and it's powerful."

Anna shook her head. "It's a ten-hour drive into . . . who knows what. No, no way."

Misty bowed her head. "Of course. I'll leave you alone with your son. I'll come back later, okay Dax?"

I NEED TO GO! STOP ZAYDEN! He yelled so loud in her head that she staggered back, catching her heel on a chair and sprawling backward into an end table, which knocked over her coffee and sent metal charts skittering across the floor tiles. Reeling, she hauled herself up.

"I'll get someone to clean this up." She hurried from the room and went straight to a stall in the ladies room, where she dug out her phone and texted her fiancé. *You're gonna think I'm crazy, but could you take off with an ambulance for a day or so without getting fired or arrested?*

I suppose it's theoretically possible, he sent back. *I could say it died and then it could 'get stolen' before the tow truck showed up. Why?*

How soon are you off shift?

You're weirding me out. Can you call?

She leaned against the stall wall, unable to believe she was about to throw away her career. *Give me a minute,* she texted, then headed up to the roof, where she'd watched Chloe fly away less than an hour ago.

Joe picked up on the first ring. "Hey, babe. Are you serious? What's going on?"

"It's Dax. He's awake, and his brother is planning something big at the Hero Academy tomorrow, and Dax is yelling in my head that he wants to go and stop him."

Silence. Then he said, "Start from the beginning, because this is making no sense to me at all."

She heaved a deep sigh and gave him the short version of the day's events.

"So you really think this kid's that dangerous?" he asked.

"I do, Joe, and so does the dragonfly girl, and most importantly, so does Dax."

"You know you're risking your career, plus kidnapping charges, and since we're leaving the state, it'll be federal."

"I know," she whispered, hands trembling.

"I'm off in two hours. Where should I come?"

Relief came with a stifled sob. "Thank you! I'll get him to the back loading dock. It should be deserted that late."

"I'll let you know when I'm on the way." He paused. "You're sure you're sure about this?"

"I've never been more sure of anything. Other than how much I love you, that is."

After hanging up, she texted her nurse friend, Rachelle, and asked her to come up. A few minutes later, the door banged shut and Rachelle emerged, holding two cups of coffee.

"I need your help," Misty told her. "The less you know the better, but in two hours, I need you to go to Dax's room and tell his mom he needs to go for an MRI, but bring him down to the loading dock."

Rachelle's eyes went wide. "What the hell?"

"Like I said, the less you know the better."

"Uh-uh." The nurse crossed her arms. "You tell me everything or no deal."

Misty sighed and began the story again—realizing she'd have to come out as para for it to all make sense. *Cat's out of the bag now*, she thought, hoping she wouldn't have to come up with some kind of ridiculous code name and costume next.

CHAPTER TWENTY-FIVE

Sunday, Sept. 11, 2016
Hays, Kansas

"The tunnels!" Chloe yelled as she woke up. The clock on the DVR said 3:47. As her brain fought its way up from deepest sleep, she understood everything. She needed to hurry.

Taking Ava's phone off the charger, she tried to get onto Parable, but it appeared to be down. No way that could be a coincidence. She called Lindsay but got an error message, so she Googled the school's phone number and called it. Same message. Her sense of impending doom grew.

Chloe'd promised to text her parents when she woke up, but she decided to give it a couple more hours. In preparation for the day's energy expenditures, she slammed down three bowls of cereal, four slices of toast with peanut butter, a cup of stale coffee, and two glasses of orange juice. Taking all the portable food and drink she could manage, she took off from Anna's back yard and headed toward the railroad tracks. By the time she could see the train, she had a plan for contacting someone at the Academy. It was a long shot, but it was the only shot she had.

* * *

"I'm sorry, Dax, but we can't drive any faster," Misty told him. She sat with him in the back of the ambulance, watching the monitors so they wouldn't have any nasty surprises.

"We should be there in about six hours," Rachelle, who'd insisted on coming with them, called from the driver's seat. Joe slept beside her.

Misty had at first refused to let Rachelle come, but then her friend mentioned that Misty and Joe would need to sleep at some point, so a third driver —and set of hands—would be helpful. "What happens if he has another cardiac event and you're asleep and Joe's driving?" she asked. Finally, Misty agreed it was in her patient's best interest to have all three of them there.

"It's five a.m. now," Misty said in response to Dax's silent question. "We should be there by eleven. That's an hour before the ceremony was supposed to start, and I have a phone number for Chloe's roommate. We should have no trouble tracking them down." She saw tunnels in her head and Zayden walking into a building with a balcony. "I know you can find Zayden, but we're better off facing him with a team than all alone."

They passed a sign announcing the exit for Hays in sixty-eight miles. "We'll be passing the town where your mom lives pretty soon."

Chloe sleep Mommy's house

"Chloe went to your mom's?" she asked. "Last night? Maybe we should go pick her up."

Choo-choo

Misty didn't understand what that meant, but before she had a chance to ask, she saw an aerial image of a freight train and realized it was Chloe's perspective. The winged girl landed on the last car just as the train started to move. She smiled to herself, thinking Chloe was a brave and clever girl. The wave of emotion she got from Dax next startled her and melted her heart. He had his first crush.

* * *

Down on the platform of the rear car, Chloe huddled against the wall and tried to focus. The noise and vibration of the freight train made it hard, but after a while she became better able to tune it out. She focused on Dax and what it felt like to hear him in her mind. Before long, she heard random snippets of conversation and knew it came from him him.

Now to see if I can send. Eyes squeezed shut, she focused on Solomon. As his face took shape in her mind's eye, she felt a moment of recognition and took it as a good sign. Either that or she was deluding herself.

Dax, she thought, *tell this boy about Zayden's plan and the tunnels. Show him the building where Zayden goes down.*

The feeling of connection came to an abrupt end. She didn't know if that was good or bad, so she could only hope for the best.

She checked the map on Ava's phone again to make sure she had it right—even though the train veered south and she needed to go north, her best bet was to ride it south to the town of Kit Carson, then fly sixty miles northwest to Limon, then either catch one heading to Denver or fly the rest of the way.

The train moved faster than she could fly, but she almost wished it didn't. At least flying, she'd feel like she was doing something. As she sat, she thought back over everything she'd learned and tried to piece it all together. Out of the blue, she remembered something about the mythical Chupacabra. It was a Mexican myth and the name meant "goat sucker."

And who sucked the powers out of other paras? *No,* she thought. *No, it couldn't be Izzy. Could it?*

* * *

Sunday, Sept. 11
Denver, Colorado

"Guys, guys!" Solomon yelled over the gaming chatter. Charlie stopped in the middle of describing a displacer beast. Sol closed his eyes and tried to assimilate all the information, but it came too fast. "This is important. Write what I say." He rattled off the message pouring into his mind and Cat scribbled it down on the back of her character sheet. At last it ended and Sol's eyes opened. He looked dazed and pale.

"Who's it from?" Bridger asked.

Sol shook his head as if to clear it. "Zayden's little brother. The one in the hospital who doesn't talk but apparently thinks pretty damned clearly. He's telepathic like me, except way stronger."

"Chloe did it!" Charlie shot up. "Come on, we have to let someone know about this."

They tried Heroes Hall, but the doors were locked and no one was visible inside. Charlie asked Cat and the other two to see who they could round up from the gym and elsewhere around campus, and he, Sol, and Bridger went looking for a security guard. It didn't take long. Charlie and Solomon, talking over each other much of the time, told him about the message and that they needed to reach Mr. Jordan or someone else on the faculty.

"I'll see if I can reach someone. You all head back to the dorms now," the guard said.

They walked away, dejected. "Why do I get the feeling he's not going to contact anyone?" Charlie asked.

"Because he thinks we're either crazy or pulling a prank and he's not about to lose his job over it," Sol told him.

Bridger paused to listen, then shook his head. "Yeah, he just radioed the other guards and told them some kids were causing trouble with a crazy story."

Back in the dorm, they went up to the fifth floor lounge, where they found Lindsay, Rhiannon, Ava, Jacob, and L.J.

"Get the others, we got a message from Zayden's brother," Charlie told them.

"This is it," Lindsay said. "Miguel and Izzy's parents got here last night, so he's with them. Lucia, too. What's the message?"

Sol recapped all the details he could remember.

"With no faculty and staff reachable," Charlie said, "and the guards not taking this seriously, we've got to stop him ourselves."

They stared at each other in silence as they took it in.

"Where did you say these tunnels are?" Lindsay asked.

"All over under campus and beyond, but he accesses them through the maintenance building," Sol said.

"What are we waiting for?" Ava stood up. "Let's go."

"We can't just go charging in," Jacob said. "We need a plan."

L.J. stood and ran for the stairs. "Be right back."

Charlie put the paper with Dax's message on it down on the table. "Tell me what everyone's powers are, starting with Zayden's."

As they listed them for him, L.J. returned with large sheets of paper—schematics of Javelin's tech.

"I thought you turned those in," Jacob said.

"These are newer ones." L.J. told him. "I made it look cooler and more modern, just for fun." He flipped through his sketch book and added a detail here and there to different weapons and bits of armor he'd drawn before. "Damn, I wish Miguel was here! Some of this stuff will be too small."

"What you've got is great," Charlie told him. "We need communication. Lucia's probably the best person to get Parable up, but . . . Kaci, Justin, you're tech savvy. Head to the lab."

"I can help, too," L.J. said, taking off with the others.

* * *

Chloe lifted off the platform and the train moved on without her. Studying the map, she decided it would be faster to make a bee-line for the school rather than follow the train tracks' wide arc. Comparing the terrain to satellite images to make sure she went the right direction, she took off, figuring she'd be there in forty-five minutes or less. Dr. Huxley had said he thought she would get faster as she matured. "Time to grow up, WyldWing," she said aloud, and pushed herself to go even quicker.

* * *

"Mr. Hutson!" L.J. yelled as they walked into the room beyond the computer lab, which was filled with electronics racks. The teacher lay on the floor, gagged and bound with hands behind his back, attempting to cut the ropes on the edge of an industrial shelf.

Kaci knelt down and removed the gag while L.J. pulled out a knife sketch, manifested it, and began sawing at the ropes.

"Dude," Justin said, "why not just carry a pocket knife?"

L.J. shrugged. "Knife laws are annoying."

"What happened?" Kaci asked the tech teacher.

"Not sure." Mr. Hutson stretched his jaw. "Something zapped me in the back of the head, and the next thing I knew, I woke up on the floor."

L.J. filled him in on Zayden's plan while cutting through the rope around his feet and Justin pried loose the knots at his wrists. "Can you get Parable up and running so we can use it to communicate?"

"Yeah, assuming we can get the backup generator running." The rope sliced in two, Mr. Hutson stretched his long legs and stood up. He rubbed at his wrists as he walked to the generator back behind the racks. He tried to start it up, then swore as he discovered it had not only been turned off, but tampered with. "This'll take a few minutes, but I should be able to repair the damage."

About three minutes later, it roared to life. Electronics all around the room hummed and beeped.

Mr. Hutson sat at one computer and directed Kaci to another, rattling off instructions for getting Parable back online.

"He didn't just shut it down," Kaci said. "Something's funky with the code."

Mr. Hutson wheeled his chair over and peered at the screen. "Oh, crap. This'll take a while."

L.J.'s eyes narrowed. "I didn't think Zayden knew enough about computers to do that."

Justin shrugged. "One more thing he's been hiding?"

"Kaci, keep on restoring that code." Mr. Hutson grabbed his cell phone from a pocket. "I'll see if I can raise Keith. Er, Mr. Jordan."

Justin shook his head. "Phones are out. Cell and landline. How'd he do that?"

"Maybe he disabled a tower or set up some kind of jammer or something," Kaci said.

"Damn. Okay, I'll jump on the code too, then," said Mr. Hutson.

"Where is the whole faculty?" L.J. asked.

Mr. Hutson's fingers flew over the keyboard. "They had a couple credible sightings, one of Zayden at a convenience store and one of Isabella in a booby-trapped warehouse in west Denver. So all the faculty members with useful powers are deployed, plus all the post-grads, half of Just Cause plus some heroes who came in for the ceremony, Denver PD, and the SWAT team. The rest of the faculty is probably at home."

"Yeah," Justin snorted. "Big mystery who called in those sightings."

"This should be up pretty fast with two of us working, but I sure wish Miguel and Lucia were here. Luce knows this code almost as well as I do."

"Sweet, thanks, Mr. Hutson," L.J. turned to Kaci. "We'll be in touch." He and Justin headed back to the others.

* * *

"I know, I know," Charlie said to the group once L.J. and Justin had returned, "we should never split the party, but there are too many of us and we've got a lot of ground to cover, so we're going to form three teams."

"Who named you the big boss?" Ava asked, arms folded across her chest.

Charlie shrugged his shoulders. "You want to take over, be my guest. What should we do?"

Ava balked. "I didn't say *I* should be in charge, I just wondered why you were."

"Anyone else want to do this?" Charlie asked, looking from face to face.

Bridger chuckled. "You're the game master, man. Lead on."

"'Cause for the record," Charlie continued, "I don't really want to lead this charge, but I figure someone's got to."

Ava rolled her eyes. "Fine, what do you want us to do?"

"One group needs to head down to the tunnels to find Zayden and stop him." He glanced down at the notes on his clipboard. "Ava, you can kick his ass, so you're on Team Tunnel for sure."

"What about me?" Jack thumped his sizable chest with an equally sizable fist and lowered his horns as if to charge.

"Tunnels, dude," Charlie said. "Small spaces. You're huge." He tapped his pen on the clipboard while he thought. "Jacob, Sol, Cat, and Ondine, you're going down there with Ava. Jacob, 'cause you can get out of there fast to get word back to us. Cat, because you can get into small spaces and you have better dark vision and hearing than anyone else."

Cat grinned and meowed, flexing her hands to unsheath long, curved claws that came to perfect points. She'd painted them neon green.

"Did you forget Zayden can block me?" Sol asked.

Charlie shook his head. "His brother showed you the entrance to the tunnels—you're the only one who knows for sure how he gets in. Plus, you can send us a message if need be. It's redundant with Jacob, but that's okay—best to cover all our bases." He swallowed hard. "Just in case."

They all eyed each other, uncomfortable with what "just in case" could mean.

"And me?" Ondine asked. "What's my role?"

"You can sense water, right?" he asked. She nodded. "Okay, I admit it's a long shot, but maybe there's water down there somewhere you could use to soak the explosives or put out a fire, or . . . I don't know. It's more likely you'll find water down there than on the quad, anyway."

She sighed, looking miserable. "I suppose you've got a point. I'm probably not much use to you guys at all."

"You're smart and resourceful," Bridger said. "You've proved in training that you don't need to use your powers to be helpful."

Ondine blushed and looked down at her feet, muttering a thank you, and Bridger's ears went red at her reaction.

"Austin and Jack—you're Team Perimeter, and Kaci, too, once she's done helping Mr. Hutson. Go by the lab and check on her, then circle the campus looking for any sign of fire, since you have a chance to stop it, or at least direct it in the least harmful way possible. Jack, you're there to protect the pyros in case you run into Zayden, and the rest are on Team Search." He looked at Lindsay, Rhiannon, L.J., Bridger, and Justin. "We'll patrol campus and look for anything suspicious. Bridger, keep your ears open for calls for help from the other teams. If my team needs the rest of you, you'll hear Rhiannon's scream. Be sure to check Parable every now and then to see if Kaci and Mr. Hutson have it back up yet, too. We'll use voice unless someone messages that they need quiet. Everyone got it?"

They all nodded and the teams split up.

* * *

"Tow-ee, Tow-ee!" Dax yelled, frantic.

"It's okay, Dax," Rachelle said, stroking his hand. "We're almost there."

"I think he's trying to tell us Chloe's nearby," Joe called from the front seat.

"Why do you say that?" she asked.

He chuckled. "'Cause she just flew over us. Damn, she's moving fast! Of course, it doesn't help that this motor home can't do the speed limit." He glared at the large vehicle in front of him, which kept perfect pace with the semi in the left lane.

Misty yawned beside him. "We'll see her soon, Dax, try to calm down."

"Crap!" Rachelle yelled. "Misty, get back here!"

The beeps from Dax's heart monitor sped up and grew irregular. Misty unbuckled the seat belt and launched herself toward the gurney. The moment her hands touched his shoulder, she sent out a burst of electricity. She and Rachelle stared at the monitor, frozen for what seemed like minutes, then let out their breath in unison as the wave evened out and returned to normal.

"That was too close," Rachelle muttered in Misty's ear. "We're so going to prison for this. Even if he survives it."

CHAPTER TWENTY-SIX

Sunday, Sept. 11
Denver, Colorado

Solomon led Team Tunnel into the maintenance building and to a dark corner. He peered around in the gloom for a few seconds before turning on his phone's flashlight.

"There." He pointed to a trap door, almost invisible, in the floor.

"Wow, you definitely have to know it's there, don't you?" Ava said. "How did Zayden ever find it?"

"Dax showed it to him," Sol said.

"Okay, I guess we should go in," Jacob said. "Cat, why don't you shift all the way? Then you can scout ahead without much chance of being seen."

Her eyes glowing red in the near darkness, Cat nodded. A moment later, empty t-shirt and shorts dropped to the floor and an orange tabby poked its head from the neck hole.

Solomon knelt down and scratched behind her ear, which earned him a hiss and a swat with a paw. He smirked, looking up at the others. "She freaking hates that, but I can never resist."

"Yeah, really funny." Ondine glared at him. "How 'bout you keep your hands off her?"

"What? I'm just goofing around."

"Touch her without consent again, and I'll knock your face in," Ava said. "Got it?"

At the word *consent*, Sol looked like he'd been slapped. He stammered in confusion for a few seconds before nodding. "Yeah, got it. Sorry, Cat."

Jacob felt around until he found a small notch just big enough for two fingers to get purchase and swung the wooden door up, revealing a ladder descending into darkness.

Cat bumped her head on Ondine's leg, then looked at the ladder and back up.

"Cats aren't so much for ladders, are they?" Ondine asked. Cat responded with a small mew. Ondine knelt down. "Would you like me to pick you up?" She shot a sharp glance at Sol. Cat nuzzled her hand, and Ondine lifted her up, settling her in on one shoulder.

"I'll go first." Ava headed down into the hole. "Ondine, you come next with Cat and I'll make sure you don't fall. Then Sol, and Jacob, you're last so you can get out in a hurry if need be."

Once Ondine's head disappeared from view, Sol leaned in to Jacob. "So, are they over-reacting about the petting, or was I really that wrong?"

Jacob raised an eyebrow. "Dude, has she told you before not to pet her?"

"Well . . . yeah, but . . ."

"And can't you sense how much she hates it?"

Sol nodded, his face pale.

"Then they're not over-reacting." Jacob motioned for Sol to head down next, then climbed down himself and turned on his phone's flashlight.

Ondine put Cat down and she ran ahead. Within a few minutes, they came to a fork. Cat sniffed down each one, then headed confidently down the passageway to the right.

"Do you guys smell anything? I mean, other than dirt and damp," Ava asked. No one did.

"We should be leaving a trail of breadcrumbs, or marking the passage, or something," Ondine said.

"I'm mapping it." Sol showed them a small notebook with a drawing of their route thus far. "I may be an insensitive ass, but I'm a good gamer." They all stared at him. "This is beginner dungeoneering. Seriously, guys, if you want to be good heroes, you'll join a game."

After the third branch, they all got whiffs of a chemical smell. At the fourth branch, Cat sniffed for a long time, sat down, and looked at them with confusion in her amber eyes.

"Now what?" Ava asked. "We can't just go blindly exploring. Who knows how lost we could get?"

Jacob snapped his fingers. "Sol, Zayden's brother showed you all this, right?"

Sol shrugged. "Yeah, but I don't remember it well enough to navigate. It was a crazy flood of images and information."

"Can you contact him and ask him to show you again?" Ondine asked.

"Maybe," Sol said. "He's a lot more powerful than me, though. I don't know if I can initiate contact from so far away, but I'll try." He closed his eyes and concentrated for several seconds, and then his eyes flew open wide. "He's close. I don't know how that's possible, but I can feel it." He started walking forward, dazed, then paused for a moment and thrust the notebook and pencil at Jacob, who took them. Sol went down the tunnel to the left, and made another left turn several yards down.

They all followed, Jacob sketching the twists and turns as best he could.

Several minutes later, the air was so thick with chemicals they could taste it. They came out into a wide area. Sol stopped short, staring, and Ava almost ran into him.

They took in the scene. Dozens of containers filled the space, ranging from flask-sized to barrels. Judging from the smell and the labels on a few, they contained gasoline, propane, and other flammable liquids. Several stout three-wick candles stood in the center of it all, with crude devices spaced evenly around the cavern.

"Um, I'm gonna guess those are some kind of bomb?" Ava gaped.

Sol gave a slow nod. "I'm thinking that's a safe bet. But where's Zayden?"

"Probably as far from this as he can get and still light the fire," Jacob said.

"How far do you suppose that is?" Sol asked.

The speedster shrugged. "No idea. He kept the pyro powers secret. Ondine, is there an underground stream or anything? Something we can use to prevent this from going up?"

She shook her head with a sigh just as her phone dinged. She pulled it out. "Hey guys, Parable's back up. There's a message from Charlie."

* * *

With assurances from Kaci they'd have Parable up soon so she could join them, Austin and Jack headed out toward the edge of campus.

"What do you make of that?" Jack asked, pointing to a telephone pole not far off. It looked charred, and a work crew appeared to be just arriving at its base.

"My guess is Zayden scorched it to take out the phones." Austin shook his head. "I want to punch that kid. My sister's had a huge crush on him ever since the stupid *Heroes* episode came out. She really looks up to him. She's gonna be devastated."

"If you seriously want him to hurt, stand back and let me punch him," Jack said. "He's earned a good beat down."

As they walked on, they saw similar damage to power lines along with trucks heading toward a cell tower on a nearby hill, but the tower itself was too far away for them to see any damage.

"Dude, he's been busy," Jack said, "damaging all this plus taking out Parable, tying up Mr. Hutson . . . Unless he's *also* got secret super-speed powers, I bet you anything he had some help."

* * *

Team Search emerged on the roof of the dormitory—the second tallest building on campus, next to Heroes Hall —so they could get a good look around.

"Hey, it's Chloe!" Lindsay yelled, pointing off to the southeast.

"I'll go meet her," Charlie said, then blushed and added, "so she doesn't miss us." He took off, moth wings glittering in the sunlight.

Chloe spotted him moments later. Her heart gave a little flutter as she zipped toward him. The noise of their wings and the wind they generated made it hard to talk mid-air, but they exchanged grins and flew together to the dorm roof, where they got Chloe caught up on everything that had happened since she'd left.

As they talked, strange popping noises came from the quad and they peered over the edge. It looked like sparklers being lit in the grass, right above where "Blayze" was burned into the lawn. One after the other, they ignited and burned in a brief, bright flash, leaving smoke clogging the air and obscuring their view.

Then the popping and flashing stopped and everything went still. A cool breeze blew through, whisking away the smoke, and revealing a new word: Lord.

"Lord Blayze. That's so He-Who-Should-Not-Be-Named. Could he be any more melodramatic?"Lindsay scoffed.

"The question is," Chloe said, "how did he know to set that off just now, when he had an audience?"

Charlie's head whipped around. "If he was on another roof, we'd be able to see him. Unless . . ."

Rhiannon nodded. "Unless he's on Heroes Hall. A story above us."

"Chloe, Justin," Charlie said, "grab a passenger and let's fly."

All of their phones made noise at the same moment. Lindsay checked hers. "Parable's back up! Kaci says she's joining the perimeter team."

Charlie opened a window and swiped in a message. *Checking roof of Heroes for Z. Will leave vid chat up. Monitor situation in case we need help.*

He handed the phone to Bridger, grabbed him from behind, and took to the air. L.J., with modified Javelin gauntlet blasters and carefully drawn jet boots, rose up next. Chloe followed with Lindsay in a death grip, and Justin carried Rhiannon right behind her.

* * *

"I'll run ahead and see what I can do to help," Jacob said as the last of them climbed up the ladder into the maintenance building. Ava had put Cat and her clothes in the restroom so she could change back.

"No, wait," Ondine told him. "I have an idea about how we can make sure that stuff never blows. The lake where I swim, it's man made and there's a hatch at the bottom."

"Do you think it's connected to the tunnels?" Ava asked.

Ondine nodded. "I know it is. Mr. Halabi says they built the lake specifically so they'd have a way to flood the tunnels where they stored chemical weapons."

"How do we open it?" Jacob asked.

She shrugged. "There's a pulley but no ropes or cables or anything. I could swim down and see if there's a way to slide the door up manually."

"Jacob, can you still run if you're carrying someone?" Sol asked.

"Yeah, just not quite as fast." He turned his back to Ondine, looking over his shoulder. "Care for a piggy-back ride?"

As she climbed on, Ava heaved a sulky sigh. "When am I gonna get to use *my* powers?"

"The minute y'all see Zayden's face, I hope." Cat, now in human form, re-joined them.

They stepped outside and Jacob sped off.

Sol stared at his phone. "Something's going down at Heroes Hall. Come on!"

* * *

Chloe flew past Charlie and spotted Zayden first. A second later, Lindsay pointed so everyone could zero in on his back as he ran across the roof of Heroes Hall toward an open door into the clock tower.

Chloe set her roommate down as gently as she could and then accelerated. She didn't have time to get between Zayden and the door, so she got a better angle and flew right into him.

Her shoulder slammed into Zayden's head and pain flared as it dislocated, as it had been prone to do in the past. She slowed and turned back to see Zayden sprawled on the ground. One hand went to his head as he struggled to get up.

"That's for the fire in my room," she muttered, wincing as her shoulder joint popped back into place.

"Stand back," Rhiannon yelled, Justin swooping low with her in tow just as Zayden got up, looking dazed. Chloe covered her ears and flew straight up so she'd be farther from the blast. On the roof, Lindsay and L.J. ducked and covered their ears. Charlie, still hauling Bridger, dipped down beneath the edge of the building.

Rhiannon opened her wide mouth and let loose. A directed blast of raw sonic power plowed into Zayden and sent him staggering sideways.

Justin flew a tight arc to get Rhiannon back in position. She opened wide and . . . nothing. If she screamed at all, Chloe couldn't hear it over her wings. Rhiannon looked confused, and Chloe followed her friend's eye line to see someone else had emerged onto the roof.

Izzy.

Chloe's heart sank as the implications set in. Angling down and folding her wings, she dove for the roof. She yelled for Charlie and Justin to land, even though she knew they couldn't hear her.

She didn't see Charlie, but Justin circled high over the roof, still holding on to Rhiannon.

Izzy threw her hands in the air, looking at the boy with black wings over her head. Chloe pulled out of the dive and looked up, hoping the pair wouldn't plummet from the sky but prepared to assist if they did.

Nothing happened and Izzy screamed with rage.

Meanwhile, a panicked L.J. fumbled with what looked like a ray gun and Lindsay shaped a fire ball between her hands.

Chloe called to Izzy. "Looks like you can't shrink a physical ability. Not as tough as you thought, eh?"

Chloe zipped over and put herself between Zayden and the stairs, wishing Ava were there.

Zayden, headed that way, stopped short and looked her in the eye. "Chloe, it doesn't have to be this way. Join me and learn what real power is. That's what I wanted all along—a good flier on my team."

Chloe scoffed. "You're sicker than I thought if you think for one m—"

Izzy plowed into her from the side, knocking her onto the shoulder that had only begun to heal. Pain flared bright.

Izzy straddled her and landed a punch on her cheek. "You. Stay. Out. Of. My. Way!" She punctuated each word with another punch. "He's. Mine!"

A popping sound came from L.J.'s blaster and a streak of light hit Izzy in the side, toppling her off of Chloe, who sat up, woozy from the beating she'd just received. She felt something hard in her mouth and spit out a tooth, along with plenty of blood. She stared in shock. *Holy crap, I hope I can grow these back!*

"Freeze, Zayden, or I'll throw this!" Lindsay yelled. She stood in a pitching stance with a large ball of fire in her hand.

Zayden turned away from Chloe and Izzy with a sinister smile marring his good looks. "Do your worst, Fireball."

Lindsay wound up and threw the roiling mass of reds and yellows like a major league pitcher delivering a fastball. Zayden flicked his head the tiniest bit and deflected the fireball toward L.J. Lindsay yelped and waved her hand to put it out, but she was too slow and it clipped L.J.'s leg.

He yelled in pain as he fell with his jeans burned away in a wide swath across one thigh. The smell of burned flesh made Chloe's stomach clench.

Rhiannon, her voice returned to full power with Izzy's attention elsewhere, screamed at Zayden, but he ducked through the door to dodge the blast. Izzy, right on his heels, slammed it shut behind them. Lindsay ran over and yanked on the knob.

"Damn, it's locked!"

Charlie and Bridger hurried to them as Justin and Rhiannon touched down.

"I can hear them racing down the stairs." Bridger held up a hand for quiet. "He told Izzy to get to the auditorium."

"Let's get down there," Charlie said. "Chloe, L.J., are you guys okay?"

"I will be," Chloe said. "I can still fly, but I can't carry anyone."

L.J.'s voice was tight with pain. "It hurts bad and that's my good leg. I can't hop on the prosthetic, so I'm only mobile for as long as the tech lasts."

Charlie nodded. "Justin, take Rhiannon down. Rhiannon, blow out the windows so we can get inside. I'll take Lindsay down then come back for Bridger." He looked at the phone Bridger had kept directed at the action all this time. "I hope to hell you guys are listening, 'cause we need you here now!"

He and Justin took off with their passengers while Bridger helped L.J. stand.

Chloe stretched her aching jaw. "Remind me to never get punched again. Ow." She looked at L.J. "You ready?"

He nodded, leaning on Bridger and powering up his propulsion system.

"Okay, I'll stay with you in case something malfunctions," she told him.

L.J. blasted off and Chloe took to the air, sticking close to him. On their way down, they passed Charlie on his way up for Bridger.

A minute later, they all stood on the ground behind Heroes Hall, except for L.J., who hovered in place a few inches above it. Everyone plugged their ears and Rhiannon prepared to scream, but then someone yelled "Incoming." Jack had arrived and ran toward the nearest door, head lowered. He rammed right through it, turning the door to kindling.

Everyone ran for the opening just as Kaci and Austin joined them.

"Zayden's inside and Izzy's working with him," Chloe rattled off as fast as she could.

Kaci froze and gasped. "Fire!"

Chloe whipped her head around but she didn't see anything.

"Where?" Charlie asked.

"All around campus—the whole perimeter." She grabbed Austin's hand. "We'll do what we can to contain it." They ran off.

"Jack, Rhiannon, Bridger, see if you can figure out where Zayden went," Charlie said. Bridger nodded and led the others toward the stairwell.

Team Tunnel arrived, minus Jacob and Ondine.

Charlie scanned the group. "Ava, Lindsay, Cat, Sol—head to the auditorium. We think Izzy's headed there."

"Izzy?" Ava asked. "You found her? Is she okay?"

"She's working with Zayden, and she did this to me." Chloe pointed to her own face.

Ava paled and the four of them sprinted down the hall.

"Fliers, let's get a bird's eye view. I'll call 9-1-1 to report the fires while you guys get a look." Charlie ended the live chat and dialed while the others took off. Chloe couldn't help but be impressed by Charlie's calm and how he seemed to have everything under control.

Chloe flew straight up over Heroes Hall and looked out toward the parking lot where she'd first arrived with her dad. She saw a slender arc of flame at least ten feet tall beyond it and her heart lurched. Sure enough, she saw as she spun in the air, it encircled campus.

Movement in the parking lot caught her eye and she flew closer. Three people unloaded something from an ambulance. No, not something, she saw—some*one*. In a wheelchair.

It's Dax, she realized with a start. He pointed up at her and she zipped down to him.

"Tow-ee, Tow-ee," he called as she landed.

"How is this possible?" She looked from a man she didn't know to a woman in scrubs she didn't recognize. Then her eyes landed on Misty, the intern from the hospital, and it started to fall into place.

"Dax was desperate to come here," Misty said. "He thought you'd need him to stop Zayden."

Chloe bent down and hugged him. "I think you're right, Dax. We're trying to find him, but he has unexpected help from one of our classmates."

"Dree." Dax held up three fingers.

* * *

Ondine jogged through the shallows, water sloughing from her blue-tinged skin. Her expression told Jacob something was wrong.

"I can't open it," she called. "The door's supposed to slide up, but the bottom's too buried and I can't get my fingers under it. We need to get some tools. A pry bar for sure, maybe a shovel, and a screwdriver to scrape algae and gunk out of the track."

He nodded. "Wait here—I'll be back with everything I can carry in, like, three minutes."

She retrieved her phone from the shore and pulled up Parable, then clicked on an invitation to a live video chat to see an aerial shot of flames surrounding campus.

First, she wondered if Jacob could run through it fast enough not to catch fire himself. Then she remembered the wind he generated and how it could spread the flames. She voice messaged Kaci and Austin.

"Jacob's running toward the south side of campus right now and doesn't know about the fire."

Kaci popped up. "On it, Ondine."

* * *

Ava charged toward the auditorium door.

Lindsay grabbed her arm. "We need to be smart about this. Let's listen at the door and see what we're dealing with before we charge in."

"It's just Izzy. You guys distract her and I'll punch her stupid face. You think Chloe looks bad?"

Sol shook his head. "Lindsay's right. We don't know what's going on in there, but I might be able to find out." He focused, eyes closed. "Izzy's there, plus five other people. I can't tell who. There's a lot of fear and anxiety, though. Nerves on edge." He opened his eyes and looked at the three girls. "We need to be careful."

"I'll slip in through the stage entrance and do some recon," Cat said. In a flash, she ran off in tabby form.

Sol went to the door—the same one they'd gone through for orientation—and put his ear to it. After several seconds, he shook his head. "Nothing. I'll see what I can get from Cat." He closed his eyes again and they opened wide a second later. "Oh, shit!"

* * *

Jacob closed his eyes and streaked right through the flame, just feeling the heat. Kaci sprinted that direction and he hoped she could keep his wind from spreading it too much.

In seconds, he arrived at the maintenance building and entered through the already-open door. He reduced his speed enough to maintain control of it as he gathered up a screwdriver set, a pry bar, and a toolbox full of miscellaneous things.

It all took only seconds, which was also how long it took for him to wonder why the door had already been open. Something smashed the back of his head and he fell to his knees, dropping all the tools with loud clatters and clangs. He looked over his shoulder to see a shovel floating in midair. Before he could accelerate to safety, it struck him again. He collapsed forward onto the spilled tools.

* * *

"Izzy's in there, along with her sister," Sol said.

"Oh, great—the one who shoots lightning from her hands?" Ava rolled her eyes. "I'm sure that'll feel good."

"They've got some prisoners, too," Sol told them. "Four who Cat can see. From the random thoughts I'm picking up, I'm pretty sure that includes Chloe's parents."

Lindsay's hands flew up to cover her mouth. "Oh no!"

"We've got to bring everyone in on this." Ava reached for her absent phone for the hundredth time since Chloe borrowed it. She made an aggravated sound. "Damn it. Lindsay, let them know."

Lindsay nodded and pulled up the live chat. "Guys, hostage situation in the auditorium. Looks like Lucia's on Zayden's side, too." She paused, nervous. "Chloe, we think they have your parents in there."

* * *

"Who's available to get to the auditorium?" Charlie asked.

"On my way now," Chloe said, "with Dax. I'll explain later."

"Me," said L.J., as he maneuvered the jet pack and swooped off toward Heroes Hall.

"Has anyone seen Jacob?" Ondine asked. "He should be back by now."

"He passed through on his way in several minutes ago, long enough that we've got the fire back under control," Austin reported.

Justin chimed in. "I saw him head for the maintenance building but haven't seen him come back out."

"We can check it out," Bridger said. "We found a tunnel entrance from the basement of Heroes and we're pretty sure that's where Zayden went, but we figured it'd be stupid to be down there when it's about to be flooded."

"Good thinking," Charlie told them. "Bridger, you and Rhiannon head over and get a listen. Kaci, Austin, what's the fire situation?"

"Under control," Austin said. "Kaci keeps getting areas put out but then they spring back up again. Weird thing is, it's not spreading on its own at all."

"Okay, Austin, stay out there for when Jacob comes through again. Kaci, move closer to Heroes Hall and standby. With Lucy and Lindsay fighting in there, we could have a fire issue." Charlie paused. "Justin, get close to maintenance and try to keep an eye on what's happening there."

"You got it," Justin said, and Charlie watched him fly that direction. He also heard sirens heading toward campus.

About time, he thought, *but where's the faculty? Just Cause?* He landed on the dorm roof and messaged Mr. Hutson. *Any luck reaching Mr. J?*

A response came back right away. *A call came into Denver PD that had them heading this way already. They should start to trickle in pretty soon. What's the situation out there?*

Fire around perimeter of campus. Fight about to break out in auditorium, Charlie sent back. *At least two students working with Zayden—Izzy and Lucy Machado, and they've got hostages. Unknown where Z is right now.*

Shit. Lucia? Damn. I'll tell them to hurry.

"Please do," Charlie muttered to himself and took a shaking breath. "You can do this." He took to the air again, wishing he could be more useful on the ground.

* * *

Chloe led Misty, who pushed Dax's chair, into the lobby with Lindsay and the others. Misty took in a breath at the sight of L.J.'s burned leg.

"Let me look at that." She peered at the burn and called Chloe over.

"Ment told me something about your powers, Chloe. Something I don't think you know."

Chloe's brows pinched together. "What?"

"You can swap your healing for someone else's power," Misty said, "through touch. That's why Dax started healing after you touched his hand."

"So if I touch L.J.—"

L.J. thrust his hand toward her. "Do it, quick."

She held his fingers. "Feeling anything?"

He didn't respond for a few seconds, then closed his eyes and breathed a sigh of relief. "The pain's fading. Thanks."

"Yeah, glad I know about that!" Chloe turned to Sol. "So, what's the plan?"

"I'm watching through Cat's eyes," Sol said, eyes closed. "Here, let me send you what she's seeing."

A moment later, Chloe's head spun as her perception shifted to a few inches off the ground. Cat slunk along next to the curtain, off in the wings. Izzy stood before a large screen, arms crossed, while Lucy paced with her head down. Random bursts of blue energy crackled around her hands.

At center stage, tied to chairs with their backs together, sat a janitor, a receptionist, and Phil and Heather Wyld. Chloe let out a single sob before steeling herself for whatever lay ahead.

"I don't know how good it is, but I think I have a plan," Lindsay said.

"That makes one of us," Sol told her, "so go ahead."

"Jack and Ava can handle Lucy's bolts, so we have you two rush in, one from each side of the stage. I'll come in behind one of you and try to get between them and the prisoners, since I can fend them off with fire." Lindsay looked around, uncomfortable in the leadership role.

"Sounds great so far," Chloe said.

Lindsay's confidence seemed to grow. "Okay, then L.J. and Chloe can fly in from over the screen. Chloe can untie them while L.J. joins me in defense. Meanwhile, Cat stays in position and transmits to Sol, who reports it all to Charlie."

"Any plans that don't involve me getting zapped?" Ava wrinkled her nose like she smelled something rotten.

They all looked around at each other. "Nope," Sol said.

Ava sighed. "Okay, fine. Let's go."

They split up, Ava, Lindsay, and Chloe on one side, Jack and L.J. on the other.

"Dax, can you see what's going on inside that room?" Chloe pointed toward the auditorium.

Dax looked at the wall and nodded.

"Once we're ready to move in, can you make something fall or bang toward the back of the seats, to distract the girls on stage?"

Dax nodded again, face blank. Chloe had to trust that he understood. "You know Sol, here. You've talked to him before. Wait for his signal, okay?"

Dax grinned at Sol like an old friend. Chloe looked at the others and shrugged. "Let's do this."

CHAPTER TWENTY-SEVEN

Sunday, Sept. 11
Denver, Colorado

"The building's quiet and Jacob's not here," Bridger reported from the maintenance building. "There's a whole mess of tools on the floor, though."

"Does that include screwdrivers and a pry bar?" Ondine asked.

"Yep. Is that what he came for?"

"Yeah." Ondine's voice cracked.

"Justin, you can get out to the lake fastest," Charlie said. "Get the tools and head out there."

"On it." Justin broke from his circling pattern and swooped down to the door, where Bridger handed him a tool box. He then took off at top speed, over the center of campus and out past the ring of flame, where a few fire engines had just arrived. The lake gleamed in the near distance.

* * *

"What was that?" Izzy asked in response to a noise at the back of the auditorium, terror in her voice. "Are the explosions starting? Do we need to get out of here?"

Lucy glared. "Chill, Iz. It just sounds like something fell. Go check it out."

"Why do I have to go?" she asked.

"Because I'm better suited to guarding the prisoners. Quit your whining and go." Lucy turned away and looked over the prisoners' bindings to make sure no one got a hand loose or tried to cut the rope on some convenient sharp surface.

Izzy trudged down the stairs and up the aisle, then stopped and looked down at something on the floor. "What the—it looks like a chair just suddenly fell apart. Zayden, are you messing with us?" She yelled the last part.

From the wings, Ava and Jack nodded at each other and burst forth on a collision course with Lucia. The purple-skinned girl saw Jack first and launched a bolt at him that glanced off a horn, leaving a scorch mark. Izzy whirled around and thrust a hand his direction just as he tackled her sister. Lucy managed to get a hand on his arm and zapped him—successfully this time. He flew several feet back and crashed in a heap on the floor. Ava dropped onto the still-prone Lucy and pinned her down. Lucy's first attempt to zap her had no effect.

Chloe and L.J. flew up over the screen. Chloe dove toward the prisoners. A wicked grin crossed Izzy's face and she thrust her hand toward L.J. His armor pieces shrank around his body, then tore apart. L.J. yelled as he plummeted into the hardwood stage with a loud crunch that Chloe hoped was his prosthetic. She knew from a wrist fracture two years ago that, even with her healing power, it took days to heal a broken bone.

She righted herself in the air and touched her feet to the boards in front of her mom.

"Chloe! What happened to your face? Get out of here. Go somewhere safe!"

"No way, I'm not leaving you guys here." Chloe set to work prying the first knot loose.

The prisoners blocked Izzy's view of Ava, so she ran toward the stairs up to the stage. Lindsay stepped out from the wings, a fireball at the ready. "Stop right there, Izzy."

Izzy froze. Just then, a loud burst of static made them all jump, and an image appeared on the screen.

"Well, well, well." Zayden's voice boomed over the speakers as his face came into focus. "It seems my guests have started to arrive."

Chloe looked up for a moment and went back to work on the complicated knots.

Ava glanced away, giving Lucy the moment she needed to buck the younger girl off, roll away, and stand up with potentially lethal hands in position for firing bolts. "Drain her, Izzy," she yelled.

Izzy focused on Ava, who panicked and ran off the way she'd come.

"That's right." Zayden's voice dripped condescension. "Run away, little heroes. Save yourselves. Because when the big guns show up, this place is gonna blow, and there's no way you can stop it!"

"The door's locked!" Ava yelled from the wings.

"Don't move, Lucia," Lindsay yelled, ignoring Zayden. Beyond the prisoners, and behind Lucy's back, Jack stood up and lowered his head. Lindsay kept both Machado girls focused on her.

Izzy swung an out-stretched hand toward Lindsay and Lucy turned to sneer at her. "Is your fire faster than my lightning? I'm guessing not."

"Take her out, Lucy!" Zayden ordered.

Lindsay sneered back at her. "I know how it works —you have to absorb power from somewhere, and I'm guessing you're about out."

Doubt flickered in Lucy's purple face and Lindsay knew she'd called it. The battery needed recharged.

Then Lindsay's fire went out and Izzy laughed. "Now whatcha gonna do, Fireball? Run off after Ava?"

Zayden's voice cackled from the speakers.

Lucy ran across the stage and put her hand over an electrical outlet. Lindsay blanched, not sure what do to next, then ran to help Chloe.

Jack bellowed and charged—but toward Izzy, not Lucy. As Zayden screamed a warning, Jack closed the distance and lowered his head to connect with her abdomen.

Izzy let out a *whoof* as the horns and skull knocked the wind out of her and propelled her backward several yards. She hit the floor, yelling in agony, clutching at her ribs.

L.J., still on the floor, leveled a roughly drawn, cartoonish-looking blaster at Lucy just as she took her hand away from the outlet and once again had electricity dancing around her fingers.

"Freeze!" he yelled as he pulled the trigger. A blast of green light streaked across the stage and hit her, and her skin took on a gray cast at the point of impact. The grayness spread out to the rest of her body, and she didn't move a muscle.

"Nice!" Lindsay called to him. She looked over her shoulder to make sure Izzy was still out of commission and saw Jack looming over the crying girl, blocking her view of the stage. Calling fire just to her fingertips, the way her mother did, she burned through the rope in seconds and the prisoners leapt to their feet.

The janitor and registrar sprinted to the nearest door. When it wouldn't open, they pounded on it and yelled for help.

Chloe's parents threw their arms around her. "Thank God you're safe," her dad said.

"Same goes for you guys." Chloe sniffed. "I'm so sorry, but I have to go. This isn't over yet. Come on." She grabbed her mom's hand and pulled her off stage with her dad following close behind. "Jack, help L.J. Everyone else, get out fast!"

Zayden gloated on the screen. "Good luck with that —you can't get out of there."

Dax, can you open the doors? Chloe thought, focusing hard. Every door to the auditorium flew open at once.

"No!" Zayden screamed behind them. "How are you doing that? Chupara, suck up some juice and fry them! Izzy, get my hostages back!"

Cat darted out just ahead of Chloe, Lindsay on their heels. Jack hoisted L.J. up into a fireman's carry and headed their direction while Zayden bellowed on the screen.

* * *

The track above the door cleared, Ondine tried to find a spot where the pry bar could grab onto something, but she couldn't get purchase. The metal was not only wet, but covered in slimy algae. The bar slipped yet again and she fought panic, choking back a sob that would allow water into her lungs rather than her gills. She thought dismally how ironic it would be if she drowned while the campus burned.

Discarding the bar, she wiped away the algae and plunged her hands into the mud along where the door met the lake floor, feeling for anything that could help. She'd about given up when she came across a small rough area. She grabbed the bar and began to pry.

* * *

On the screen, Zayden's live image had given way to the video Lucy had helped him make. "Welcome, faculty, staff, heroes, and hero-wanna-be students!"

Immobilized on the stage with several broken ribs, Lucy didn't understand why it started playing before anyone important arrived—after all, he should still be able to see through the web cams they'd put up. For people who'd once been responsible for national security, the administration was awfully lax about security right here on campus. Zayden and his allies came up through the floor at night and had their run of the place.

Zayden's recorded voice continued. "Don't bother trying to leave—I've sealed you all in. You cannot escape my wrath, and this day will forever be known for the greatest single parahuman massacre in history!"

The pain in her ribcage beyond anything she'd experienced, Izzy gasped for breath. No way could she stand, or even sit, to get a better look at her sister. She didn't know if she could drain the effect of a weapon created with parahuman abilities, even if she could see her. She lifted her head enough to catch sight of Lucy's hair, its burgundy replaced with a dull gray. Izzy raised her shaking left hand two inches off the floor. The motion sent fresh shooting pain through her chest.

"No longer will that pretender, Destroyer, take credit for that," Zayden went on. "Today marks the ascension of the greatest super villain the world has ever known. Witness the power of Lord Blayze!"

Lucy felt terror at those words, knowing they heralded explosions ripping the building apart. She willed her sister to do something, anything, to get them out.

Is it possible to hurt this much and not be dying? Izzy wondered. Summoning all of her will, she splayed her hand in Lucia's direction and focused. She heard strange popping and hissing sounds, then red tones rippled through the drab locks. She collapsed as Lucy yelled her name.

Wondering again if she was about to die, Izzy shut her eyes, too tired even to sob in pain.

"Oh God, Izzy, please don't be dead," her big sister wailed.

Izzy cracked open her eyes and whispered, "Can't you see . . . I'm busy passing out?"

The auditorium's rear door swung open to admit not Principal Jordan, but MetalBlade in full costume. Former Just Cause leader Doublecharge flew through the doorway behind him. More faculty and heroes followed. Zayden's message began again, and this time, Lucy knew they'd be dead if they couldn't get out of there before it ended.

* * *

Clear of the building, with her parents heading for the edge of campus where fire crews had gained control, Chloe zipped at top speed toward the maintenance building. In her mind, Dax took her up a staircase, through a door bolted from the inside, to Zayden standing before a bank of security monitors showing the auditorium, tunnels, and several other places around campus.

Zayden swore and raged at the image of the auditorium. On a recording, his voice said, "Witness the power of Lord Blayze!" Moments later, Lucy screamed Izzy's name.

Tell everyone to stay out of the auditorium! she mentally screamed at Dax. She heard him relay that to Sol, but she didn't know whether Sol responded. She almost turned back to deliver the message herself, but she knew finding Zayden was the best way to stop something horrible from happening.

She arrived at the maintenance building well ahead of everyone, wondering what in the world she could do on her own. *Distract him if nothing else,* she thought, refusing to let her fear take over.

* * *

From his vantage point on the dorm roof, Charlie saw Chloe zip around the maintenance building and directed everyone listening to head her way, then asked Justin for an update on Ondine.

No idea, Justin replied. *She's been down there a long time. I'm heading back to campus now.*

The group from the auditorium—including Misty pushing Dax—rushed after Chloe. Kaci and Austin weren't far behind them. Charlie lifted off and swooped that direction as well.

With a start, he realized he'd heard nothing from Bridger since he'd handed the tools off to Justin.

* * *

Chloe flew into the workshop through the open back door and landed in a deserted room. Through windowed doors, she saw the other rooms on the first floor were dark and empty as well. Zayden's broadcast had come from a well-lit room with white cinder block walls, so not from a tunnel, but, she suspected, from this building. She spotted a staircase tucked behind a tall tool cabinet and ran for it. Just after her foot hit the first riser, she heard yelling from above.

* * *

Lying on the floor of a dusty storage room, Bridger heard Chloe's wings buzzing toward the building. He opened one eye a slit to see if Zayden had noticed, but he didn't appear to. In fact, he appeared frustrated and angry as he stood before a table strewn with electronics, including several security monitors.

On one monitor, Bridger could see several faculty members surrounding something on the auditorium floor while a group of heroes closed in on Lucy, dodging, deflecting, and absorbing her energy blasts.

Zayden also hadn't noticed the soft sound Jacob's fingernail made as it scratched at high speed through the thick rope, wearing away the fibers and snapping them one by one. A quick glance that direction showed him Jacob's hands would be free soon.

From the whispering of air currents, he could tell they were in a large and somewhat empty space, but he couldn't see far due to a barricade of old dressers, desks, mattresses, and other assorted furniture that stood between them and the door. The ceiling soared high above him, which seemed odd considering this used to be a dorm, but then he realized they must've taken out a floor in order to create this huge, warehouse-like space.

The buzz of Chloe's wings cut out and footfalls approached the stairs. The loud, creaky stairs, he knew from when Zayden dragged him up, bound and no longer unconscious but pretending to be. He knew the would-be villain would hear her approaching. He turned off the super hearing.

"What the hell, Zayden?" he yelled, making Zayden jump and whirl around to face him. "Where am I? Why am I tied up?"

Hearing back up to maximum, he heard Chloe's footfalls cease and the soft clicks of her sending a message on her phone. He also realized several more people headed toward the building, hearing their feet thudding against the ground, some loud whispers being exchanged, and the beat of large moth wings. Something also seemed to be rolling through the grass, but he couldn't make out what.

"Why are you awake so soon?" Zayden, red in the face, bent over to check the bonds on Bridger's wrists and ankles, then went to check Jacob's, as well.

"Dude, did you drug me? What's going on?" Bridger asked, hoping to distract him, but Zayden looked down and saw Jacob's rope almost sawed through and his eyes widened in fury.

"Get in here and bring the rope!" Zayden yelled through an open doorway into another room.

* * *

Charlie's commands came in, one line at a time.

Chloe hang back

Ava Jack take point

LJ Lindsay Rhiannon back them up

Sol get in Bridger's head and tell me where he is, I can't reach him

Sol responded moments later. *He's in with Zayden, tied up on the floor*

Stay with him and send me what he sees

Flattening herself against the wall so the front-liners could get past, Chloe swiped in a message. *Sol should send Dax what he sees*

Chloe's right do that, Charlie replied.

* * *

Bridger knew several people now stood right outside the door, beyond the barricade.

Look around for me, Sol's voice said in his head.

Bridger scanned the barricade, then the table of electronics, the open doorway, and Zayden standing over Jacob, who glared up at Zayden and moved his thumb even faster in full view of the would-be supervillain.

Bridger's eyes flicked toward movement in the doorway, and through it stepped Miguel, looking like he'd just woken up from a nap, holding a coil of rope.

"Tie his hands better," Zayden said, "and make sure to bind his fingers, too."

Miguel knelt down and whispered a soft, "Sorry, man," as Zayden went back to his monitors. The second airing of the video was almost complete.

"I need a boost in thirty seconds. You ready?"

"Yeah, just say when," Miguel told him.

Zayden stayed focused on the video player time display. "Twenty-five."

Something bashed into the door on the other side of the barricade.

* * *

Jack rammed his horned head into the thick wooden door. It splintered, but it didn't give.

"I think it's barred or something." Jack took a few steps back, got a running start, and slammed into it again.

A rough, rectangular hole opened up, but the door itself didn't budge.

"Twelve, eleven . . ." came Zayden's muffled voice from inside.

Jack leaned against the wall, a hand to his head. Ava darted forward and reached through the gap.

"It's over, 'Lord Blayze,'" she called as she groped for the bar.

"Nine, eight, seven . . ."

She found it and lifted it from its cradle. It fell to the floor with a clatter. "God, that's a dumb name."

A message from Ondine flashed up on Parable. *I can't move this thing. I need help.*

Omw, Chloe sent back.

* * *

Zayden shot an angry look at the barricade in response to Ava's taunt. "You're too late! Everyone in the auditorium's about to die!" A cold smile crossed his face. "Now, Miguel."

Miguel put a hand on Zayden's shoulder. On the monitor, flames shot up along the sides, front, and back of the auditorium, penning everyone in. Zayden switched focus to the image of the tunnel, took a deep breath, and forced it out with a low grunt.

Bridger didn't need super hearing to know the two bricks were breaking their way through the barricade. He stayed focused on Zayden's back, which blocked the monitor, and hoped Dax could see what he needed to.

"Why the hell isn't this working?" Zayden spat. "Miguel, max boost, now!"

Miguel, standing beside Zayden now even though he hadn't done much about Jacob's hands, squeezed his eyes closed and grabbed Zayden's shoulder.

After a few seconds, Zayden went pale. "Someone's blocking me. Who's blocking me? How is this possible?"

A heavy filing cabinet grated across the floor with a metallic groan and Jack and Ava burst through the narrow opening it created. Zayden spun to face them and mind-yanked a large metal desk from the barricade. Ava went down beneath it and Jack staggered off to the side.

"Ears off, bro," Bridger heard Rhiannon whisper. A moment later, she stepped into view and let loose with a scream that made him wish he were deaf. Zayden and Miguel stumbled back a few steps, covering their ears and wincing with pain. Windows shattered and monitor screens cracked.

Jacob realized he'd covered his ears—the reflexive jerk of his body had broken the rope's last fibers and freed his hands. Everything around him seemed to freeze as he kicked into high gear.

Taking in the scene, he saw the blast had knocked over a soda can and several drops appeared to be suspended in the air just outside the mouth. A dresser teetered precariously atop the barricade next to the empty space left by the fallen desk, and it threatened to hit Jack.

Jacob loosed his feet, ran over and pushed Jack away from the barricade, and plowed into Zayden, knocking him into Miguel. Those three went down in a big pile, the impact painful enough to pull Jacob out of speed mode. The first drops of soda hit the ground just after him, splashing on his arm.

The bookcase crashed to the ground a foot from Jack, who spun around, startled and confused.

A moment later, Zayden flicked his hand and Jacob flew through the air and crashed into the barricade, then fell to the ground, the wind knocked out of him and searing pain in his arm.

Ava lifted the desk up just enoughto wriggle out from under it. Despite her ability to withstand damage, she had scrapes all over, a bleeding lip, and a large knot on her forehead.

Lindsay stepped into the opening in the barricade, a fireball at the ready. As Zayden picked himself up off the floor, she wound up and threw it. A foot from its target, it froze in the air and came hurtling back toward her. With a surprised yelp, Lindsay waved a hand and it poofed away into nothing, leaving wisps of smoke in its place.

"Want to play with fire, do you?" Zayden sneered at her. He waved a hand and a wall-to-wall line of flame rose up from the floor. Bridger upped his hearing just a little and heard Lindsay calling for Kaci and Austin.

Zayden, smirking, turned back to the monitors, cracked from Rhiannon's scream but still functioning. "Now why can't I make it work down there, like when we tested it? Come on, Miguel."

Miguel took his place next to Zayden once again, looking with wide eyes at the fire and the injured students beyond it.

"Hurry," Zayden shouted, "before they're out of the building!"

Miguel's eyes went to the auditorium monitor. The fire still burned in neat lines and firefighters tried to battle it from the main door as a flying hero lifted people over the flames to the safety of the stage, one by one. A couple of costumed heroes had Lucy in handcuffs and his twin writhed in pain on a stretcher. "What happened to Izzy? You didn't tell me she got hurt!"

"Shut up and boost me, dammit!" Zayden yelled.

Miguel put one hand on Zayden's arm, but his eyes stayed locked on the monitor.

* * *

As fast as her wings could carry her, Chloe raced to the lake. She would have to be Dax's eyes. She saw Ondine in the water next to the concrete structure, tucked her wings in tight, and let herself freefall.

Below, Ondine dove under the water. Chloe took a deep breath, arms outstretched with her hands coming together in a point. A moment later the cold water enveloped her as she broke the surface with barely a splash and plummeted toward the bottom. Ondine streaked along beside her.

When Chloe's momentum began to run out, Ondine grabbed her hand and kept swimming at top speed, heading toward the metal sliding door. Chloe's body moved in new and fluid ways and she realized she could now swim as fast as Ondine, but she still couldn't breathe under water.

Her lungs ached, but she ignored them and allowed Ondine to keep pulling her deeper. She felt Dax in her mind, looking through her eyes, and urged him to hurry. They reached the lake floor, Chloe fighting panic as the pain in her lungs mounted and her body screamed for oxygen, desperate to let out its captive breath and take another.

She almost dismissed it as wishful thinking when the door jerked, just a little. Then it happened again, and she could feel the water being sucked through a small gap.

Got it? she asked Dax, wondering if she'd pass out before they could reach the surface.

Got it. Go, Chloe!

Chloe gave a sharp nod. Ondine grabbed her hand and launched herself off the bottom of the lake. She headed straight for the surface, pulling Chloe behind her, racing against the turbulence the opening door would create behind them at any moment.

Dark spots swam before Chloe's eyes. Her lungs burned and her heart ached with every beat. At last, she couldn't hold it any longer and the air burst forth. She tried to close her mouth before too much water rushed in, but against her will, her body gasped for air that wasn't there.

Dax tore open the door below, creating a powerful vortex beneath their feet as lake water rushed into it.

* * *

The two pyros raced up the stairs and to the opening in the barricade, where they could see the fire. Austin closed his eyes and chanted under his breath while Kaci squinted and stared into the dancing flames. In moments, there was a *whoomph* and the fire vanished without a trace, save for a straight, shallow trench burned into the floor.

"Ignite, dammit!" Zayden yelled at the monitor, not seeming to register what else happened in the room.

Kaci and Austin fell back as Cat, in feline form, shot in and L.J. hopped forward on his good leg. He'd removed the remains of the prosthesis so his pant leg hung empty below the knee.

"Stay back," he yelled. Cat dove behind Bridger, still on the floor, and Jack and Ava put their backs against the barricade.

Zayden didn't see L.J. raise the cartoonish-looking ray gun and point it at him, but Miguel did. As L.J. fired, he lunged forward, pushing Zayden out of the way, and took the blast himself.

"No!" L.J. yelled, seeing his friend go stiff and gray, just as his big sister had.

Zayden stumbled a few steps before recovering his balance. He saw Miguel frozen, waved a hand, and L.J.'s gun flew across the room. With another gesture, the barricade shook and rumbled ominously.

L.J. lunged after the gun but fell, sprawling on the floor. Lindsay and Rhiannon rushed in to help him but he waved them away and pulled himself toward Miguel. Jack and Ava both ran toward Zayden, and Cat leapt over Bridger, flashed her claws, and attached herself to Zayden's leg. With a scream, Zayden grabbed the scruff of her neck and hurled her at Ava. He pointed the other hand at Jack, who flew backward through the air and into the barricade. Furniture rained down, burying him.

Ava moved toward Zayden once again, but with a wave he threw her into the air—where she froze, hanging for a few seconds as Zayden stared in shock, and descended to the ground.

Zayden motioned toward a dresser and it started toward her, then stopped dead. "Who's doing this? This isn't possible!" he yelled.

* * *

Charlie's wings shimmered in the sunlight as he descended. He saw Justin off to his right, on the same trajectory, black wings cupped and held close to his sides.

The girls had just broken the surface not far from the concrete hatch and he could see the water's smooth surface dip like a draining bathtub as it rushed into the tunnels below, threatening to pull Chloe and Ondine back under.

His heart clenched as Ondine hoisted a limp Chloe up onto herself and streaked away from the center of the lake.

Seconds later, but too many for comfort, he got into position above them and reached down, slipping his hands underneath Chloe's shoulders and pulling her up. He struggled to manage the dead weight and the tip of his right wing dipped into the water, just for a second.

No, no, no, no, no! his mind screamed. He shook the wing, flinging water droplets in all directions, and pulled Chloe's limp form up against his chest. He managed to stay aloft as he got his arms around her and counted himself lucky.

He veered off to the left, careful to keep that wing out of the water just inches away, to make room for Justin to swoop in for Ondine. He didn't look back to see if his friend was successful, though—all he knew was Chloe wasn't breathing, and with his wing not fully functional, he might not get her to dry land in time.

* * *

As Ava realized Dax was blocking Zayden's telekinesis, a victorious grin crossed her face. She launched herself toward Zayden again.

Zayden turned tail and ran into the small office, slamming and locking the door behind him.

"Ignite, ignite!" he yelled as Ava slammed into the door again and again. It crunched, but not as loudly as the other one had when Jack rammed it.

"Maybe I *should* work out more," she muttered as she switched shoulders and prepared for another bash. Cat paced behind her, tail twitching. Ava lunged forward and the door crunched again, caving part way in.

"Yes! I feel it burning!" Zayden shrieked. "You can't stop it now!"

Bridger's eyes went to the security camera image of the tunnel. Flames sprang up on the candles between propane barrels. A glance at the auditorium feed showed paramedics around Izzy's gurney, halfway up the aisle, using a defibrillator. A handful of faculty and costumed heroes, plus firefighters, still battled the flames.

Still bound and on the floor, Bridger had a dim awareness that Ava's third attempt to bash in the door failed, that Jack had managed to dig his way out from under the collapsed barricade, that L.J. had retrieved his gun and now pointed it at Miguel again, that the room's opening was once again blocked. None of it mattered, though. He couldn't draw his attention away from the two monitors.

He wasn't aware that in the hyper-focused state he'd increased his hearing—until he heard it: a low rumble from the south, growing louder. Coming closer.

As he watched, a torrent of water rushed into view on the tunnel monitor. It overtook the flames. It stole the barrels from view. And then, as it ripped the camera and its mount from the wall, the feed went black.

Feeling his flame extinguish, Zayden roared in fury while Bridger whooped and cheered.

* * *

Charlie fought to beat his wings, but the water-damaged tip just wouldn't function. He kept veering right and losing altitude. Tears clouded his vision and he screamed in frustration.

The water was too close for comfort but he couldn't pull up no matter how hard he tried. The tips of both wings would dip into it soon, he knew.

A few flaps later, the left one skimmed the surface, sending up spray that splashed big drops all over the wing.

"I'm sorry, Chloe," he whispered, feeling himself drop, "I'm so sorry."

The backs of his hands brushed the water, which he knew wanted to pull them down under the surface. Then, something jerked on his back from above. Stunned and confused, he looked up to see Justin's powerful black wings. Relief washed through him—at least he wouldn't fail her completely.

Seconds later, they touched down on the shore and Ondine rushed over to them. Charlie started chest compressions, but nothing seemed to happen. Even when it seemed futile, he couldn't stop.

The next thing he knew, a shock sent him flying backward, hands tingling. Water gushed from Chloe's mouth, shooting up into the air. She choked and sputtered, then rolled onto her side and threw up.

Charlie ran back to her and knelt down. "Oh thank God, Chloe! Are you okay?"

She spat into the dirt and wiped her mouth. "Tastes like I licked a fish tank."

Charlie laughed, anxiety and adrenaline making him sound a little unhinged.

"So . . . wow, what just happened?" Ondine asked.

Justin nodded, hands on his hips. "Yeah, that was crazy."

"Dax," she said. "He kind of zapped me and forced the water out. I think Misty helped somehow? He was in my head, screaming at me to breathe."

"Sure am glad he's on our side." Charlie helped her up and hugged her before realizing what he was doing. She hugged him back, though, so he had no regrets. After reluctantly letting her go, he pulled out his phone and looked out over the diminishing lake. "Status check. What's going on at maintenance?"

* * *

One more bash and the door exploded into splinters. Ava and Jack rushed into the small office, Lindsay and Cat on their heels.

Charlie's voice came over Kaci's phone, asking for an update. "I can't see anything," She called from behind the collapsed barricade. "Someone tell me what's going on."

"The tunnel's flooded, the fire's out, and Zayden's about to get his ass handed to him," Bridger yelled. As Kaci repeated that into her phone, Bridger heard his sister outside, yelling toward Heroes Hall that they had Zayden cornered in the maintenance building.

In the office, Zayden sent the desk sliding toward his adversaries. Jack leapt out of the way, Lindsay hit the wall, and Cat jumped right over it, landing in a menacing position just feet from Zayden. The desk clipped Ava's side and sent her sprawling.

As Zayden raised his hands to attack, Lindsay hurled a fireball and he stumbled back, trying to get out of its path. As it lost altitude, it connected with his leg and his jeans burst into flame. He screamed and beat at the fire, trying to put it out.

Cat pounced and landed on his back, claws out. Zayden screamed again as she scrambled up his neck and swiped at him, leaving long bloody scratches over his cheek, ear, and neck.

Zayden went rigid and stared in horror at a spot high on the wall. Ava and Lindsay looked up at it, then at each other in confusion as Zayden howled and waved his hands frantically at . . . nothing around his face.

Jack yelled for Cat to get clear. As she leapt away, he lowered his head and charged. The ram horns connected with the side of Zayden's head, sending him crashing into the wall, and then falling to the floor unconscious.

Ava straddled Zayden's back and twisted his hands behind him. "What the hell was he freaking out about?"

In their minds, they heard Sol chuckle. *I owed him a little messing with his mind. Did you know he's deathly allergic to bees?*

Ava shrugged. "Whatever works. Jack, get his feet, in case he's faking or comes to." Jack sat on his legs.

Lindsay clicked on voice chat. "We've got him, everyone! Zayden's unconscious. It's over!"

Then she speed dialed her mom. "Hey! We've got Zayden, uh, detained, I guess you'd say, in the maintenance building. Can you get someone here with a sleeper set?"

"What's a sleeper set?" Ava asked after Lindsay hung up.

"It's a helmet thing they use to transport para prisoners. Keeps them comatose."

"Hey," called Bridger from the other room. "If this thing's over, can someone untie me?"

* * *

Miguel headed toward the auditorium as fast as he could, one arm around L.J., who hopped along beside him. Tears streamed down his face. "I'm sorry, L.J., I'm so sorry, man."

"What the hell were you doing, going along with that psycho?" L.J. clung to his friend for support.

"Zayden got into Lucia's head, she got into Izzy's, then Izzy fell for him." Miguel shook his head. "I dunno. Damn, I was an idiot! And now Izzy's hurt . . ."

"Dude, leave me here and just go. I'm slowing you down way too much."

"You sure?" Miguel asked.

"Yeah." L.J. thrust the gun at him. "Take this to reverse Lucia, if she's still frozen."

Miguel helped L.J. sit down on the grass. "No way, man! Brown kid shows up with a gun?"

"Good point. Send somebody else to get it. I'm not going anywhere."

"You're a good friend, L.J. I wish I was half as brave as you." He turned and sprinted toward Heroes Hall.

* * *

Justin insisted on flying Chloe back to campus. They touched down behind Heroes Hall as two paramedics pushed Jacob out of the maintenance building on a gurney. Moments later, another pair wheeled out a bleeding, bruised, and scorched Zayden wearing a bulky helmet. Chloe winced at his injuries, even though she couldn't find it in herself to feel bad for him. She recognized the sleeper set keeping him in an induced coma from footage of prisoner transports to Deep Six.

"Hey, that's Desert Eagle," Justin said, pointing. Chloe recognized the Native American woman with white and brown wings who led Just Cause Dallas. "I've always wanted to meet her! I'm gonna see if she'll come with me to get Charlie and Ondine." He jogged off.

Chloe flew over to maintenance. As she rounded the corner, she saw Dax in the chair, which Misty had parked just beyond the open door. His all-white eyes now contained traces of red whorls.

Chloe landed and hugged him. "Thank you, Dax. You saved my life, along with preventing the explosion."

He didn't say anything, but his face and neck turned scarlet and he ducked his head, not looking her in the eye. Next, Chloe threw her arms around Misty. "And thank you for bringing him. I don't know how you managed it, but even knowing the plan, I don't think we could've stopped Zayden without Dax."

Mr. Jordan emerged from the building, still wrapped up in his MetalBlade armor, leading a gaggle of students and faculty members along with a few costumed heroes, firefighters, and police officers. He brought everyone to the stadium for a briefing, since the auditorium was an official crime scene as well as soaked and full of extinguisher foam. The fliers and Ondine, back from the lake, joined them as everyone got settled in and Mr. Hutson hurried to hook up a PA system.

Microphone in hand, Mr. Jordan surveyed the assembled students. "First, I want to commend you for taking action in my absence and preventing a heinous act. Who wants to come up here and fill in all of us johnny-come-latelys?"

All eyes turned to Chloe, who froze.

"Come on, roomie," Lindsay said. "You're the one who figured it all out." Chloe stood on shaking legs. Lindsay stood with her, and Charlie appeared on her other side. Together, they walked onto the field and Chloe started telling the story. Lindsay and Charlie chimed in to fill in blanks, and before long Bridger and Ava joined them, too.

After they finished, Chloe realized her parents were there, as was Lindsay's mom—and Dr. Huxley and Anna Lord, as well, standing behind Dax's chair. At some point, Dax had curled up and gone to sleep, an IV in his hand.

Chloe's heart seized at the thought of what Anna must be going through. Misty and the two people who'd come with her stood apart from everyone. Their anxiety was palpable, but she didn't know why.

Chloe started toward her parents and they ran forward, meeting her half way. Inside a big family hug, she broke down and cried.

"Our daughter's a real hero, Heather. I suppose we should get used to scenes like this." Chloe couldn't help but grin through her tears.

"What happened to that tooth?" Her mom grabbed her chin. "Did it get broken?"

Chloe felt the spot where Izzy had knocked her tooth out and discovered a new one growing in its place. "Huh, guess I do grow new teeth. Good to know."

* * *

"You realize you're not only fired, but likely going to prison." Dr. Huxley shook with anger as he reprimanded Misty and Rachelle outside the stadium. "I'm certain that applies to you, as well," he said to Joe. The three of them looked at the ground and stayed quiet.

"Dr. Huxley, if I may . . ." a tentative Anna came up behind him.

He bowed his head and gestured for her to join them. "Certainly, Anna. As the mother of the abduction victim, you have every right to give them a piece of your mind."

"Who are these people, who helped you take my son out of the hospital and bringing him here?" Anna asked Misty.

The intern swallowed hard. "This is my fiancé, Joe Newton, and this is Rachelle. She's a nurse and a good friend."

Anna pulled Misty into a hug, then hugged Rachelle and Joe. "Thank you. Thank you, all. You saved all those people in there and who knows how many more." Tears streamed down her cheeks and her voice wavered. "You stopped my son from becoming a murderer. Knowing what he'd planned, what he almost did—" Her voice broke and she struggled to keep herself together. "I don't know how I'll live with the knowledge, Dr. Huxley, but how much worse would it have been if they hadn't brought Dax here to stop it?"

Dr. Huxley gaped. "But, Anna! They kidnapped your son, put him in significant danger. You were worried sick all the way here."

She turned to face him, nodding. "That's all true, Doctor, but it's also true they—and Dax—are heroes. Misty told me Dax wanted to come and I said no. I should have given her permission, and if the police or school or Just Cause ask me, I'll tell them she *did* have my permission. I can't stop you from firing the two who work for you, but if you try to turn them in, it'll be your word against mine."

Jaw clenched and nostrils flaring, he nodded in acquiescence. "Very well, Anna. He is your son, so I'll defer to you in this."

"Uh, excuse me, sir." A dark-haired boy had walked up, unnoticed, and stood next to Dax. "My name's Solomon Fromm, and Dax wants me to tell you that you can't fire Misty. He'd be sad and lonely without her, and since she'd be sad and lonely without Rachelle, he says you can't fire her either."

Dr. Huxley crossed his arms and opened his mouth to speak, but Sol cut him off.

"He says he knows a secret of yours, something about . . . Victor? I'm pretty sure he's willing to blackmail you to get what he wants."

Alarm flashed across the doctor's face for an instant before he composed himself. "Very well, Dax. They can stay. However—Misteya, you'll be doing more grunt work than you can imagine."

She gave him a rapid nod. "Yes, Doctor. Thank you."

"Uh, did you contact the ambulance company, by any chance?" Joe asked.

"I didn't. My only concern was reaching my patient. And yes, in light of the lives saved by your actions, I will refrain from reporting you." He turned and stalked away.

"Thank you, both of you," Misty said to Anna and Sol. "I can't believe Dax was going to blackmail Dr. Huxley."

The corner of Sol's mouth curled. "Well, I may have embellished that part a little. I have boundary issues."

CHAPTER TWENTY-EIGHT

Charges Filed in Hero Academy Terror Attack

DENVER, COLO.—Zayden Lord, the 14 year old accused of attempting to blow up a building on the Hero Academy campus in east Denver last week, today was charged with multiple felonies involving terrorism, theft, and attempted murder. A judge ruled earlier this week that Lord could be tried as an adult. He is the first juvenile to be held in Deep Six, the prison for parahumans in rural Montana.

Lucia Machado, 16, an alleged accomplice of Lord, is scheduled for a court appearance tomorrow. She is expected to face similar charges and also is being held in Deep Six.

Her sister and suspected co-accomplice, Isabella Machado, 14, remains in serious condition at a local hospital. She was injured during the attack by another student, whose name has not been released, and suffered internal injuries along with shattered ribs. The district attorney's office has not yet released the charges it expects to file against her.

Isabella Machado's twin brother, Miguel Machado, is said to be cooperating with investigators. A spokesperson for Just Cause says Miguel regrets his decision to assist in Lord's plans and has helped them piece together how Lord acquired explosive devices and materials and placed them in tunnels beneath the campus. It is unknown at this time what, if any, charges he will face. However, Hero Academy principal Keith Jordan (a.k.a. MetalBlade) has said Miguel Machado will not be returning to the parahuman high school, regardless of whether he faces criminal charges.

Meanwhile, the investigation has uncovered more on the para-supremacist recruitment efforts of Lord and the Machados, finding messages on multiple parahuman websites believed to be left by Lord under the user names LB, Lord Blaze, or Lord Blayze; by Lucia Machado as Chupara; by Isabella Machado as iGirlie or Menos (Spanish for "less" or "minus"); and by Miguel Machado as M&M.

Jordan says the Hero Academy plans to recognize the students who uncovered and foiled Lord's plot but declined to say when that would take place. He also declined to release the names of the students involved but said their actions "herald a bright future for superheroism."

* * *

Saturday, Sept. 17, 2016
Kansas City, Missouri

Dax looked up and smiled when the door opened and Misty walked in.

"You're both looking uncharacteristically cheery," she said to him and Ment.

"Dax is making exceptional progress," the psionicist told her, then turned to Dax. "Show her what you can do."

His hand shaking, Dax reached out and, after a few tries, picked up a pencil off of the table over his bed.

Misty made an excited sound. "Wow, that's great, Dax!"

Ment held up a finger. "Wait. That's not it."

His face pinched in focus, Dax put the tip of the pencil down on a sheet of paper. Misty wanted to move forward and watch but she didn't want to distract her patient. She knew from recent brain scans that Ment was succeeding at something she'd have thought impossible—healing Dax's brain, not just randomly in the way Chloe's borrowed healing power had, but strategically, starting with the areas necessary for communication. Dr. Huxley was certain no one else on the planet could do it.

After a few minutes, Dax dropped the pencil and looked up at her, grinning. "Cuh zee!"

Come see, she heard in her head. Misty hurried to his bedside and looked down to see squiggles on the paper. It took her a moment to realize what it was, and when she did, she gasped and her hands flew up over her mouth. "My smart boy, look at you, writing your name!"

* * *

Sunday, Sept. 18, 2016
Denver, Colorado

Chloe opened the door to see her parents in the hallway. Her face lit up. "What are you guys doing here? I thought you couldn't make it."

They grinned. "We wanted to surprise you." Her mom pulled a large gift bag out from behind her back and Chloe stepped back to let them in.

"Hi, Mr. and Mrs. Wyld," Lindsay said from her desk, where she worked on her makeup for the awards ceremony.

They greeted her and Heather handed her daughter the bag. "I'm dying for you to see this, Fly Girl."

Chloe smiled as she dug into the many layers of colorful tissue paper, at last uncovering a bundle with white paper taped around it. She tore the paper off and found herself holding a what she first took for a purple and lime-green leotard. Then she unfolded it and realized it was a bodysuit. A costume, in fact, with insectoid-looking panels on the chest and down the outsides of the arms and legs.

She gaped, not sure she liked it. "What's this for? We don't get costumes until junior year."

"We checked with the principal and he said it was okay, under the circumstances," her mom said, giddy. "We thought you could wear it to the ceremony."

Chloe's heart leapt into her throat. *Up on stage, in front of everyone, in this?* She gave Lindsay a desperate look.

"This is so cool, Mrs. Wyld!" Lindsay got up to look it over. Chloe felt betrayed. "It's the same colors as the evil fairy makeup Rhiannon did on you."

Heather beamed. "That's right! I loved the picture she sent me and thought those colors were perfect on her."

"I'll give you some space to try it on, Chlo." Phil Wyld stepped out into the hall and Chloe slipped into the costume, hoping it didn't fit.

Lindsay squealed. "Oh my gosh, it's perfect!"

Chloe's mom threw her arms around her. "You look so beautiful. I'm so proud of you!"

"Thanks, mom." She looked at herself in the full-length mirror on her closet door and thought she looked ridiculous. "It's . . . I don't even know what to say."

Heather opened the door to let her husband back in and Chloe's heart thudded to see him standing there talking to Charlie. They both turned and saw her at the same time.

"Ah, honey, you look great," her dad said.

Charlie's jaw dropped. "Wow, Wyld. You look . . . wow."

Chloe blushed and turned to look at herself again, thinking maybe it wasn't so bad after all.

* * *

"While today's ceremony is about honoring the nine-eleven victims, both human and parahuman, it's become a tradition here at the Hero Academy to also recognize outstanding members of our community." Mr. Jordan addressed the students and family members, faculty and staff, and several costumed heroes in the stadium. "We had planned to honor our own Salena Tibbets—Mustang Sally—with a lifetime achievement award, but she asked us to delay that for a couple of reasons. First, she says she's far too young for it, and second, she didn't want to distract from what's coming up next. As I'm sure you all know, we have a group of students who could not be more deserving of recognition. Their courage, quick thinking, and leadership saved who knows how many lives, and that bodes well for the future of superheroes in this country. Please come up here as I call your name."

He went on to list those who'd participated in the battle against Zayden and the others: Lindsay "Fireball" Malone, L.J. "DaVinci" Vincent, Jacob Cotton, Ava Zhang, Rhiannon Adkins, Bridger Adkins, Clara "Ondine" Sato, Solomon Fromm, Cori "Cat" Linwood, Justin Sharp, Jack "Ramage" Marlo, Kaci Taylor, and Austin "Firebird" Mann. They assembled on the stage as the audience applauded with enthusiasm. Mr. Jordan waited until it died down to continue. "Two others stand out even in this crowd of young heroes—one for putting together the pieces and rallying her friends to help, and the other for organizing and leading them. Chloe "WyldWing" Wyld and Charlie O'Neal—who I understand has recently chosen the moniker Meta Moth."

Both of their faces beat red, Chloe and Charlie climbed the stairs to the stage as everyone in the audience gave them a rousing standing ovation.

"Meta Moth? Really?" Bridger muttered as they passed.

Charlie shrugged. "It was that or Super Geek."

Mr. Jordan gave them each a medal and wrapped up the ceremony. Everyone filed out of the stadium and toward the dining hall, where a feast awaited them.

Chloe and Charlie held hands on the way out. She pulled him aside as the crowd dwindled. "I don't feel like being crammed in a room with a bunch of people right now. Do you?"

He grinned. "What did you have in mind?"

"I thought maybe we should fly off into the sunset. Or at least make a lap around campus before being stuck in chairs that aren't built for us."

Charlie squeezed her hand. "As long as you're there, I'm in."

She smiled up at him as they both put their goggles in place, got her wings buzzing, and lifted off the ground until she looked him straight in the eye. The last of the throng had filed past them, so after a quick glance around, she kissed him on the cheek. With a grin, he fluttered his wings and lifted off.

"Wanna race?" she teased, yelling over the sound of their wings.

He rolled his eyes. "I thought I was done having to chase you, Wyld."

Together, they rose up and flew out to the lake, then circled around until they approached the dining hall, flying west. The sun would set in that direction eventually, but at the moment, it shined down on them and warmed their wings.

ABOUT THE AUTHOR

Adrienne Dellwo is a novelist and award-winning indie filmmaker from Washington state. She's ecstatic to be playing in the Just Cause sandbox and looks forward to many more stories in that universe. In other arenas, she has two books out in an urban fantasy series— *Through the Veil* and *Traveler Lost*—and is working on the third. She also writes horror and traditional fantasy.

Adrienne's had short stories published by Local Hero Press, Alliteration Ink, Siren's Call and others, has one published poem, and has seen two of her stage plays performed. (Three, if you count one from third grade.)